The Quicksilver Settlement

Andrew Ballantyne

Dedication

To Gill Ince

Acknowledgments

Thank you JJ Thomas, Kate Hardy and Gerard Loughlin for your responses to the text, which helped it develop.

Thank you Rachel Armstrong, Stafford Critchlow, Rolf Hughes, Gill Ince, Pat Kaufman, Harriet Lane, Kate Levey, Mark Lockett, Juliet Odgers, Sophia Preston and John Stathatos for your different sorts of encouragement over the years.

About the Author

Andrew Ballantyne grew up in Lancashire in the UK. He trained as an architect and has worked with archaeologists in Greece. He has written books about architecture. This is his first novel.

1

Alekos was still thinking about the shapes of branches in the thicket near the cypresses, even now that he was walking home between orderly rows of lemon trees with dense glistening leaves that blocked the view to left and right. He saw someone on the path: a stranger a couple of years older than himself, dressed in khaki, a gun slung over his shoulder. As they drew close, their gazes met and locked and would not let go. Neither of them knew what to do with this moment. It might have been a moment to panic, but each seemed well aware that the other wasn't hostile, just wary. The gun was there, but the stranger didn't reach for it.

"Matthias," said the stranger, by way of introduction, holding out his hand. Alekos took it without looking away from the stranger's eyes, which were blue and intense. Alekos became a moth, transfixed. The gem-like eyes seared his soul. At that moment, there was nothing in Alekos's world beyond the stranger's face with its cautious smile. Alekos had a feeling that he was being visited by destiny, but he was lost in a present that had become formless around him. He couldn't move, and Matthias didn't move. He seemed equally locked, and they stood there, unable to break away from an unexpected instinct that held them in its grip. But then the spell was broken. The flame went out. The stranger's eyes looked troubled. His mouth opened. No sound came out. His dull shirt darkened and glistened.

Old Dinos was there. He did his best to wipe his knife on the ground.

"Come on, Alexakis," he said, "We'll get you home. They can deal with him later."

Alekos was numbed. He saw the body lying on the ground, the life bleeding out of it, and reached down to hold the guy's hand.

"Matthias," he said under his breath, but he knew there was no point expecting a reaction.

2

You'll see the brass plaque that says Lantern of Demosthenes by the door if you notice the door. It's between shop windows. Stationery on one side, mainly shirts on the other. If you take the lift to the sixth floor, that's where you'll find the reception desk. If you've arrived for one of the institute's famous cocktail parties, you go straight out onto the terrace, and it feels like you've arrived in another world, away from the dust of the street and the traffic's noise, with a not-too-distant view of the Acropolis framed by small olive trees in timber tubs painted pale olive green.

Charles Winchester first came to the institute in 1953 when it was still in its old building. He was newly married and in need of a job in Greece because a school friend, Luke Zimbrean, had suddenly died, and his parents asked Charles to take charge of his excavations, hardly begun, at Ziros on Crete.

3

Alekos felt numb, somehow distant from the world. He could hear his own blood throbbing in his head, but other sounds were muffled. The brightness went from the day. He could see that it was bright, but it was bright like in an under-exposed photograph. The only thing that was real was that gaze. He had to hang on to it.

At home, he went from the courtyard into his darkened room. The shutters closed already as they always were. He closed the door, lay on the bed, and closed his eyes, not to sleep but to call to mind what he now remembered. He could hear Dinos in the yard just the other side of the door, talking to his parents, explaining how he'd saved Alexakis's life from a Nazi paratrooper. The whole story sounded wrong.

Alekos knew that if Dinos hadn't been there, everything would have been all right. Maybe he'd have hidden the guy and brought him some food, and no harm would have come to them.

"I'll go into Chania," said Petros, Alekos's father, "See what gives."

"Is it safe?" said Hannah, Alekos's mother.

"I don't know," said Petros, "I'll keep my eyes open."

Alekos had no appetite. His mother brought out the black cherries preserved in honey, which she kept for feast days.

"They don't taste of anything," said Alekos.

"My baby," said Hannah, and she came to hug him, but it didn't seem to be the right thing to do just then, not so far as Alekos was concerned. She kissed him on the forehead. He looked miserable. Withdrawn.

When Charles Winchester looked back, he saw 1951 as the great summer of his life. He'd spent it with Luke Zimbrean, traveling in Greece after they'd both done their National Service. Luke and Charles had been together when Luke found the place that he decided he must excavate. Later, when Charles told the story, he said they'd both of them together found the land, but he knew it was Luke who had gotten excited about it and said he could tell there was a ruined city there waiting to be found near Ziros. He seemed convinced of it, and he definitely wanted to do something about it. Charles wasn't convinced there was anything really there. He didn't try to talk Luke out of it, but he couldn't waste his time on it. He needed a salary in a way that Luke didn't, so it was easy for Charles to make excuses for not doing more about archaeology. They'd met a friendly Cretan lad who spoke good English and said he'd help. The archaeological evidence seemed flimsy, and frankly, the lad seemed to be a more compelling reason for Luke to go back to the place.

Charles started work as a prep-school teacher back in England, and he and Luke didn't really keep in touch after that. Luke, with his grand family's money behind him, came back to Ziros to get things moving. Charles didn't visit the place again until he came with Luke's parents to visit after Luke's funeral in England. The little group of outsiders came in a gleaming car to the dusty little village. Mrs Zimbrean wore heavy makeup and had a cigarette holder. Her black hat had a veil. She did not connect with these people in homemade clothes, even though the lawyer from Chania was translating for them.

Charles recognized the lad, Alekos, who seemed to think he was in charge. There was a ghastly moment when he introduced a girl who said she was Luke's bride-to-be. She must have been hoping for some money from them. Mrs Zimbrean looked at Charles. He looked startled and gave his head a very slight shake, and closed his eyes.

"Are you pregnant?" said Mrs Zimbrean.

"No," said the girl.

Mrs Zimbrean looked at her without smiling and said, "You're very pretty. You'll find a husband in no time."

5

The day after briefly encountering Matthias, Alekos was in the workshop. It had been a forge – a tall space, dimly lit so you could see how hot the iron was and know when to hit it. Now that they worked wood there, they stayed close to the door where it was light.

"Alexakis," his mother called from the yard outside, "Run!"

She said, "Run and hide."

"Why?" said Alekos, "What?"

She said, "My baby, I don't know what's happening."

She said, "I don't like it."

She said, "Go to the woods."

Alekos set down his plane and ran as he was, with flappy sandals that made him feel feebly unathletic. The house was at the edge of the village, and low lemon trees came right up to it, so he was quickly lost in view. When he heard people up ahead on the path, he ducked away among the trees. He crouched and could see their legs. Khaki trousers, pale hands. If one of them crouched, they'd see him. They weren't from the village. He couldn't properly hear their voices, but the sound was different – a different rhythm to it. They sounded excited. He stayed still until they'd moved on. Should he try to run ahead of them to warn the village? Mother already knew something. He took a deep breath, heard her voice in his head, and thought he'd better do as he'd been told.

He went to the stani – the sheepfold with cypresses growing in it. It felt like a safe place as if a natural sanctity there would protect him. He went up the steps, and, standing on top of the wall, he could see the back of Dinos in the enclosure. He thought he'd found him pissing, but it wasn't that. He was dressed up in a colorful old waistcoat and a hat with a tassel and looked like an old Cretan brigand. He had cut his left forearm and was letting the blood trickle down his fingers and drip onto the ground.

"I'm going into battle," he said.

"How does this help?" said Alekos, gesturing to the arm.

"I'm mixing my blood with the blood of kings," said Dinos, "I mustn't get blood on the coat. It's my great-grandmother's embroidery."

There was a sound of firecrackers in the distance.

"You stay here," said Dinos, "You'll be safe. It's important that you live. Remember that. You're the future. I've had my day. I'm going to fight."

"Stay here," said Alekos, "You won't stand a chance. There's no reason for you to die today."

"Oh yes, there is," said Dinos, "There's every reason. It's what I must do."

He drew his sabre, which looked dangerous enough, but he knew it would be drawn against a machine gun. With his left hand, he touched Alekos's forehead and left a blood fingerprint there like a blessing. He solemnly gave Alekos his zig-zag walking stick, presenting it like a scepter, horizontally, using both hands. He went with a fierce, determined look, ready to unleash savagery, unsteady on his feet. Alekos curled up on the ground. His tears mingled with the blood of kings, and he trembled. With his head on the ground, the wall around the stani made a horizon of his world. He could see some trees beyond it, but the cypresses within were his sentinels. He knew in his bones that he couldn't be seen even if someone passed by, and he felt safe here, so he stayed, and time passed in a way that didn't make sense to him. He could feel the heat of the afternoon building up and ebbing away, and he did not move. He could smell the earth and hear the cicadas, and he did not move. He could see the light dim in the sky, and he did not move. Then the moon began to show, and it was as though a spell had been broken, and he could move now.

He got back to the house, and there was no one there. He went to the plateia, and there was activity in the failing light, but it was silent. They'd be preparing for the market in Chania tomorrow. Sacks were arranged against the church. More than usual.

There was Maria.

"Hi Maria," said Alekos, "Have you seen my mother?"

Maria looked thunderstruck. She stayed still and said nothing, which was not at all like her.

"Varvara," said Alekos when he saw Varvara.

Varvara turned and looked at him. She started to cry.

Alekos felt panicky. What was going on? He wished he could see better. There was his mother.

"My baby," she said. She kissed him and murmured into his ear, "You're the only man in the village now. They've left us to deal with the bodies."

It hadn't been a fight. It was a mass execution.

6

Alekos showed the Zimbreans the village hall, built with money they'd sent. It was still incomplete. Alekos was directing the works.

"We call it the megaron," he said.

"There should be something to say it's from the family," said Mrs Zimbrean.

"Formally, we call it the Zimbreanion," said Alekos, "We can do the lettering in the concrete."

"We should have our crest," said Mr Zimbrean, "I'll have something made. It can go inside."

"Thank you," said Alekos, "We will make it a good place."

"Luke told us you were a great help. Thank you," said Mr Zimbrean, "We want to see Luke's project succeed, so we've asked Mr Winchester here to take over."

Alekos looked more shocked than the young woman had been.

7

The young commander had said something that sounded angry and spiteful, spat out his words, loud and broken. There was a translator – a mild-mannered man who seemed to want to calm things down, but the words wouldn't let him.

"How dare you," he said, "How dare you."

He said, "If you kill our paratroopers, then you're not civilians."

He said, "You've made your village a battle zone."

But it wasn't a battle. The men from the village weren't armed.

Alekos felt that it was all his fault, but he didn't say. He thought about Dinos, who had felt that it was all his own, Dinos' fault. He had killed the soldier and brought on the storm. Dinos had seen to it that he himself had perished. His wielding of the sabre wasn't futile. It brought the sentence he'd passed upon himself. Alekos internalized his own guilt and lived with it. He'd prompted Dinos' deadly deed. Alekos knew nobody blamed him, and he didn't know who knew that Dinos thought he'd saved Alekos' life. Everyone now was numb in the way that Alekos had been since the encounter, and there were questions in the air that never would be asked.

8

Charles Winchester didn't have high expectations for the excavation. He set it up in the 1950s so he could work comfortably, and he went there each summer for the next thirty years with a small party of students, helped by hired excavators who did the actual digging. As he approached retirement, he had no expectation that anything much would be found, but his team did regularly find minor things, and the students could learn the proper procedures. The find that had really established Palioziros as a genuine Bronze-Age place and a promising place to excavate had maddeningly been made by Alice Cyprian, who was a disruptive influence. She didn't follow proper procedures and caused havoc in 1953 by uncovering a tholos tomb – a vaulted underground chamber definitely from the Bronze Age – that hadn't even been on the official site. She wasn't allowed back. As director of the excavation, Winchester, of course, took credit for the find, and it helped him later when he was appointed as director of the institute.

When he took on the role of directing the excavation, Winchester didn't know much about it. He knew that Luke had persuaded his parents to buy a plot of land that he was convinced had an ancient settlement on it.

He had no idea how tricky the purchase had been. That wasn't because of money but because it wasn't at all clear that the land could be bought. Luke's father didn't want to

14

part with money until he knew that something had actually been bought with it. Luke made a deal with the village that said he'd be recognized as having the rights to the land if he brought electricity into the village and built a village hall. The Greek lawyers drew up title deeds, and English lawyers thought they had made it watertight, so with some misgivings, Luke's father agreed to it and made payments for builders and the electric company. Luke set everything in place but then died on the island. He suddenly wasn't there anymore to do the work that had been going to make his reputation, but everything was in place for it to be done. Mr Zimbrean owned the land and couldn't really sell it, and there might be buried treasures in it, so would Charles take over? Then, at least, they could salvage Luke's vision and keep his reputation alive.

The Zimbreans didn't think of paying Charles a salary, and to ask for one from them would have made him their servant. He liked to think that they thought of him as their son's friend, not as hired help, so to keep himself afloat, he took a low-grade administrative job at the Lantern of Demosthenes.

"It's not an academic job, you understand," said Sir Alcuin Cowie, the director.

"I understand," said Charles, "But I need to be in Greece to organize things for the project."

"We can't pay you much," said Sir Alcuin, "But you and your wife can live here, and we can give you a good title. It will help when you're making invitations. You know how these things work. At Paleoziros, you'll have to pay the workforce that does the heavy lifting, but the academics just get expenses. I'll explain it all to the Zimbreans if you like."

So, on his thirty-third birthday, Charles Winchester found himself well-placed for a brilliant career. He was Director of Palioziros, Deputy Director of the Lantern of Demosthenes, and had two adjacent rooms in the old Cantacuzene house, where he and his wife would live, eating in the school when they wanted. Cowie was already working on the new building, discussing with anyone who would listen what it should be like and where it would be. Winchester caught his mood.

"We need proper residential accommodation on the site at Palioziros," said Charles, "It would make sense. The students could stay in our own set-up."

"Do you think the Zimbreans will pay for it?" said Sir Alcuin.

"I think they would," said Charles, "It would save on expenses down the line."

"There'll be lots of empty houses there, though," said Sir Alcuin, "Those villages are depopulated. You could just let people sort themselves out in abandoned houses."

"It doesn't sound safe," said Charles.

Sir Alcuin shrugged.

"It's an adventure for students. It's a very benign climate," he said, "They'd be OK in tents if you have some shade to put them in."

"It's the plumbing that worries me," said Charles, grimacing.

"What plumbing?" said Sir Alcuin.

"Exactly," said Charles, "Luke stayed with a family in the village when he was there. It looked reasonable. His books are still there. It wasn't until I nearly stayed there myself that I realized there wasn't a lavatory. They use a pot and then dig stuff into the ground. They say it's good for the soil."

"It is," said Sir Alcuin, "They're quite correct. It's traditional."

"Well, I couldn't face it," said Charles.

Sir Alcuin smiled and raised his eyebrows.

"We need to build accommodation with proper facilities," said Charles, "or we'll frighten off our volunteers. We can leave the hirelings to sort themselves out in the village."

"Imagine what your great-grandparents would think of you," said Sir Alcuin, "Young Zimmers must have been OK with the arrangements."

"Oh, but he was in love," said Charles, "or at least besotted."

"Oh yes," said Sir Alcuin, "the fiancée."

Charles looked shifty. He would have to ask the Zimbreans for money to build facilities on the site, and he'd first have to go to that lad Alekos to find out how to get the work done and how much money to ask for. He'd better get moving with it, or the excavations wouldn't ever start.

9

The coins came one by one, each a disappointment. When little Alekos saw one, he reached down, picked it up, and hoped it would be the sort of coin that would buy something sweet when he went to the market with his dad. He had found small coins in the street in Chania, and then it was money you could spend. Dad always let him keep things he found himself. In the fields, if he found a coin, it was always a disappointing coin that you couldn't spend.

"That's Turkish," said Mum, "You should keep it. It will bring you luck."

She grew up in Istanbul, so it meant something to her. Alekos put the coins in a jar. Dad brought one in from time to time.

"I think this one's really old," he said, "D'you think it could be Roman?"

"I don't know," said Mum, "It's not Turkish."

It went in the jar.

Alexakis developed a reputation as a coin collector. People who found old coins didn't know what to do with them. When Dad was visiting a client about a new table, an old coin on the mantelpiece caught his eye.

"My son collects old coins," he said.

"Take it," said Mr Phi, "I don't know what to do with it."

Later, people Alekos didn't know would occasionally leave a coin with Costas at his shop in Chania. Dad had an arrangement with Costas. He would collect messages and orders there. One day, when there was enough business, he thought he'd open a workshop there, but for now, he was OK with his base in the village. He could use the family forge as a workshop, so his overheads were low. The family could live off the land around them. Money was nice to have, but it wasn't absolutely needed. They could have enough to eat by picking food off the trees or digging it up from the ground. Sometimes, there were more lemons than they would ever be able to eat, so in principle, they could sell some at the market, but when that happened, it was always when lemons were in season on the island, and everyone else was trying to sell them too, so it wasn't worth the trouble.

"It's best to do something no one else can do," said Dad, "You're good with your hands. You're a natural. It's better to get paid for that and just pick the lemons you want to use."

Alexakis looked dreamily on and might have heard.

10

At Paleoziros, Charles put himself entirely in Alekos's hands. What else could he do? At first, Alekos felt he was working not for Charles but for Luke, whom he called Loukas, which annoyed Charles. Still, Charles thought Alekos would get the job done. They fenced off the site to make it secure, and at the edge with a good view across where the excavation would be, Alekos arranged a long, narrow timber stoa – one long side of it an open veranda with sleeping rooms off it, toilets, and showers at one end, and the director's suite at the other with its own facilities, and in between them a deeper space with a long narrow table, a run of cupboards and a basic kitchen. It would only be used in summer, so the shared space with the big table wasn't closed in but open as a verandah that ran into the corridor verandah that went the whole length of the block. From outside, it was approached from the middle of the closed long side, which faced the padlocked gate of the compound, and anyone moving across from the gate to the doorway walked over, without knowing it, the first septic tank to be installed anywhere near the village – a miracle of ingenuity that put visitors from England at their ease without them even noticing.

It was Luke who first took an interest in the coins as a collection. He'd been living in the house a few weeks, and by then, he and Alekos were sleeping together. Mum had been pleased to welcome Luke in, and he was paying them more in actual money than they'd ever had as a regular income. So it was right that he had the best bedroom, which had been the parents' room with the double bed. Mum moved herself up to the room on the roof, which was actually over the house next door, but no one was living there. There were steps up to the roof from the yard and then a door into the room. Mum had fixed it up nicely, covering up the cracked plaster by hanging fabrics around the walls so it felt like the inside of a tent. She was often in the yard and the kitchen, but at night, she was quite separate from her son and the lodger.

Alekos's room opened into the yard. It was the biggest room in the house, but it had to double up as more than a bedroom. There were some shelves and a table that they moved out into the yard when they wanted to eat at a table that was bigger than the very small one in the kitchen. They used the big table outside all the time with Luke. They ate better, too – more things that had been bought rather than grown by neighbors. The things the neighbors grew were good, but there wasn't much variety. Vlita, courgettes, tomatoes – all good things – but they're better if you have them with fish or sausages. Alekos knew the butchers in Chania because they gave him skin and bones to boil to make glue and bristles to make brushes. They thought he had a dog and gave him scraps. Jael knew what to do with the scraps to bring out good flavors for a sauce, but with Luke's money coming in now, they could have proper meat.

Luke and Alekos were at the table, thinking about a visit to Heraklion.

"It would take too long to go there and back in a day," said Luke.

"Costas has a car," said Alekos, "We can borrow it."

"I should buy a car," said Luke, "You'd be able to drive it, wouldn't you?"

"Of course," said Alekos, "but you should get a van. A van is more useful."

"OK," said Luke, "We'll get a van. It will be useful when I want to deliver furniture. I can see that."

"You'll see," said Alekos, "It will be good."

"I don't mind," said Luke, "I want to make you happy."

"Costas will find one," said Alekos, "He knows people."

"We'll take the bus this time," said Luke, "We'll want to stay in a hotel."

"We can borrow the car," said Alekos, "It's not a problem."

Luke shrugged. His eyes scanned the shelves. There were small boxes and glass jars with rusty tops that seemed to have been undisturbed for decades.

"What are these things?" said Luke and Alekos didn't know how to reply. They were his treasures, but he knew they wouldn't look like treasures to someone like Loukas. It wasn't like they were worth anything.

"That's a stick my father made," said Alekos.

"It's very crooked," said Luke.

"It was a bit of a joke," said Alekos, "in a way. It's a traditional joke. It's stronger than you'd think. It follows the grain of the wood. You have to look for something where you can cut off the branches where it changes direction and then polish it up. Dad made it for our friend Dinos. Dinos had it with him the day they died."

"And what's this?" said Luke, "A turkey baster?"

"Maybe that's what it is," said Alekos, "Dad said that when he was a child and was constipated, it was filled with olive oil and squirted up his bum."

Luke laughed uproariously.

"Your dad had a sense of humor," he said.

"I believed him," said Alekos.

"Yes, of course you did," said Luke, "I expect it was used for other things too. What about this jar?"

"That's picture hooks," said Alekos.

"Oh," said Alekos. There were no pictures in the room they were in and only one in the rest of the house. An icon in the kitchen. Mum had taken the family photos from her room and hung them upstairs.

"If you want to put up something in your room, we can use them," said Alekos.

"Thank you," said Luke, "We might do that. It looks like I'll be here for a while. You're sure that's OK with your mum?"

"Definitely," said Alekos, knowing how much she appreciated the money coming in. She also seemed to think that Loukas was a good influence. She could see that Alexakis was becoming more confident and that he and Loukas were becoming inseparable.

"And is this a jar of coins?" said Luke.

"It is," said Alekos.

"Can we look at them? I know about coins," said Luke.

Alekos shrugged.

"I'm not sure the top comes off the jar," said Luke, but it did, with a bit of coaxing.

"They're the coins you can't spend," said Alekos.

"They're interesting for archaeologists," said Luke. He laid them out carefully, sorting them into groups, "These are Turkish," he said.

"My mother likes those," said Alekos, "She grew up in Turkey."

"The island was in Turkey," said Luke, "or at least in the Ottoman Empire, so they used Turkish coins here. You have a history of the island here in your coins. Do you know what this one is?"

Alekos shrugged.

"I wonder if it's Venetian," said Luke, putting it on one side, "This one's definitely Roman. When we go to Heraklion, we can find a book about them. Look, this one has Greek characters. It must be Byzantine."

"Is it valuable?" said Alekos.

"You wouldn't want to sell it," said Luke, "It's interesting enough to keep but not worth enough to sell. You could throw the Turkish ones away."

"My mother would be upset," said Alekos.

"Of course," said Luke, "I was forgetting." They were about half the coins in the half-full jar, and he kept them apart in a heap. The others he laid out in rows by type.

12

Sir Alcuin Cowie had the gentle, world-weary manner of someone who had retired into his job rather than clawing his way there by ambition, but he was conscientious about doing the things he should do. He enjoyed talking with the brighter students and radiated bonhomie when there were visitors. He was ambitious for the school and would talk with animation about the projected new building, especially if he was talking to someone who might be able to give the project some money. He often spoke about it with Charles, who came to him for advice about his own building project on Crete – a much more modest affair that moved much more quickly, but still, there was a need for permissions as well as for the actual building work. There were more technical things to keep an eye on in the school, which Cowie did quietly when he wouldn't be interrupted. He didn't want to look as though he spent his time with the drudgery of accounts and rotas, but he knew what was going on. Or at least he thought he did. It was late one night in his bedroom when he was looking at the accounts and realized that there was something wrong. In the entries for fees for the new building, there were sums of money that were much higher than the bills coming in from the consultants. It went back to the very beginning of the project, and now the sums of money were significant – not enough to ruin the school, but enough to double the accountant's official salary, which was already more than anyone else's. He would have to ask the accountant about it, and he would want a witness.

He was in his office in a supervision with Alice Cyprian, which was a free-ranging conversation. Alice was his favorite student of the moment, but he tried not to let it show. He would choose an object from the clutter on his desk and ask her to speculate about it to get the conversation started and to gauge what he might expect her to know. There were little figurines, Cycladic, Roman, and Classical, some of them genuinely old, others reproductions from the museum, and others made of plastic or resin and kitsch. There was a fluorescent octopus that might have come from a keyring and an Owl of Minerva from a tourist-tat stall in the Plaka. Alice's thinking was similarly all over the place. He handed her a small Cycladic figurine.

"It's real," she said.

"There's no need to sound so surprised," said Sir Alcuin, "How can you tell?"

"It's cold," she said.

"Very good," he said.

She was skeptical about everything the archaeologists said about anything, and she knew her stuff. She could always point out just how flimsy their evidence was, so he knew she had tracked down the evidence. She had spent some time on Crete worked at first at Knossos, but she was impatient with the reconstructions of the place and dumbfounded by the way everyone there seemed to believe them. She had a quiet manner and a way of becoming invisible when she wanted by wearing dust-colored clothes, and she could pay close attention to things in her peripheral vision, seeming not to be interested in the things that mattered to her most. Her current enthusiasm was Voodoo, which she was convinced was more like what was going on in the ancient shrines than anything Hollywood has yet shown us of classical Greece.

"The trap with these," she said, "is to think that they look modern. If I think it looks modern, it means I'm not understanding it right."

Cowie's phone rang.

"Yes, OK. Show him in," he said, and to Alice, "Now dear, this is the school's accountant. Sorry for the interruption. I'd like you to stay if you don't mind. He won't be here long."

After he had gone, Alcuin said, "So. What did you make of that?"

"He's definitely guilty of something," she said, "You didn't accuse him of anything. You asked him to explain. An innocent man would have wondered what you were getting at, but as soon as you asked, he said you were accusing him. It was just bluster. How dare you accuse him when you hadn't."

"I'll have to think what to do," said Alcuin.

"What do you think he's done?" said Alice.

"There are some irregularities in the accounts," said Alcuin, "I wanted a witness when I confronted him. If he comes clean, maybe we turn a blind eye to it."

He wasn't expecting the call he had that afternoon from Tom Harley, the chairman of the trustees. The tone was friendly but grave.

"He says you've humiliated him and ruined his reputation, old boy," said Tom.

"That isn't true," said Alcuin, "I have a witness."

"Ah," said Tom, "That's part of the problem. He says you accused him in front of a member of the public, and now the whole world will know."

"The witness is someone I trust," said Alcuin, "I don't trust the accountant."

"This is going to be a problem," said Tom, "but leave it with me."

After the world had rocked on its axis, and Loukas wasn't around anymore, Alekos was with Alice on the roof of the Megaron Hotel in Heraklion, looking out across the Venetian harbor to the sea. Alekos was wearing a machine-sewn shirt. Alice was in one of her dust-colored dresses and gold seahorse earrings.

"I'll be able to help you," said Alice, "I know people."

Alekos said nothing. He was always close to tears in those days, numb and hyper-alert at the same time.

"You don't know whether you can trust me," said Alice, "but you can, and you know you're going to have to trust someone."

Alekos sat awkwardly at the table, squirming without actually moving. Alice was relaxed in herself but fixedly attentive.

"You should talk with my mother," said Alekos, his eyes scanning the horizon, and then he turned and still quietly but angrily said, "We haven't found anything. There might be nothing."

"I have a feeling that you know," said Alice, "I know that you think you know."

Alekos looked wary. He looked away. The horizon was somehow soothing, but he couldn't sharply see it. The graded tonality of the sky and the sea were blurred together by a haze that made it impossible to tell where one began and the other ended.

"There's no need to worry," said Alice, "but I already know way more than you think I know." She paused and waited for a reaction that didn't come, "I know that you have some old coins in a jar in your room," she said. That made him flinch.

"Did Loukas tell you?" said Alekos, "or my mother? It doesn't matter."

"You told me," said Alice.

"I know you don't think you told me," said Alice, but you did."

He was looking at her now, and while their eyes were locked, she said, "When you find your treasure – your real treasure – it would be a good idea to leave the coins in there as if they'd been dropped."

"I don't know what you mean," said Alekos.

"You will know," said Alice, reaching for an olive.

When Doreen, the administrator, brought Sir Alcuin his instant coffee, she said, "You're not going to want to see this, but you need to take a look," and she gave him a newspaper, folded to show a picture of himself taken for a passport several years ago. It made him look like a criminal, the way passport photos do.

"It seems to be saying that I've resigned," said Alcuin, "It's the first I've heard of it."

"You can't believe everything you read in the papers," said Doreen.

"Can you call Harley for me?" said Alcuin.

The school couldn't have the bad publicity that would continue for as long as Sir Alcuin remained in post. He couldn't work with the accountant. The school had to accept that the accountant hadn't done anything wrong. There was money missing, but the accountant said it was just that there were receipts missing. All the money had gone out legitimately, and he had friends in government and the media, and the future of the school was threatened if the allegations against him weren't retracted in full.

Cowie accepted that he couldn't work with the accountant after this. He denied that he had made an accusation at all, and if anyone had set out to ruin the accountant's reputation, it was the accountant himself. He was the one who had made everything public. It was the accountant who had invented the allegations and taken them to the press. Cowie was not going to resign, and he had done nothing that was any reason at all to dismiss him. He had the law and reason on his side, but he had caused an employee from the host nation to take offense, and the consequences had to be resolved. It wasn't a question of winning an argument, said Harley, but of practical politics.

Work continued on the new school, and it wasn't far from completion. The trustees resolved that since the director and the accountant had to work together, and since Sir Alcuin and this accountant could not work together, either one or the other would have to go. It couldn't be the accountant for reasons of practical politics, and it couldn't be Sir Alcuin because he had not breached his contract, which was theoretically permanent but actually could be terminated in five years. So he would stay on his salary for the next five years and would live in the new apartment that was built for the director of the school, but he would not be the director of the school. He would be there but disconnected except at an informal level, and visitors might suppose him still to be in charge.

"It's a funny old world," said Alcuin to Charles, "One guy embezzles money from the school, and I notice, and so I'm sacked."

"Not sacked exactly," said Charles, "and the new building is going to be your legacy."

"I was hoping it would be my platform," said Alcuin.

"It still will be," said Charles, "You'll live there and preside over the cocktail parties with the view of the Acropolis."

When Alekos found the tomb and liberated the gold octopus masks from it, he scattered a handful of coins in the sooty vaulted space. He knew for sure that Alice had uncanny ways of knowing, and he knew he had to trust her whether he wanted to or not. The tomb didn't stay open for long. Less than a day. The women put the earth back, and by the time Charles Winchester arrived to start the official excavation, there was nothing to draw attention to it. In fact, Charles didn't even see the grove of cypresses as being part of his site. The first thing he oversaw was making the site secure. Alekos sorted it out with some friends of Costas that they'd come and put up a tall chainlink fence. That would be enough. Where would it go? Alekos acted as the guide to show the workmen where the fence should go, with Charles in attendance.

"It's bigger than I was expecting," said Charles.

"We should include the stani here," said Alekos.

"Fuck off," said one of the men, in mumbled Cretan Greek that Winchester did not understand, "The trees are close together there. Tell the creep it will be expensive."

"They say the fence gets complicated around there," said Alekos, "They don't mind doing it, but it will cost a bit more. It's worth doing."

"I wouldn't bother," said Charles, "We have plenty to go at without it. Remember, I'm an archaeologist, and I can tell just by looking at them that they're modern walls. They're just agricultural. They don't matter."

"Are you certain?" said Alekos, "They might be modern but built over something older."

He was appalled and triumphant at the same time. He knew, and Charles did not know, that the site's greatest treasure had come from that spot and that it had gone, but the underground chamber was still there, and surely it would eventually be found again by the official excavation. But maybe Charles was so completely clueless he never would find it. It was at that moment that Alekos realized he despised Charles. The roiling envy, jealousy, and sense of injustice were simplified into a scorn that could not be expressed. He had had his problems with Loukas, but Loukas had always had an instinct for the site. It was an imprecise instinct, but he had known that it was important in some way. Charles had no idea at all. He was in charge because Luke's parents knew him as Luke's friend, not because he knew anything at all about what he was doing. If Charles had approached Alekos differently, they would have cooperated, and things would have turned out well, but Charles treated Alekos as a servant without paying him. Loukas had treated Alekos as a friend and lover and had also quietly been generous with the money in a way that had transformed his life. Alekos wanted the project to succeed for Loukas's sake, but he didn't like the idea that Charles would get all the glory. He was glad that the gold masks were safely back at the house under his bed.

16

Sir Alcuin Cowie was thunderstruck when he found that Charles Winchester, of all people, had been appointed as the new director.

"He's not up to it," he said to Harley, "He knows it, and that's why he didn't come to me for a reference. Of course, he's a nice guy, and there's no one better when it comes to dealing with the photocopier, but he doesn't have the social reach that will bring people in, and he's not going to be able to supervise research."

"But you'll still be there for all that sort of thing," said Tom, "You'll be on the premises, and you'll have your salary. You can keep doing whatever you're interested in so long as you don't deal with the accounts. Look over them by all means and point out where Winchester needs to keep his beady eye. He interviewed very well. We asked him about his vision for the school, and he was very convincing."

"He's just told you my vision for the school," said Alcuin, "I kept telling him about it because he works here, and I need him to be on board. He doesn't think himself."

"He gave very good answers to the questions we asked, and he had a very impressive reference from Zimbrean, so he brings some good connections with him and Zimbrean-funded research."

"You're making a big mistake," said Alcuin, but he knew the trustees had made up their minds.

17

It took direct action on Alice's part to bring the coins to light.

"He's a slave to his method," she said.

There was a trial square that Alekos had dug with Luke, mainly to see how difficult it would be to dig. They set out before dawn with spades and a pick.

"We should have a ground-breaking ceremony," said Luke. They saluted the low sun with water. They raised their hands to embrace its rays. Luke turned north, west, south, and back to the east and threw a capful of water from the flask in each direction. He pulled Alekos to him, kissed him on the mouth, and said, "This is our future. This is where it really begins."

The ground was harder than they expected, and they didn't manage to do much.

"It'll be softest in spring," said Alekos, "after the rains, but it's had a few years of being baked hard undisturbed. Since the war, no one's been working the land here."

"We can come back tomorrow," said Luke. And they did come back. They made a square about a meter across. It went down only a little way, but it was enough for Charles to be able to see it when he came the next year to take charge. He treated it as the authoritative setting-out point. He had people stretch the string to define two of the edges at right angles to one another and continued those lines to start a grid across the site. The surveyor would draw a plan, and they would plot each thing they discovered when it came to light.

"It's all very well being methodical," said Alice, in a kafeneion in Chania, "but he really misses the point of things. He seems to think the method is the point of it all. He's not going to discover the tholos for years if he discovers it at all."

"Do we care?" said Alekos. He had discovered the tholos. He had the gold masks from it. It didn't bother him if Charles never found anything.

"The problem," said Alice, "is that the project needs to be taken seriously. At the moment, when they look at it from Athens or London, it's just a field with archaeologists in it. There's no evidence that they're excavating anything that matters. They might as well be digging up the field to plant lemon trees. They'd better have a reason to think it's worth doing, or it'll just fizzle out."

"Charles believes in it," said Alekos, "and the money's coming from the Zimbreans."

"The problem," said Alice, "is that Charles is a cretin, and the trustees are going to realize it sooner or later. We don't want them to step in and replace him with someone intelligent. He needs a helping hand."

"He's put the stani outside the site," said Alekos.

"He won't mind if I dig there then," said Alice.

"He'll be angry," said Alekos, "especially when you find the tholos."

"I'll ask him first," said Alice, "I'll tell him to excavate there. He'll refuse. Then I move in. How can he object then?"

Alekos drily laughed.

"He'll hate you," he said, "He already hates me. He needs me, and he hates that."

18

Alekos had some builders to help with the stoa – a sophisticated cabin with rooms to sleep in and the director's chalet at the other end. It was carefully made, for Luke's sake, like an over-scaled musical instrument that sat light on the ground so as not to compromise later excavation. Charles could settle in here with the students and avoid the awkwardness of dealing with the village. That meant that in the village, Alice and Alekos could organize as they liked. The paid people who did the digging all stayed in the village and ate together in Luke's megaron, the Zimbreaneion. The unpaid archaeologists were young and were hoping to land a job at a university. Palaeoziros wasn't their first choice, but once they got there, it was quite agreeable. The beach was a short walk away. Charles was older than them, and they accepted his authority, which grew with each passing year. No one ever came back for a second season, but they could say that they'd had some experience on an archaeological dig, so the students stayed the same age – around about 20 – while Charles started in his thirties and continued into his sixties with the same routine. The students enjoyed each others' company and imagined while they were there that they were doing something that would help their careers along. Charles saw to it that they had something to cook and a roof over their heads, and he shared his wisdom, such as it was.

Alice was an anomaly. Alekos kept Charles at a distance, knowing that Charles thought of him as a rustic laborer who, by some miracle, could speak English. Alice was harder for Charles to place. She had had dealings with the Lantern of Demosthenes and would come to the site and chat with the students in a way that made it impossible not to invite her to stay for the meal. She clearly knew the site well and had an authority that the students respected, and that made Charles uneasy.

"You should excavate below those cypresses," said Alice when they were eating.

"That's outside the site," said Charles, "we have plenty to do inside the fence."

"I'm sure there's something there," said Alice.

"It's just a nineteenth-century wall," said Charles, "we want to find things that are older than that."

"I have the feeling it's marking the spot of something much older," said Alice.

"Well," said Charles, "You have your feelings. I have my method. We'll excavate square by square on the grid, and in the fullness of time, everything will come to light."

"If you go down there and look up the hill, you get the sense that it all builds up to where the cypresses are," said Alice.

"Thank you," said Charles, "but I'm in charge here. We have two more weeks this summer, and then we'll pack up. Everything has been there for thousands of years, and it's not going to go away all of a sudden now."

"It will be decades before you get round to it," said Alice.

"Yes," said Charles. He had his career before him, and if this site kept him going for forty years, it would take him to retirement. If he didn't find anything much, then he would have had a respectable life's work tending an unimportant site, "We might not find much, but the students will have a good grounding in the method."

19

How do I explain to Loukas? Smart enough to look respectable, but not so smart, you look like you've come from another world. His clothes mark him out right away, and it would be better if he spoke better Greek, but people like him well enough. The first time he came to the village, he made the mistake of thinking Maria's house was a café. There's a table set up in the shade of a tree outside the church on the plateia, and when he looked towards Maria's door, he saw boxes – cardboard printed with familiar names – Metaxa, Persil, Brillo – piled up inside. He thought it was a shop. He and Charles sat down at the table. Maria came out to welcome them, and they ordered beers. In case you're wondering – the boxes aren't Maria's idea of furniture, but they make themselves useful and, well, they hang about. Cupboards have to be thought about and paid for. You'd think that the box was just going to be there for the week while you used up a few things, but then there it still is a year or even a decade later. Maria doesn't have the money for new cupboards, and anyway, she thinks about other things. Maria looks rather fleshy; her habitual black blouse has ruffled fabric around the collar, and she always wears strongly colored lipstick. She looks like she could be a singer in a bar and somehow has an expansive personality, with a voice that carries an air of being in charge. She brought Loukas and Charles a glass of water each and a homemade biscuit, and they thought she hadn't understood but went along with it.

It was a moment later that Eleni stopped by and said hello. Maria took her indoors, and there was a lively conversation, after which Eleni left. She returned with two bottles of beer from before the war. Maria put them on a tray with two glasses and took them to the table.

When I arrived with my mother, the glasses were almost empty, and Loukas was asking for the bill.

"Good evening," I said in English, "Would it be possible for me to help?"

There was a look of relief on Loukas's face.

"How do you do," said Loukas, "We need to get back to Chania, and it's getting late. We should say goodbye, but I don't think I'm getting through. I've asked for the bill, but the nice lady here doesn't seem to understand. She just wags a finger at me."

I laughed.

"You're her guests," I said, "You should thank her and wish her well. She would be insulted if you gave her money."

A look of alarm crossed Loukas's face, and he didn't say the thing that first came to his mind.

"Thank you for explaining," said Loukas, "That's embarrassing. So this isn't a kafeneion?"

"This is Maria's house," I said, "We all come to eat at her table, so you're welcome – especially welcome as strangers. We don't see many."

"I should introduce us," said Loukas, "I'm Luke, and this is my friend Charles. We're exploring. Looking for archaeology."

I translate for Maria and Eleni.

"You won't find that here," I say, "That's in the east, at Knossos."

"Yes, we know about that," said Loukas, "we want to find things that haven't been discovered."

"Good luck," I said.

"We've had a good time," he said, "We were traveling around the Peloponnese with a copy of Pausanias, and there were times when we got off the bus, and we could see traces of ancient things – a theatre – maybe a big rectangular patch of dried up grass that hinted at the stylobate of an ancient temple below the surface."

"Of course, we'll never be able to check up on it to see if our guesses were right," said Charles.

"That sounds good," I said, "but what brought you here? We're not on the main road."

"All the excavations are in the east of the island," said Loukas, "I'm sure there must have been something in the west. I could just imagine from the map and from walking along nearer the sea that this would be a good place for a town. The ground's a bit higher. You have a good view out. It's a place you could defend. I thought it was worth a look."

"And did you find anything?" I asked.

"No," said Charles, "Nothing."

"Steady on there," said Loukas. He looked me in the eye and said, "We saw a possibility. I saw enough to make me want to come back." It was a look that brought back an unbidden memory of Matthias. It was the same sort of moment. The same sort of look. The same feeling of collapsing space. The same feeling that this was a pivotal moment. I had a moment of panic, fearing for his safety, but as our eyes locked together, I knew that this was all that mattered in the world.

"You'll need to leave now if you're going to be in Chania before it goes dark," I said, "but you could stay here. We'll find you a room."

"We must go," said Charles, "Our things are at the hotel."

I'd forgotten he was there, and I resented him being there, even then.

Loukas shrugged and looked as if he might have a different view, but he wasn't going to argue.

"It will be difficult in the dark," I said, "If a car passes, wave for a lift. They'll understand."

"I do want to come back," he said.

20

The next season, Charles arrived at the stoa and unpacked his suitcase. When he came out of his room, thinking it might be time for an ouzo and wondering whether there was some already here from last year, he found Alice sitting at the table, one of the laborers with her.

"You should come and see something," she said.

She led Charles to the cypresses and showed him where the spade had hit the stone. Cut stone. The outside of a vault.

"How dare you!' he said, "You have no authority to do this."

"It's a find," said Alice, "and it isn't on the site. It's nothing to do with you, but I thought you'd want to know."

She went away and left Charles to work out what he was going to do. He sent a student to ask Alekos to come to see him as a matter of urgency, and Alekos went, but not until the evening the next day when the students had arrived and were preparing the meal. A big pan of water was heating up, and there were tins.

"We have made a discovery," said Charles, "and we'll need to move the fence to include the sheepfold within the archaeological site."

"I can see to that," said Alekos, "I'll have it done by the time you return here next summer."

51

"It's urgent," said Charles, "It must be done before I go away."

Alekos gave him a quizzical look. On the surface, you might think he looked mildly surprised, but perhaps he was gloating as he realized he had Charles again completely in his power.

"You know that everyone's away at this time of year," said Alekos, "Will you stay on for a while?"

"I can't do that," says Charles, "I have commitments. It must be done now."

He seemed to be infuriated by the way Alekos remained relaxed and by the way he smiled.

"I'll have to see whether it's possible," said Alekos.

"We can ask the diggers to do it," said Charles.

"It's not their kind of work," said Alekos, "It really isn't."

"What about the people who put up the rest of the fence?" said Charles.

"They're the right people," said Alekos, "but they're on holiday now."

"Are they on the island?" said Charles.

"It's possible," said Alekos.

"Then we can pay them time-and-a-half, and they'll be able to take a better holiday afterward," said Charles.

"That's not how it works," said Alekos. He shook his head and looked amused, but as if he was trying to conceal his amusement, "You think a holiday is something to buy. You think a holiday is when you go away and stay in a hotel," he shrugged, "It's not like that for us. Some people will go away to stay with family, but often, the family is here. Crete's a nice place. The family who aren't already here work in Athens, and they come here for the summer. If you're asking someone to work this week, you're asking him to turn his back on his family. His mother will be there, and she'll be angry. You'd need to pay him enough to make it worth a fight with his mother. He won't win. He'll hear about it for the rest of her life. If you offered him ten times as much as usual, he'd take the offer seriously, but I can't guarantee you'd be accepted."

"You people!" said Charles in a whisper.

"There are things that are more important than money," said Alekos.

"But I need it done," said Charles, "The diggers are here. They're working at this time of year."

"They weren't easy to find," said Alekos, "and we gave them plenty of warning so they didn't make other plans. I'll ask around. What are you eating this evening?"

"Aubergines," said one of the students, a stern, bespectacled girl with startlingly pale skin.

"Very nice," said Alekos, "Melitzana. We fry them in olive oil."

"We don't like oil," said the student, "We're boiling them."

"And sardines," said the other, who might have been a sister, gesturing towards the cans as yet unopened.

"Well, enjoy them," said Alekos.

"I've been thinking," said Charles, "Let's get the diggers to open the place up. They can stop their other work. We'll see what's there, make it safe, and then the fence can go up when the holidays are over."

21

And now here he is, Loukas Zimbrean. He is no longer a stranger who deserves random hospitality but still a visitor in the eyes of the village, even though he feels like a permanent addition to our household. At least, that's how I feel it. He has conversations with my mother, and it's her insistence that Loukas should come with us to meet other people. Our routines changed when he arrived, and we ate three-together at the beginning, in the yard, but we had a routine: the volta two or three times a week, Maria's at least once a week, and church on Sunday. He's now met Ariadne, who's shy with strangers because skin-cancer treatment years ago left her with no nose. She alarms strangers and keeps a low profile when they're around. So meeting her – and her pig, Grylla – is a rite of passage into village life. She often walks the pig, which is a companion for now and will have her big day in October at the Thesmophoria.

"Varvara's gone for bread. She'll be back in a moment," says Eleni, who always seems rather well-groomed and tightly self-controlled. She holds herself to high standards but is kind and understanding when other people don't meet them. In fact, she expects it of people to fall below her standards. She would never let herself go the way Maria has, but they're the best of friends all the same. I hand over the basket of courgettes we've brought from our garden.

Here's Varvara with the bread. She's sturdy, walks with a slight limp, and will clearly stand for no nonsense. Varvara's the only one here who regularly fires up an oven. It's outside her house. Bread's become her thing. Next time we come, the courgettes will have been cooked in the oven unless Maria takes it into her head that they'd be better grilled on her charcoal. Maria comes out from her kitchen with a big bowl of spaghetti dressed in olive oil so it slithers as it should. She's very particular about it. The cardboard boxes are still there.

I'm accustomed to the village being the way it is. Loukas asks questions that make me see it afresh.

"A lot of the houses look very run down," he says, "They're solidly built. They're not going to fall down, but they do look neglected. Even here on the plateia, there are abandoned houses, and Maria's isn't exactly in great shape. They're perfectly nice inside."

"It's the men's work," I say, "Painting the house. It's not being done."

"Because there's no men," he says to himself, "How tactless. I should have realized. What about water and electricity? You don't need men to have them, but there's none in the village."

He's seen the cistern at the house and the hand-pump on the roof. I go up in the morning to re-fill the tank that's up there, and the water warms up in the heat of the day. You can take a nice warm shower through the summer. Summer showers are good. In winter, it doesn't get really cold here, but the shower – attached to a wall just outside the yard, kept private-enough by trees – doesn't get used so much.

"You need money," I say, "Money to get the electricity here. Money to pay for it once it is here. Costas has electricity in Chania. It's a contaminated blessing."

"In the future, it's going to be different," he says, "They're working on nuclear power stations that will make it so cheap they're not going to have to measure how much anyone uses. Imagine the power of the atom bomb tamed and run into millions of homes."

I laugh because it seems so far-fetched.

"I don't see it coming here," I say.

"It'll happen sooner than you think," he says.

"Where's Stasia?" my mother asks Eleni.

"She's staying in Chania this week," says Eleni, "There's work at one of the clothes shops. She's staying with Argyro."

I translate for Loukas: "Anastasia, Eleni's daughter, is staying with her aunt in Chania. Her uncle, too – he survived the war. Stasia's good with clothes. She's really good at cutting dresses so they fit, and she can sew. She doesn't like doing that so much, but she'll do it for money."

"I'm surprised there's tailoring going on in Chania," says Loukas.

"You need to think ahead with clothes," says Eleni, "There'll be a need for warmer things in a little while, so they'll be copying the new designs in the new fabrics. When they're in the window, we can go and look."

"Ah, clothes!" says Maria, and perhaps because Loukas is there, she stops at that.

"Loukas was asking about painting the houses," I say, and there's a murmur of reaction.

"Everyone's doing them white these days," says Eleni, "and blue for the doors and shutters."

"Why's that?" says Loukas.

"National colors," I say, "The flag."

"I remember the old colors," says Varvara, "The men used to know where to go for the red earth and the yellow earth. Does anyone know about it now?"

"Not round here," says my mother.

"Yes," says Varvara, "They'd start off bright – garish pink and yellow – but then they fade over a few years and become really beautiful. Then they end up sort of stone color, like we have now."

"I remember," says Maria.

"Yes," says Eleni, "The new colors didn't look good, but when they were a bit older, they blended with one another very nicely. My husband used to say you could tell when a wall needed painting from the state of the color. You'd see patches of bright and mellow color around, and that looked good."

The women rarely mentioned their husbands, not just out of tact but because they hadn't really known each others' husbands. In the old days, the men met each other much more regularly in the kafeneion, where women weren't allowed. The women stayed at home and heard about things through their husbands. The way the village worked had changed since the men were killed, and the women had become different people. The former kafeneion is abandoned now, on the other side of the little plateia. Maria's house is where everyone meets.

Maria puts some tomatoes in the basket for us to take home. Everyone has tomatoes at the moment – that's why we don't grow them ourselves. Maria's always taste good in that watery way of big tomatoes – you can't hold more than one at a time in a hand. She's left their stalks in – the part of the tomato with a scent. They smell fresh but powdery as if they're carrying a secret from long ago. I raise this beautiful golden orb to my face. I inhale, and it envelops me in its perfume, holds me in its world, and tells me nothing has ever been so beautiful. It's like a tautly upholstered pin-cushion – something from the Ottoman court – a condensation of sunlight and luxury here in my hand. I hold it out to Loukas, who takes it, breathes in, and looks back at me. He knows that good things can happen here.

22

What Charles found, as Alekos and Alice knew he would, was a tholos tomb that had been visited before. The vaulted space was not huge, but there were stone plinths with three skeletons on them. There were plenty of things for Winchester to document, including the coins, which were valuable evidence of the presence of the tomb-robbers. He would publish a paper that explained how the tomb had been robbed in the third century by Romans who had broken in through the vault near the top. Then there was a later visit during the twelfth century when the same opening had been used, but those Byzantine visitors had probably found little to interest them as the Romans would have taken the real treasures. Charles had found his way in through a new opening high in the vault, and once inside, one could see where the original doorway had been. In the future, they would excavate from the outside to open up that door, but for now, they would plot the place on the site plan and continue with the orderly, methodical excavation following the grid.

It was the most exciting thing they had found, but Charles was angry that his instructions hadn't been followed. The article came out the following Easter in *Fos: the Journal of the Lantern of Demosthenes*, which was edited by the school's deputy director, Charles Winchester.

"You should have said that I found the place," said Alice when she saw the article, "You haven't even mentioned me."

"That's the way it works," said Charles, with a tight little smile, "I'm the director, so the work is credited to me. We all know there's a team behind it, and you're credited as part of the team. You're there in the footnotes."

"I'm in an alphabetical list with the students," said Alice, "You wouldn't know that I pointed you to the place and dug it up when you refused to look there."

"You shouldn't have done that," said Charles, "I could have had you arrested."

"Fat chance of that," said Alice, "It wasn't on your site at the time."

Charles looked indignant and pompous.

"It's my dig," he said, "Who do you think you are to talk to me like that?"

"Oh Charles," said Alice, "You silly little man."

He never saw her set foot on the site again.

23

The taxi driver points to the meter, where there's a number in thousands on the display. It's about half the money I was allowed to bring into the country. The rest, which should be enough, is in travelers' cheques, and I'd better find out how to change some, but first, here's the institute: the Lantern of Demosthenes. I can see the name on the brass plate by the door. The driver takes my suitcase from the boot and puts it on the pavement. He drives away, and I feel that I'm a long way from home. There's a hotel just along the street. That's reassuring to see – but I can't afford to stay there. I've just started as an academic in the UK, bought a flat, saw interest-rates rise, and now I have no furniture, hardly any disposable income, but the freedom to research over the summer. Word reached me that someone at the Lantern of Demosthenes needed someone to do some architectural drawings. I thought, "I can do that," and thought it would be good to visit Greece. There was an exchange of letters, and I'm here, but I still don't know what to expect. I certainly didn't expect the heat. The lobby seems underlit and dusty. There's a door to some stairs that no one's expected to use and a lift that seems to take you to small businesses designated by personal names, all in Greek characters that I can decipher if I take the time – I guess they're lawyers or accountants or something – and then the Lantern of Demosthenes is up above. You need to have a key

62

to use the highest floors. The lift doesn't inspire confidence, but it works. The lobby on the sixth floor is quite small. There are two doors, one on each side, and a wall of reeded glass that lets some light in from an office on the other side. You can see the shapes of filing cabinets against the light, cut up into vertical stripes by the corrugations in the glass. One door is unmarked. The other has a buzzer and a brass plaque with the institute's name on it again, so I know I'm in the right place.

I press the button. I can hear a distant buzz.

I wait.

Nothing happens.

I buzz again.

Nothing happens.

I start to think of alternatives. What do I do? I don't know the city. I don't know the language. I don't know how things work around here. What are my alternatives? Go to that hotel? My flight back to the UK is in two months. I'm supposed to have a month here, being fed by the institute, and then a month on Crete working with the archaeologists. If I don't link up, then I guess I go to a hotel for long enough to find out how to change my flight, and then I go right back home.

I buzz again, in a more prolonged and despairing way, and this time, after a pause, the door opens. There's a thin young woman in a pale grey dress. She looks a bit dreamy, and she's holding a white rose in her right hand – casually, not showing it off. She's not wearing shoes.

"Hi," she says, "there's no one around at the moment."

"Ah," I say, "I'm supposed to be staying here. I've just arrived."

"Come back at five; they'll sort you out," she says.

"Could I leave my bags here? Could I wait here? I don't know my way around yet."

She smiles wanly.

"Welcome to Athens," she says, "Your best bet's to find some shade on the terrace. Come in. Your bags are OK here. You'll hear when people start up again." She smiles again. She is not unfriendly, but it's not her job to sort me out, and she doesn't want me to think it is. "This is the office," she says, pointing to a closed door with reeded glass in it and not much light coming through. There's a bust on a plinth – "Demosthenes" carved on the plinth – and an old engraving, nicely framed, of the Lysicrates Monument, and old photos – good photos – of two people, a man and a woman.

"There you are," she says and gestures to the terrace. I follow her gaze, and when I turn back, she's gone.

"Thank you," I say, a bit too loud, imagining my voice will reach her, and the space is quite resonant with hard surfaces everywhere – echoey. On the terrace, there's a view over the rooftops of the Plaka to the Acropolis, which isn't far away. There are olive trees in planters, tables, and chairs. It's hot. The view's fantastic, shimmering with heat and car fumes. From here, it seems as if the institute must more or less own the city. I will, of course, take a photo, the invitation's irresistible, but I'm going to be here for a while, so I needn't do it right away. I can just drink it in – experience it for real rather than through a camera lens. I can identify the two main buildings – the Parthenon and the Erechtheion. I've been showing slides of them to the students. Here they are for real – talismans of excellence down the ages – details copied and recopied, time after time, all over the world. It feels like such a privilege to be here. I want to internalize the link so that I feel it forever, whether I'm here or not. It's quick to take it in as a view: there it is. I could photograph it in a moment. But this is different. I want to be here, with it, in it, as a living connection. It has to take time, and it has to be prolonged. There are some places I've been, and when I see a photo of them, I know exactly where it is. I can feel the feeling of being there even though I know I'm not. I want this to be one of those places, but I don't know if I can make the connection or if it's something that just has to take me by surprise. Maybe I can do it with my sketchbook. I can look intently for an hour or more without it seeming like a strange thing to be doing. In fact, I've been here only a short time, and already, I can feel my forehead beginning to burn. I'd better find some shade. I'd better buy a hat. It's a shame there isn't a pool up here. It's a shame I don't have my room yet. I want to change out of these clothes, which feel contaminated by the flight. I want to wear something lighter. I do need to find some shade. I should have brought a novel up here with me. What was I reading on the plane? Michael Ayrton. I'd have to go in to get it. Are there other, shadier places to hang about? Downstairs maybe. I'm looking across the terrace – there's shade on the other side of it, but what's beyond the windows? They're shaded and look shuttered at the moment – floor-to-ceiling roller blinds. It must open up, but at the moment, the only part I can see open is the section where I came out. Up above the shutters, there's another terrace, and I can see a hat palely moving into and then out of sight. Somebody's about, but there isn't a way up to that terrace from here. I don't really want to read. I want to doze. There's nothing to lie on or lounge in, but there are chairs. I move one of them further into the shade and sit in it. I try to zone out the clutter, so it's just me and the acropolis here. I almost close my eyes.

24

On the roof terrace of the Megaron Hotel in Heraklion, Luke and Alekos are having breakfast with a view across the Venetian harbor to the sea. Swallows swoop with confidence beneath the awnings, turning up to land in their muddy little nests tucked almost out of sight. Luke is wearing a white tennis shirt with a laurel wreath embroidered by a machine on the left of his chest. His sunglasses are on the table. He has an omelet with bacon, mushrooms, a salad of mainly tomatoes, and a pile of toast. Alekos, in his loose-fitting smock-like shirt, looks wrong-footed when he sees it come to the table.

"You're hungry," he says, "We haven't been giving you proper breakfasts. I should have thought of it. English breakfasts are famous."

"I'd never eat like this at home," says Luke, "and if I did, we'd call it a Romanian breakfast. It's just a thing with hotels. I don't know why. You have too much to eat. It feels like it's all part of the fun. I ordered with two of us in mind. There's plenty here for both of us."

Luke is familiar with this sort of place from holidays with his parents, and it comes as no surprise to him that he can order in English. For him, it's more like being at home than it is at the Ziros house. Here, he's the host.

"I'll just have coffee," says Alekos, "and some toast." The water beyond the harbor shimmers. The light trembles. The swallows swoop. There's a gentle breeze.

"It's good being away from the house," says Alekos, "When you make me want to moan, I can moan."

"What goes on in the bedroom stays in the bedroom," says Luke, "Don't talk about it out here – or anywhere. You never know who's listening."

Alekos smiles and pours the coffee. He raises an eyebrow and tilts his head to one side. He opens his mouth but then thinks better of speaking.

"Don't," says Luke, earnestly in a stage whisper, on the edge of laughing.

They look into one another's eyes and smile.

In the library, Luke is hoping to find out how Sir Arthur Evans managed to buy his land – the site at Knossos. Alekos is the go-between, asking for odd little pamphlets and then skimming the text to look for information. Some of the documents are in English, and Luke can deal with them himself. There are large, sturdy tables, big enough for reading a newspaper spread out flat, and card-index drawers – ranks of dozens of them – to leaf through. This is local history, and the documents must be there somewhere, but Evans' own papers will be somewhere in Oxford. What Luke's hoping for are legal documents from this end to see what he did to get the land. Maybe they'll be in a lawyer's office, and maybe the lawyer's name will be mentioned somewhere here.

"Oh yes," says the archivist, an elderly man with a kind face who doesn't seem to have much energy, "You need to find the lawyer's name, and then we can find the papers."

It's going to take longer than Luke imagined, but then everything takes longer than Luke imagines. By the end of the day, things aren't exactly clear, but Luke now knows that it took Evans ten years to get his hands on the land so he could excavate it. He and Alekos are talking in the street and go to sit at a café table.

"It's more complicated than I thought," says Luke, "Schliemann wanted to excavate there; I knew that much. Things had been found there. I thought Evans bought the land to snatch it away from Schliemann, and now I know it wasn't like that at all. Schliemann wasn't outmaneuvered. He died. So, he must have been excavating while the land still belonged to the farmer. Maybe he'd already made the farmer an offer. He must have been paying him off. The farmer must have done well out of it – compared with farming."

"He must have been rich," says Alekos, "Schliemann."

"He discovered gold mines in America," says Luke, "and after that, he could do what he liked, which was archaeology. Impetuous, fanciful archaeology. He went to Mycenae, dug up a grave, and said he'd looked Agamemnon in the face, and then he did Troy and sent his wife out dressed in the jewels of Helen-whose-face-launched-a-thousand-ships.”

“And here he found the Minotaur,” says Alekos as a waiter appears – an undernourished guy, no longer young, who seems to have come outside expecting to smoke a cigarette. “Two beers,” says Alekos.

“Fix?” says the waiter.

Alekos nods.

“He didn’t find the Minotaur,” says Luke, “He was convinced he would find the Minotaur, but he died. Evans took over – years later – and found what he was determined to find. He wasn’t as rich as Schliemann, but he wasn’t short of money. He wanted to buy the land at a fair price. The farmer knew there was buried treasure there because of Schliemann and wanted to be paid for the buried treasure, so it took ten years of wheeling and dealing before Evans got the land. Ten years! I’m surprised the state didn’t just claim the land. You wouldn’t find the Acropolis being bought and sold.”

“Remember, Crete wasn’t part of Greece then,” says Alekos.

“I was forgetting,” says Luke.

“1913,” says Alekos, “every school-child knows.”

“You must teach me some proper Greek swear words,” says Loukas.

"They say if it had been discovered later, all the treasures would be in Athens now," says Alekos.

"I expect they're right," says Luke,

"Whatever he paid, it was a bargain," says Alekos.

"Cost him ten years of conniving and bribery and extortion," says Luke.

"He was English. I expect he wanted to do it all with lawyers, the way you do," says Alekos, "You know the type. He comes in with money and expects to be able to get what he wants. Look at the difference with Schliemann. All he needed was to get the farmer to like him. I bet he promised the farmer a share in the glory. With Evans, you don't get that. You sell him the land and get nothing except the money, so it had better be big money. You only get it once."

"I wish I understood the legal framework better," says Luke.

"Oh Loukas," says Alekos, "Why do you need the law? All you need is for everyone to fall in love with you. I'm on your side already. Learn from Schliemann. He must have been charming. The farmer let him start excavating even though he hadn't sold him the land. He must have said the farmer could have a share of anything that he found."

"You're so right," says Luke, "Schliemann's money came from gold mines. He went to California and found gold in the Gold Rush. Of course, he could tell tales about that and convince people that he could be trusted to find buried treasure. But what he actually found here was bits of stuff with writing on them that no one could understand then. I don't suppose the farmer was very excited about that."

"Not by the things," says Alekos, "but by Schliemann. He'd have seen how excited Schliemann was. Schliemann knew they were little signs of something big. His face would have lit up like someone in love. The farmer saw it."

Luke laughs quietly and looks at Alekos, entranced.

"How do you know these things?" he whispers.

"I see it in you," says Alekos, "and in me. I know your dig is going to work because you know it. I can see you believe in it, and I believe in you."

"I know there's something there in the ground," says Luke, "but I don't know quite how I know it. Maybe the important thing is that I've found you."

Of course, they would have kissed if they'd been in a less public place.

"Two beers," says Alekos. The waiter nods.

"You must do up a house in the village," says Alekos, "You're going to be here for years. Once you're a villager, you can do what you like."

"Is that expensive?" says Luke, "I suppose not."

"It's the same as with the land," says Alekos, "There's so many abandoned houses. You just move in and do it up, and it becomes yours. I'll help you."

"What if the owners come back?" says Luke.

"That doesn't happen," says Alekos, "If anyone ever did come and say that some house or other had been their family's, then they'd have to respect the fact that someone else had spent money and made the place habitable. If they wanted to move into the village, they'd start on another house. There's plenty of them. There's no documents in the villages. The towns are different."

"Can you sell a house?" says Luke.

"I don't see why not," says Alekos, with a shrug, "if you can find someone who'll give you money for it. Then you'd need somewhere else to live. No one in the village has any regular money. We're subsistence-people. You can stay with us for as long as you like, of course. We love the rent, but normally, we live by growing things and doing things for one another. If people want to make money, they move away. All the villages have empty houses. You know that."

"So I should move into an empty house," says Luke, "and have it done up. Are there people to employ?"

"Not in the village," says Alekos, "There would have been before the war. But we'll find someone. If you look like you've settled in the village, no one will be bothered by you doing the dig. They'll know who you are, and you'll show them what you find. They'll feel that they're part of your success."

"First things first," says Luke, "Where are we going to eat? Do you want to go back to the hotel?"

"The food doesn't taste of anything there," says Alekos, "but I like the place."

"The glamour," says Luke, as though he's joking, but for Alekos, the glamour is real. He's never stayed in a hotel before and never crossed the threshold of such a swanky place. With Luke, it seems like the natural thing to do. The doors just open. It's easy to feel comfortable there. The obstacle is feeling that you're allowed in in the first place, and that feeling comes with having the money to pay the bill they're going to give you.

"There'll be a taverna near the harbor," says Alekos, "We could eat properly there and then go up for a drink on the roof terrace."

"We should have that drink first," says Luke, "and take it from there. Let me introduce you to the Negroni."

25

It's only when I wake up that I realize I've been asleep. It's five fifteen. I go to the office and try the door, which opens. There's one person there. A youngish man, older than me, I'd say, with gold-rimmed spectacles, fairly long hair, and a droopy mustache.

"Hello," he says.

"Hello," I say, "I'm Ian Bell."

"Ah, the architect," he says, "I'm Dan. Daniel MacLeish. Deputy Director."

"You wrote to me," I say, and I feel a rush of relief and gratitude. It's the first sign I've had that anyone here is expecting me.

"You're staying here for two weeks, is it?" he says, "and then joining them on Crete."

"That's the idea," I say, "but it's three weeks here."

"That's fine," he says, "I'll show you your room – it's up one floor. Charles hasn't left yet. You should meet him."

"Charles?" I say.

"Winchester," he says, "The Director – you'll be with him on Crete."

"Oh yes," I say, "We haven't met yet."

"I'll tell him you're here," he says, "He'll want to meet you."

My room is a small study bedroom with a window overlooking the street. It feels familiar – institutional and old-fashioned – the bathrooms are across the corridor. I wonder why they paint everything pale grey. Maybe it's to stop dust from showing, but it makes the place feel dowdy and unloved. Of course, the location's brilliant – the view from the terrace tells me that – but otherwise, I might think I was in a student room in the UK before they started to give them their own bathrooms so they could let them for conferences.

"I'll leave you here," says Dan, "When you're ready, come back to the office, and I'll show you around."

It turns out, when I go to the office, that I have an invitation to dinner with the director.

"You're honored," says Dan, "That's not what normally happens. Everyone's away, you see. His wife's in the UK, and Charles is setting off for his dig tomorrow. All the others are at their digs. The artists have gone to be inspired by scenery or whatever. We've only got an epigrapher left. He works in the library. You can meet him if you want to."

"There was someone who opened the door when I arrived," I say.

"That was Cassie," he says, "She's my wife. You'll meet her again at dinner. A tie would be a good idea." He gestures to his neck. He's not wearing a tie himself at the moment.

Luckily, I packed one. A plain khaki tie with an open weave that might have been part of a military uniform and that doesn't look too dressy with summer clothes. It's too hot for a jacket, but maybe if a tie's expected, a jacket goes without saying. I've only brought one pair of shoes, desert boots, chosen for the excavation, not for looking smart in the city, but they're quite new, and they'll have to do. Nothing to be done about that. It feels at first like a job interview. I've already got the job, but Winchester wants to know the right decision's been made. Maybe he's just being considerate and helping me out with a meal on my first evening here.

26

"We could have breakfast sent up," says Loukas, "but even so, you'd better dress. We can't have food delivered with you looking like that."

He opens up the shutters, and it's very clearly day. I stretch and yawn. The sky is harshly bright in my eyes, so I close them.

"Why? How do I look?" I say. I feel relaxed and profoundly calm and in no hurry to break the spell. I'm tangled with the sheet, my face half in the pillow. Loukas quietly chuckles.

"You look debauched," he says, "You look like the Barberini faun. Now pull yourself together."

I half open my eyes and smile at him. I don't know what the Barberini faun is, but it sounds as if it's a good look. I'd like Loukas to get back into bed, dressed or not, but he's not open to persuasion; he sounds businesslike.

"I must go to the museum," he says, "You know I must. I'll go up and order my omelet while you have your shower. The roof is a good place to sit, and you'll have to behave yourself there."

27

The jacket was a good idea. Unnecessary but expected, and ceremoniously taken from me on arrival and hung up.

"We like ouzo here," says Winchester, "The Greeks dilute it with water, but we like it on the rocks. Try it. I think you'll find it very nourishing."

"Thank you," I say.

We take our drinks out on the director's terrace, which is a private personal garden. There are plants in metal tubs – the big cans that olive oil comes in here – a hibiscus plant with big red flowers. Jasmine. Roses. There's a small round table with a bowl of olives on it. They're passed around. I wonder what to do with the stones and keep them in my hand. I wonder whether to try to put them in my pocket. Winchester theatrically throws his away over the parapet, not in the least worried where they might land. He's sixtyish, red in the face, grey hair that's white at the temples, and he's quite lean. I don't know whether to follow suit and wait to see what the others do. Nobody else seems to like olives. I don't have the confidence to throw my stones. I don't think I've earned the right to do that yet. No one seems to notice. It seems like a minefield, but I don't know whether it is or not. The ouzo's good in the heat, the aniseed taste is sharp and refreshing, and the liquid goes cloudy as the ice melts, and it grows colder, milder, and easier to drink as the drink dilutes itself.

"Let's go to the table," says Winchester, "We have a waiter this evening. I hope you're impressed."

"Very smart," I say, thinking it's just someone who works at the school, and why would I be impressed by that? But his presence contributes to the formality of the occasion. There's a big glass case near the dining table, separating it from the main living room. It seems strange that it's there, and Winchester can see that I'm looking puzzled by it.

"That was Sir Alcuin's aquarium," says Winchester, "He used to keep octopuses in it. One at a time. They don't get on."

"Oh," I say, "That must have been quite something."

"He used to talk to them," says Winchester, "It was like a séance. They kept escaping, though. They could find their way from here to the bathroom and down the drain."

"Incredible," I say, unsure whether to believe him.

"Is there anything you want to do while you're here?" Winchester asks me.

"I haven't been before, so I should do the most obvious things first," I say. This prompts him to start telling me things about the principal monuments. They're in my lectures, so he's saying completely familiar things. I know the facts. It's the experience of what the places feel like that I want. I hope he might say something interesting if I let him go on, but he doesn't. The waiter puts a plate of tomato soup in front of each of us. I wonder if it's come from a can.

"I was thinking I'd try to get to Eleusis," I say, thinking that might nudge him toward raising his game. To judge by his appearance, if he's indulged himself, it's been in moderation. He has the primness of someone who's always held himself in check: correct and very proper but dull. The whole apartment's like that. Everything here is what ought to be here – bookshelves with proper serious-looking books, sober furniture that might have been inherited, pictures that might be family portraits. All beyond reproach, but with no sign of personal idiosyncrasy about it that might have made me warm to him, and yet I'd like him to like me, so I listen politely.

"Ah, the mysteries," he says.

"I was looking at Sir William Gell's drawings in the British Museum," I say, "He walked from here to Eleusis and kept a notebook. I thought it might be interesting to compare it today."

"You wouldn't want to do that," he says, "It's all industry now. You wouldn't find your way. There's nothing to recognize."

"Maybe the hills in the panoramas," I say.

"I doubt you can even see the hills," he says.

"Oh," I say, "but is Eleusis worth visiting?"

"It's easy enough to get there," says Dan, "There's a bus. There's a good Byzantine church nearby at Dafni if you're interested."

"Thank you," I say.

"There's a small museum," says Winchester, "but you should see the museums in Athens first."

Cassie hasn't said anything at all. She looks demure and seems fascinated by the tomato soup. The ties the two men wear haven't been chosen for the way they look but for what they signal, and I'm not quite sure what that is. They look formal enough but might have come from old school uniforms, and maybe I've failed by not wearing a tie that signals a school or a regiment. Nothing to be done about that. There's a settled game in play, and the others know how to play it.

But here's the thing about Eleusis: the initiates there were drugged and fell asleep. When they woke up in the dark, they saw apparitions. They were convinced that they'd died and were coming-to in the afterlife. They met spirits, and at a climactic moment, some shutters in the roof fell open, so the whole space was flooded with dazzling light. This was all long before there was any stage lighting. I bet there was music, too. It must have been an intense and overwhelming experience, a total work of art, and the initiates were sworn to secrecy about the rite, on pain of death, so the accounts had to be pieced together from things that were obliquely said, and maybe the guesses were all wide of the mark, but there was something extraordinary going on – something really amazing – , and the point of going to Eleusis isn't to look round the museum and be disappointed by it or regret that the temple isn't standing. The point is to stand at the spot where these things happened and be thrilled by them in the imagination, to feel a connection with them because you're there in the actual place, even if you can't be initiated these days. There's something human and vital that they were waking up to in that place, and Winchester shows no sign of knowing about it or being curious about it, still less responding to it. I don't want to know if the museum's any good. I want to be struck by a thunderbolt from the distant past – a crackle of electricity to tell me something thrilling happened here in the minds of men. Maybe I haven't passed his tests, but I'm sure he's failed mine. I'll be polite, of course, but I won't expect too much from him.

The waiter takes the soup plates away and brings us each a slice of roast beef with mashed potato.

"I'll be leaving for Crete in the morning," says Winchester, "I imagine you'll fly, will you?"

"I thought I'd do some island-hopping," I say, "see some sights and arrive by ferry."

"I wonder which port that will be," he says.

"I haven't worked it out yet," I say.

"Ah," he says, "You see, the problem is, there's no way to get a message through except by post. There's not many phones. The mayor has one in the village near the site, and we have our name down for one at the site, but we've not yet been seen as the most deserving case. We're not there most of the time. Locals take priority. Doreen will give you the number in the village in case there's an emergency."

I don't like the sound of this. He must see the anxiety in my face.

"People on the island are good at offering lifts," he says, "but whichever port you come in at, there'll be a bit of a walk. If you leave your bags somewhere, we can come and pick them up."

"It's his first time in Greece," says Dan, "It might be a bit of a challenge."

Again, I feel a wave of gratitude.

"Well," says Winchester, "You're most likely to arrive at Heraklion early in the morning. There's a big hotel near the waterfront, the Megaron. It's a good place to wait. If you're there at 12 noon on Saturday the third of August, someone will find you. How about that?"

"That's tremendously reassuring," I say, "Thank you." It's a precise appointment, four weeks away. Three weeks in the institute, one-week island-hopping, ending up at 12 noon at the Megaron Hotel.

"You'll find timekeeping's a bit relaxed on the island," says Winchester, "An hour adrift counts as being on time. If someone's two hours late, they don't apologize. We try to do better than that. Make sure you're there at noon, or your lift might have been and gone."

"Is there any reading I should do before I get there?" I say.

"You won't be expected to know anything," says Winchester, "We want you to come to the site and draw what's there. The last time it was surveyed, there wasn't much to see, so at the moment the plans just have trees on them and contour lines. Things have progressed. We have some building lines to plot, so we thought an architect would be appropriate. We don't need you to know about history."

"I'm teaching architectural history, though," I say, "so I'll be wanting to find out."

"You must start with the Parthenon," says Cassie, breaking her silence.

"That goes without saying," says Dan.

The waiter brings a fruit salad, clearly from a can. The little cubes of peach and pear and one wan red cherry each are all too familiar from when I was a teenager. Is this chic in Greece? or is Winchester importing comfort food?

"I'll leave you to it now," says Winchester, "I have an early start. Dan – help our guest to a brandy – you know where everything is." The evening winds down, and we stay on our best behavior. The brandy is Greek, not French. We go outside with it and have an unobstructed view of the

Acropolis, floodlit against the hazy night sky. No stars. It's still very warm.

"The pollution looks beautiful at night," says Dan.

28

As a local, I don't have to pay to go into the museum, but Loukas does. It's only just reopened, newly arranged after the bombs. The rooms are spacious and well-lit, and I feel proud that it's here.

"There's something not right about it," says Loukas, standing in front of a big mural of young men with muscular thighs and slim waists, carrying big pots, one hand underneath to take the weight, the other on the handle to balance it.

"Why? What's wrong?" I say. These are the things that everyone comes to see. I've grown up knowing that they're wonders from the dawn of Greek civilization and the envy of every nation in the world. You can't go around saying there's something wrong with them, but Loukas has the look of someone who's troubled. "Don't you like them?

"Oh, they're lovely," he says, "They're amazing. Spectacular."

"What's the problem then?" I say.

"It's just that they're too good to be true," he says, "Much too good to be true. When you start paying attention to which bits are genuine, you start to realize it's not very much. It's hardly anything. They're lovely things, but I don't trust them. Not the first impression of them."

"Why? What's wrong?" I say.

"Well," he says, "What are we looking at? This all looks very fresh, and at first, you think, 'Wow! It's way ahead of its time! It could have been done yesterday!' but actually, when you look at it, it was done yesterday. It's all new paint. Look for the old dark bits – the lumpy bits. They're original. You see, there's some feet over there, but you can hardly make them out. There are some corners of skirts. I don't think there are any jugs, and there are whole figures added in, including that – er – arresting figure of the woman with her tits out. If you take away all the modern painting, you don't have much of a museum."

"That's my heritage you're insulting," I say.

"No, no, no," he says, "I'm not insulting anything except the English archaeologists. They've been doing dodgy things with your heritage. The original things are precious, and it's amazing that there's any sort of painted walls survived from way back then. I just wonder what they were really like. Everything here's over-restored when you look closely. Look at that bull's head. When do you think it was actually made? It looks like new – so fine, the gold so shiny. You're not telling me that's over 3,000 years old."

"It is!" I say, "That's what the label says."

"That's what's wrong," he says. He peers at it more closely, "OK. I'll believe the main casting is ancient, and you can see where it's been worked – it's astonishing – but then they've re-gilded it so it looks like new."

"You're being unfair. If the museum only had the dark, lumpy bits in it, no one would come," I say.

"Quite so," he says, "There's good reason to make restorations, but it should say, 'Here's a painting done in 1935 based on an idea suggested by a tiny bit of something over 3,000 years old'. We shouldn't come away thinking we've seen the real thing, but most people do. But look at these. These are real."

They're seal stones – pale stones about the size of a fingernail, displayed in cabinets behind glass. It would be easy to walk past them without noticing them.

"They're so small they haven't broken," he says, "but look how fine the detail is."

You need a magnifying glass to see them properly, and they're much clearer in the blow-up photos. They are amazing.

"What are they?" I say.

"You'd press them on to cooling wax, or maybe lead, to leave a picture in the seal, so you'd know who sealed the thing. They'd have been expensive things. Only important people would have had them."

Each one has a little scene on it – figures dancing, animals fighting – that sort of thing.

"The stones aren't really the things they'd look at," says Loukas, "They were made to produce the impressions. Look: they've done them in plaster here."

"Ha!" I say, "We get a better idea by not looking at the original."

"Just look at them!" he says, "They're incredible. Could you make something that detailed that small?"

"No," I say, "I couldn't. Maybe a jeweler could. I suppose they must have had magnifying glasses."

"They didn't know how to make glass till later," says Loukas, which seems to settle it, but a bit later, I notice something that looks like a lens. It's rock crystal that's been polished up.

"Look at this! They did have lenses," I say.

"Wow!" says Loukas, "That's extraordinary! I bet there weren't many of them. I've never seen anything like that before. That's made my day."

"There couldn't have been many craftsmen doing those fine stones," I say, "How many people could have had that sort of skill in one generation? You can share a lens around a group. You wouldn't need it every day. And once you have the lens, you can pass it down from father to son. It's not the sort of thing that wears out." Loukas looks at me as if I've said something unexpected and profound. He doesn't say anything, though. I feel like I've won an argument, but we weren't having an argument. There are lots of people here by the time we leave. It was good that we came early.

"I'm really glad we spent time with the seal stones," says Loukas, "They're the things that really matter here. The rest of the stuff here gives me a feeling that it's kind of bogus."

"And the crystal lens," I say, proud to have noticed it.

"Yes, that too," says Loukas, "That's a good thing. That's an amazing thing. That's the star of the show."

"You're going to hate Knossos," I say, "We shouldn't go there. It will take an hour to walk, and the day's hot now. We'll both be miserable."

"We can take a bus," says Loukas, "What the heck. We can take a taxi. I want to be familiar with the place. It's my warning about what not to do to an archaeological site."

<h1 style="text-align:center">29</h1>

I've arrived at Heraklion by bus, desperately short of sleep. I didn't know the arrangements on the boat and didn't book a seat to sleep in. The moon was shining, and the sea was spectacular as we chugged along. More than one dolphin came to see what we were doing there. I sat on the deck, and other people, probably students, who, like me, lacked foresight or money or both, were sitting drowsily or leaning against one another, hoping to sleep. Everyone was silent. I didn't know I'd slept until I looked at my watch and saw how the hour had jumped ahead. The day hadn't dawned when we landed, and the buses had their headlamps on. Now I'm in the heat of the day, and my body's telling me to go to sleep. There's the Hotel Megaron, prominent and expensive-looking. My appointment isn't until the day after tomorrow, so I'll look in a back street for I place I can afford to stay in. I'll do that first so I can drop my bag there, sauntering past shops and cafés, peering down narrow alleys for likely-looking places.

30

On the way to Knossos, we rehearse the story of the Minotaur. Asterion – born of the stars – to Minos and his crazy nymphomaniac queen.

"It's all Schliemann's doing – and then Evans's – the linking of this place, Knossos, with the Cretan legends. If you think about what we saw in the museum, what was there that would connect? There's some bulls, but no bull-human hybrids on show. There are no ancient images of a Minotaur in the museum. None at all. If you take away all the restoration work and start again, I wonder where you end up – if you're not determined to make the link with the old stories. Suppose the stories were about a different place – one that hasn't been found yet. Suppose you tried to work out what was going on at Knossos just based on the complete images we get on the seal stones. What would we have then?"

I can't do more than shrug. He's not expecting an answer from me. Actually, being at Knossos has never excited me. There's crowds of people, and it's like a playground with low school buildings around it, built in stone with concrete columns and beams. I know it's important and all that, so I don't say much. Of course, the stories are real. I know the stories are real. I know there have been times when I've felt the Minotaur wasn't far away. It might be breathing down my neck, but it's not happening now. I've never had that feeling at Knossos. When did I have that feeling? When I was alone, I suddenly fearful, wanting to go home or at least be with other people. In the lemon groves, where I couldn't see far and there's no sense of direction – a moment's panic. In the pine forest where, suddenly, the ground shelved away, and I was looking into the depths of a gorge. By the sea in winter when a storm blew in, and in the rain, I walked past the turn for the path back and lost my way – in a place that was familiar enough but where I felt bewildered. The Minotaur was there then. I know it as a living presence, not as something in the museum. Now, I have my own companion monster instead. Matthias appears and wants to undermine me. He's my Minotaur. Beautiful Asterion turned terrible but wanted to be loved. He's not with me now. I'm just remembering. I'm wide awake. I'm just remembering the Minotaur. I'm not feeling it at all. Loukas is here at Knossos, really in the place, but my mind is going for a wander as he repeats himself.

31

Here's the Hotel Alpha. One star. It's kind of terrible, but it will do. The shower is along a dingy corridor, but there's a wash basin in the room. It's small, barely twice the width of the single bed, on a corner at the first-floor level. There are two large windows on adjacent walls. I open the windows and the shutters, and it feels like I'm sitting on a balcony in the street. The arresting thing about the room is the frantic wallpaper, which turns out not to be wallpaper at all but a pattern that's been repeatedly printed on the wall with a carved block. The wall was white. The printed paint is dark blue. It's an abstract pattern, rather sinuous, and it's vigorous and insistent. It's been printed on the front face of the pipes that run through the room. There's a kind of mania here. The door's thin. With the windows open, I can hear everything from the street – mainly voices and motors. Goodness knows if I'll be able to sleep. I'm not sure that the noisiness of the wallpaper will go away when I close my eyes. I have a shower, try to doze for a while, and then set off with my Blue Guide to find the bastions.

I want to see the tomb of Nikos Kazantzakis, so I find my way there. The Blue Guide says very little. It tells me I'm on the Martinengo Bastion, but I do not know what that means. Kazantzakis died in 1957. The inscription – written with a stick in wet concrete, not carved – means "I hope for nothing. I fear nothing. I am free." The Blue Guide writer hasn't been inspired by him, but I feel inspired by the tomb. It's very raw – unfinished stones, a stark timber cross that seems already to be distressed by the harsh sunlight – its grain standing out like on the doors of neglected old farm buildings. I think he's saying that he's free from religion – doesn't hope for heaven, doesn't fear hell – but yet it seems a profoundly religious place. From here, I can see the roofs of the town and see how it's positioned between the sea and the pale mountains that rise up inland in the distance. There's a wild rose growing over the concrete block – which might be too pretty – but it's wild and has thorns, and its flowers are small. He's at home here, but in exile – not in a churchyard – or if not exiled at least alone – set apart – standing with geology and the elements to see out over the heads of the everyday goings-on of the town, lost in the alleys and under roofs, while I see the horizon and the mountains and I'm in a place where gods were born and myths took shape.

32

"This is supposed to be where King Minos held court 3000 years ago," says Loukas, "but you'd think we were in the foyer of a 1920s cinema. It's lovely to look at, but old? Come off it. When was the reconstruction done? Oh. In the 1920s."

"It's good to hear some heresy round here," says a gentle voice so close to my ear that, for a moment, I wonder if it's from inside my head. I have an uncanny feeling that this might be a new demon. It's a young woman, very slight, dressed in dusty colors that might have been chosen as camouflage against the stone here. Her eyes are startling – the color of a straw hat – but her arrival has been so quiet that we haven't noticed that she's there. I don't want to take the chance that I'm imagining her, so I hold back and wait for Loukas to speak. In fact, though, Loukas doesn't say anything. He looks at her, then at me, and he smiles at both of us.

"I've just started working here," she says, "Most people believe what they're told. I've been told off. Apparently, I've been causing confusion."

"What are your ideas?" says Loukas.

"Oh," she says, "I don't know that I have ideas. So far, I just have questions."

"Such as," says Loukas.

"Well," she says, "here they'd have you believe it's a throne room with baths in it. But the floor is made of gypsum, including the baths. If it had been used regularly, there would be signs of wear. It's a very soft stone. The builders knew their stones. They wouldn't have used gypsum for a floor that was ever going to be used. It's like deciding to plaster your floor. It's crazy for anything that actually gets used."

"So why was it built?" says Loukas.

"I can't tell you," she says, her gold seahorse earrings glinting as she moves her head. They match the color of her eyes when they catch the light, "but I can tell you it wasn't used. It's the sort of thing you might do for a stage set. But this is supposed to be a palace that would have been in use for maybe hundreds of years before the civilization died out."

"That doesn't make sense," says Loukas.

"Correct," says the woman, "I've heard it suggested that this isn't a palace for the living but a necropolis. So then you might have a symbolic throne room waiting for the king of the underworld to come and preside. It could be that."

"What," says Loukas, "some kind of ghost palace?"

"If you like," she says.

"What do you think about the bulls?" says Loukas, "We're noticing a distinct lack of Minotaur images. Is there even a tiny seal stone with an image of the Minotaur? I don't think there is."

"Oh," says the woman, "They miss the point. They get excited about the bulls. I think the bulls were just sport. There were snakes in the religion here, and they've picked that up, but I think they made a big mistake with the marine life. They think the octopuses and dolphins are just decoration."

"And they're not?" says Loukas.

"You know they're not," she says. Then she hesitates and turns to me, "No. It's you! You know they're not."

I don't know what to say. She looks me straight in the eye, and she knows this isn't the time.

"Of course, they do work as decoration," she says to Loukas more than to me, "but think how much this decoration costs. One of those big octopus pots would cost more than most people who lived in the Bronze Age could ever scrape together. If you're doing something of that scale and complexity, you don't just put things on it to make it pretty. Your decoration means something."

"What would it mean?" says Loukas, "An octopus."

"It would take some work to find out," says the woman, who glances in my direction again, "but we can educate our intuition."

"If it was a burial place," I say, "wouldn't there be some bodies or at least a few bones in the pots?"

"Ah," she says, "there's a story that Evans had all the bones carted away in dozens of wheelbarrows before he started the excavation. I don't know if there's any truth in the story, but it's a story I've heard. Nowadays, you'd do all sorts of tests on the bones. You could learn a lot from them. But he just saw them as something that was getting in the way. He wanted to find a labyrinth, so that's what he found. He wanted to find the Minotaur, and there he failed, but he did make the bulls here very visible and restored ambiguous little things into spectacular exhibits. He destroyed a lot of evidence. Threw bones away. Poured concrete over real remains. You wouldn't be allowed to do that now."

"Who are you, by the way," said Loukas, "I'm Luke Zimbrean. This is Alexander Ziros."

"How do you do," says the woman, "My name is Alice Cyprian."

33

On Saturday, I arrive cautiously early for the rendezvous so I can settle near the Megaron's lobby with a book and have at least a coffee and maybe a snack if they'll bring food to that part of the hotel. They're very accommodating and hide my rucksack away so I look more respectable. Noon comes and goes, and now it starts to feel as if I've been here long enough. I order another coffee. What if no one comes to find me? Do I go back to the Hotel Alpha? Can I find something better that isn't ruinously expensive? Maybe I should think about taking a bus to the west of the island. That would be the thing. If no one shows up, I can make my own way to the dig. I came through Chania on my way here, so I know I could get back to the bus station there. If I went there, maybe things would become clearer. I have my prescription sunglasses ready and my broad-brimmed straw hat that I was told I'd need. People come and go, dressed more for the beach than the town, and in my own mind, I look more like the kind of person the hotel was designed for than anyone else here, except the staff, who seem to be happy to accept me as a fixture for as long as I want to stay here.

"You must be the architect," says a thin young woman with freckles and mousy sun-streaked hair.

"Ian Bell," I say.

"Jem Broadbent," she says, "Sorry I'm late. In fact, round here, this isn't late, but I did intend to be on time. It's just that it turns out to be impossible."

"My bag's at reception," I say, wondering whether or not that was an apology.

"We can come back for it," she says, "First, we have to find some food. The car's parked a bit away. We can come back here in the car to pick up your things. What do you like to eat? We need some new ideas. There's something like a riot brewing. There was an incident yesterday."

I haven't had to cook anything since I arrived. Since I set out from the Lantern, I've eaten in tavernas and had occasional conversations with tourists.

"Someone," I say, "told me about some British people with a restaurant here who were fined for not putting enough cucumber in their salad."

"Cucumber!" says Jem, "brilliant idea! What goes with cucumber?"

"Well," I say, "round here it goes with tomato, a little raw onion, a few olives, and some feta cheese – and olive oil, of course."

"Genius," says Jem, "Let's get those things for a start, except for the olive oil. We don't like olive oil. There'll be some fruit, and we always get custard creams."

34

Loukas and I are making our way along a narrow street – more of an alley, really – in the old part of Heraklion. There's something spectral about the light. The buildings don't seem solid. There's a shop window in among shuttered houses at a corner that might look like a dead-end, except there's sunlight streaming in at that point. I'm noticing reflections in the window – the render that needs re-doing, the shutters that were painted a while ago. It's old paint that doesn't peel. It just loses its color. Loukas has stopped and is looking in, holding his hands up like blinkers by his eyes to try to see past the reflections.

"Galanakis," says the sign-board, which might have been done in the 1930s. It would have looked modern then.

"Light-drawing," says Loukas, reading a label.

"You're over-translating," I say,

"You mean photography."

"I like it as 'light-drawing,'" he says, "It makes you think about what's going on."

There's an abundance of photos on display – weddings, portraits, groups of children, solemn faces, strong chiaroscuro. The pictures all belong together: they have a certain look about them, grave and still and roundly present.

It's not that the sitters have anything in common – they're all quite distinct in their own way, but the images all seem serious and monumental. It's something to do with the way the light falls. It makes them look more solid than the buildings in the street. The settings are different from one another – here, in a schoolroom, there is a forest or a stagey painted backdrop. No one's smiling. They were relaxed, maybe attentive, maybe not. When the shutter clicked, they hardly knew it.

"They're really something," says Loukas, "Look at those twins."

The twins, sullen teens, are dressed alike in baggy dark dresses and plaited hair, each holding a homemade bouquet. They have a lumpish, almost beauty, gazing at the camera as if they're waiting for the photographer to ask them to pose, but he's turned them into an implacable presence. In another picture, a small child in a traditional costume stares steadily and looks as if he could kill. His hat sits oddly on his head and pushes his ears so they stick out. Then there's a group of six languid young men in woodland, one of them holding a violin to his chin. They are carrying or wearing leafy twigs. The violinist is wearing a peaked cap. Five of them are looking at the camera. The sixth is in profile, with a broad-brimmed straw hat on his knee and the leafiest bunch of all at his buttonhole. They're not dressed in their best clothes, and their shoes are scuffed and muddy. Four of them have waistcoats. It has the gravity of a group portrait – it's not a snapshot – but why was this occasion so seriously recorded?

And what were they doing? I watch Loukas by looking at his reflection in the window glass. He's absorbed with the images and doesn't notice me.

"I want to meet this photographer," says Loukas, "He's good. Let's see if he'll do us a portrait."

He opens the door, which makes a bell jingle. The shop is empty. To the right, there's a mirror covering the whole wall. Straight ahead and wrapping around to the left, there's a floor-to-ceiling photograph of woodland, with three chairs in front of it. There's a table with a book and a telephone on it, and a woman comes out from behind the woodland, sits at the table, and says, with a smile,

"Hello. Can I help you?" She has a neat appearance and a cool, professional manner.

"My friend is very impressed with the photos in the window," I say, "and he wonders if he can have his portrait made."

"Of course," she says, "We can make an appointment." She opens the book. Today's page seems to be blank.

"Could it be now?" I say.

"He's in the darkroom at the moment," she says, "but you can come back later." She gestures to the empty page, "Whenever you like, but let's say a time, so he knows when to be here."

"What time should we say?" I say to Loukas, and he's looking in the mirror. I meet his gaze there.

"Look at us," he says, and we see ourselves against the background of woodland, and already we're almost in a photo, "We should go and get a haircut. Would he be open if we came back after that?"

"I'm sure he'll be open if we make the appointment," I say.

"Then let's say one-thirty," he says, "There'll be somewhere round here, won't there."

35

It's quite late in the afternoon when Jem and I arrive at the site, and the others are pleased to see us – especially to see what we've brought.

"Chris, Toby, Phoebe, James," says Jem by way of introduction. They know who I am. I instantly forget their names, and they seem quite interchangeable. A polite and good-natured pack of nicely brought-up young people, happy to oblige and all with the same ideas about what to wear: flimsy vests and shorts. They go in for baseball hats rather than straw hats like mine, and their hair, however, it started out, has been lightened by the sun, so they look like they've all had the same streaks done. There's a long table that would seat twenty or more. We're in a long, low building with a verandah along one side that overlooks the site. The director's house has two or three rooms at one end, and Winchester must be in there.

"Does the director eat with us?" I ask.

"He does when the food's good enough," says Chris, who's younger than me, lean and tanned, like all the others. They're all volunteers with hopes of academic careers of one sort or another. I'm the only one who actually has a post, so I find I have some standing in this little community.

"Toby," says Jem, "Can you show Ian to his room?"

"Sure. This way," he says, and he leads the way, his sandals flapping against the boarded floor, to a room that's furnished with two pairs of bunk beds, "The showers and lavs are down the end. They're easy enough to find."

"Is anyone else going to be in here?" I say.

"No. This room's for you," says Toby, "Once upon a time, there must've been some idea of packing people in, but now the workers are in the village, so we have a room each."

"Who are these workers?" I say.

"Oh, they're Greek," says Toby, "They turn up in the morning, and we tell them what to do. They're helpful, but they don't say much. I'll leave you here to unpack a bit. Come and find us when you're ready."

When it's time for an aperitif, Winchester comes out of his house and is instantly the center of attention. Phoebe pours everyone an ouzo.

"Splendid," says Winchester, giving his tumbler a shake so the ice rattles, and he watches the liquid go cloudy around the clear cubes, "Bottoms up." He's dressed in pale khaki shorts and a patterned short-sleeved shirt that makes me think of pajamas. He's had a shower and looks a bit disheveled. He seems like a benign grandfather here. He's not as stiff as he was in Athens. He sits with his drink at the end of the table, and there's some olives in a bowl. The habit of throwing olive stones away comes more easily here. Maybe when he throws them off the terrace in Athens, he's imagining his domain here. There are rather good chairs round the table – traditional, with rush seats, nicely made, and the table itself is sturdily built. Along the verandah, there are roller shutters – all the way along – and they're all up at the moment. They'll drop when we go to secure the place, but presumably, they're open for the summer while the building's in use. It's a neat arrangement. The place is well-designed. The table's in the one big space, which goes right through the building from front to back. Against the back wall, there's a counter with two sinks and a gas hob, and a run of cupboards and drawers beneath it, including two fridges. On the wall above the cupboards, there's a pinboard with a calendar and rotas for this and that, and to the right of it, centrally placed, there's a substantial framed photo of two young men. They're maybe eighteen, dressed alike but not in uniform – tweed jackets with different patterns, open-necked shirts with big collars spread wide over the collars of the jackets.

"We bought some sausages," says Jem, "Ian's a genius. Full of ideas."

"I'm really not," I say, and I mean it, "it's just that I had some sausages at Monemvasia. They were very good. They served them with lemon to squeeze over them."

"That sounds strange," says Toby.

"Just try it," I say.

"I bought lemons," says Jem, who seems to have been lacking in inspiration to a quite remarkable degree, "And … tomatoes!"

"At least it's going to taste of something tonight," says Winchester quietly. He looks at me with an expression that's so serious it might possibly be a joke, "There were some issues with the food yesterday."

"So I hear," I say.

"Who's on mosquito duty this evening?" he says.

There are mosquito spirals to light – they give off a protective gas as they burn.

"We light them before we put the lights on," Winchester says, and I look out and see the light beginning to fade from the always-cloudless sky. "I'll show you in the morning what we need you to do. You'll be OK working on this table?"

"Yes," I say, "This looks fine." I can tape the drawings to the tabletop and run a T-square along the edge – it looks like a good straight edge, and that's all I need from it. Then, I can plot points using a scale rule and compasses. It should work. "I'll work down the other end – it looks as if that never gets used."

"That's right," he says, "These days, the diggers prefer to stay in the village most of the time. We only ever use this end of it eating. Sometimes, it's used for sorting pottery shards, but that's for a specialist. At the moment, we're just gathering the pottery and putting the pieces in the drawers over there."

"Why did the living accommodation get built here?" I say, "Wouldn't it make sense for everyone to be in the village?"

"Two reasons," he says, sounding well-rehearsed on this issue, "One: for security. It's good to have someone here night and day while we're digging in case something valuable turns up. The word might spread. Two: when it was built, there was no plumbing in the village. They have it now because we brought it in, but honestly, it was unspeakable."

"Noisome?" I say.

"Unspeakable," he says, pulling a face and then going on hastily, "It's not like that anymore. The village is prospering. You should go take a look one day. We put up a village hall. They call it the megaron – the Zimbrean Megaron – they've turned it into a café of sorts." There's a hint of his eyes rolling as if they've missed the point, like the people who used to keep coal in the bath.

"I'd like to see it," I say, "Maybe tomorrow."

"Sausages!" says Jem.

"Hurrah!" says Toby. James has made the salad. There's a plastic container by the sinks with a tap on it that dispenses low-grade wine.

"Do you have any aubergine recipes?" says Jem.

"Not really," I say, "You can do moussaka if you have an oven."

"No oven," says Chris.

"Then you'd fry them," I say, "they absorb olive oil. You've discovered olive oil?"

"We don't use it," says Jen.

"You should. It's good for you," I say, "They use it all the time here. They pour it over vegetables when we'd melt butter on them at home. They fry chips in it."

"Chips! Could we make chips?" says Toby.

"If you're prepared to use olive oil," I say, "It sounds as if you haven't been in tavernas much."

It astonishes me that I'm being treated like an expert after my very brief exposure to the place.

"No. We stayed at the Lantern in Athens and then came here," says Toby.

"We can't afford to eat in restaurants all the time," says Phoebe. She looks unhealthily thin.

Winchester, on the other hand, looks very comfortable and settled. He's not overweight, despite his apparent indolence. His hair is grey and combed over, so it's not too clear how far it has receded. He wears glasses for reading and has a pair on the table beside him. I wear glasses all the time, except very occasionally when I'm doing close work. Taking off my short-sight glasses is like putting a strong magnifying glass there. It's no good for seeing normally, but

I can see every carefully placed spot of printer's ink in a published photo.

"How long have you been coming here?" I say.

"Well," says Winchester, "I set it up, so I've been coming here for as long as it's been here to come to. It's over thirty years now."

"It's a young team," I say, "Do they keep coming back?"

"Oh, people come and go," says Winchester, "There was a lot of excitement early on when we found the tholos, and in those days, there were hopes that we'd find some significant treasures," He took a swig of his ouzo, "but we can see now that what we have is an architectural site. There's plenty to uncover, as you'll see, but we're only getting a few small finds. What we're doing – methodically – is sampling the soil and taking that to the lab in Athens. If you count the pollen grains and analyze them, you can tell quite a lot about who was here, what they were cultivating, that sort of thing. And, of course, as we go, we're finding walls that are definitely old. That's where you come in. We're reaching a stage where they need to be plotted so we can understand what's going on."

36

I'm the one who has to find the barber. I know they're around and about, but I've never paid attention. I've never been to one. Mum normally cuts my hair, and she's the one who says when it's time. I've never taken the decision to have a haircut. They feel like things that just happen to me. I feel suddenly self-conscious about my appearance. I try to see myself in shop window reflections. I'm really scruffy. My clothes look wrong. They're homemade and don't have the look of the smart shop-bought clothes that everyone wears in the towns. Loukas's shirts have labels on them.

"I should buy a new shirt for the photo," I say, thinking we'll have the money now there's rent coming in, but that, too, is something I've never done before.

"Your shirt's fine," says Loukas, "You look great in it."

"But it doesn't feel right," I say, "Yours is so much better."

"That's not true at all. This is very ordinary. Yours is made by hand. In England, at a shop, I'd have to pay much more for your shirt than mine." But he can see I'm not happy, and there's shops around that would sell me a shirt. "I know. Let's try each other's on. That might work for the photo. We'll buy you a shirt if you want, but there's no need for the photo."

"Should we go back to the hotel?" I say, but Loukas has taken off his shirt right there in the street and slipped it over his head with the buttons done up. I do the same, and before you know it, there we are, cross-dressed, as it were, as one another, laughing at the silliness and feeling of abandon, the recklessness of the impulse. At the barber's, feeling slightly giddy, we have our hair shaved short as if we're starting in the army. My face is still the same, but with the severe trim – electric clippers – and the machine-made shirt, I'm feeling more sophisticated. We have a shave, too, so our faces are raw and smooth and tender to the touch, and there's a cologne that seems to be part of what's going on. There are people waiting for haircuts on a row of chairs, and stepping off the cutting-chair with its levers and hydraulic pistons, I smile, half expecting a round of applause. The barber flourishes the cloth that's been draped over me to catch the clippings, like a matador flourishes a cape, inviting admiration. There's a big pile of my hair on the floor, less of Loukas's. Loukas looks neat and dapper, and the matching cuts make us look like brothers. Something's happened to unite us, something intimate that can go on in public, something superficial that suggests what's going on within and helps my feelings catch up with the change that's overtaking me – and not only me.

37

In the morning, I wake up quite early. I lie dozing, piecing together what I can see with my memory of where I am – my sense of the room. It's dark, and at first I could be anywhere. I have a sense of a window to my right, with a lightproof curtain hanging over it. But light from the street should be finding its way round the edges. No. I'm in the hotel with shutters on the windows, but no sounds from the street. I can hear some mumbling voices and then some footsteps of bare feet padding past. No. I'm at the stoa in one of the four beds, a door facing me and a shuttered window behind me. The sense of the space is secure. It's too warm for bedding but cooler than it was when I went to sleep. I'll need to turn on a light to see the time, but people are stirring. Of course, I didn't pack a dressing gown – who would? – so boxers and tee-shirt will have to be OK for visiting the bathroom.

The electric light by the sinks is on. They're making coffee in the kitchen area. There are tea bags, but only evaporated milk or milk-powder, which don't taste right in tea, so instant coffee's the better bet, even if it isn't really coffee. I have a peach with it and an industrially produced biscuit. I sit at the table and look out across the site as the sun comes up and rakes the ground with rich golden light, showing up every bump with unbelievably long shadows for a moment and then, in moments, becoming normal and bright. Around the site, there are trees – mainly dark-leaved citrus, but also some olives, paler and more delicate-looking. At the top of the slope behind the stoa, there are pines and cypresses, which are much taller, but the crop-trees are low, and from here, you can see over the top of them and the land gently shelves to the sea, which looks darker as the sky brightens.

"They're here," says Chris, calling out so everyone can hear, and the little group makes busy little movements to tidy up. They'd brought their notebooks with them to breakfast – and their baseball hats.

"Are you coming to meet them?" says Jem.

"Later," I say, "I'm waiting for Winchester. He's going to show me round," and he appears a moment later as if he'd been waiting for the students to go. We go down three steps from the verandah to the earth of the site. There's a well-trodden path that descends to a stone square with a square brass plaque set in it. It looks like a gravestone, and the plaque has a cross incised across it and a date, 1950.

"This is the place to start," says Winchester, "X marks the spot. It's our datum point for the surveys."

I look up the slope and see that the stoa is aligned with it.

"Is that due south?" I ask.

"It is," says Winchester, "We stretch string to set up the grid when we need to. You'll find everything you need in the cupboard. There's a theodolite if you want it, but our surveyors have been more interested in the tape measures and string. Tent pegs, too, if you have a use for them."

The site is fairly clear, with one or two trees, quite a few scrubby bushes, and a lot of scorched sage plants that release a powdery perfume when you brush past them. There's a perimeter fence – just simple chain-link, three meters high, like you'd find round a tennis court. Not exactly high security, but enough of a discouragement. Beyond the fence, there are groves of agricultural trees, and within it, the main thing you notice is a tent the size of a smallish marquee that seems to be the focus of activity.

"I suppose you drop the shutters, and everything's secured in the stoa when you're not here," I say.

"That's right," says Winchester, "but we take the finds to the ephoreia at the end of each season. We can borrow them back if we need to study them."

"They go to Heraklion?" I say.

"Chania," he says, "and this," pointing to the brass plaque, "is the original spot where Luke Zimbrean and I dug a trial for the excavation before we bought the land."

I try to look properly reverent. This is holy ground. As a datum point, it's as good as any other, so I can go with that. I can see from here that there are some pits dug in the ground, some of them quite extensive. The part they're working on this summer has a tent erected over it to give the team some shade – an aluminium frame, unbleached canvas cover, open at the sides, except on the south. Under the cover, there are stretched strings close to the ground – those grid lines on the plans – but no one's really been keeping track, so I've to make sure they're properly positioned on the drawings and then also plot in a systematic way the lines of the walls that have been uncovered over the years. It doesn't look systematic, but Winchester says it is.

"You're uncovering walls," I say, "but you're not following the lines of the walls with the excavation."

"No," said Winchester, "we're following a sampling methodology. We do a random square here and there. It's what they want for the samples in the lab, so we follow that with the excavation while we're taking the soil samples."

"It doesn't help us to understand the buildings," I say.

"Ah," he says, "but that's where you come in. If we plot the parts on the plan, you'll be able to infer what's going on in between. It's not the treasure-hunters' method, but it's properly scientific. You'll make sense of it, I'm sure. "

"I can we have a stretch of wall here and some over there," I say, "Wouldn't it be better to do a trench following the line of a wall? You'd bet a better idea of the shape of the buildings much quicker."

"I've had to re-think what we're about," says Winchester, "In the early days, I was hoping there'd be gold statues, or at least regular seal-stone finds, but it's been disappointing from that point of view. We started with field-walking and seeing what that produced – which was a few Turkish coins and a few shards of peasant pottery – no identifying features date-wise. Then people started taking an interest in pollen and carbon-dating, and I realized we'd better change tack, so for the last ten years, we've been taking systematic soil samples and testing them in the lab. Now, at least we know that the site was inhabited in the Bronze Age, which was the assumption we'd started with and which we already knew conclusively when we found the tholos, but it's always good to have these confirmations as a check. I don't think we're going to find any great treasures here – the tholos was robbed in Roman times. That would have been a great thing. I think the interest's going to be in the architecture – that's why we've brought you in. It's obvious that the city-plan isn't like Knossos. Not at all. You can see – we keep turning up these curving walls. So the first thing we want you to do is to plot all the walls on one plan so we can begin to see the shape of things as we uncover more."

"Are you hoping to do reconstructions?" I say.

"Not on site. Not like at Knossos. That wouldn't be allowed now. No. We want to uncover what there is and then – well, ideally – how are you at drawing? You've seen the views that Piet de Jong did at Knossos, of course. If you could do something like that for us, we'd be very happy."

"I'll see what I can do," I say, thinking there's not much to go on here. Winchester's "method," from my point of view, is idiotic, but he's the expert, and he's in charge.

"Of course, that's not something that'll come immediately. You'll have to get your eye in. And Piet was amazing. You could give him a fragment of a pot, and he'd hold it for a while and go into a sort of trance, and then he'd do a drawing of a whole room with the pot in it – it was like he could just see into the past."

"It doesn't sound very scientific," I say.

"He was a genius," he says.

"I don't suppose I am," I say and leave it at that. "Did you meet him?"

"I did. He came to look at the tholos, but he wouldn't do a drawing of it. He thought it didn't feel right. There was something about it he wasn't happy with – I've no idea what. I think he wanted there to be bulls or double-headed axes or something he'd seen at Knossos. The masonry's more like at Mycenae than at Knossos, and he seemed quite put out by that."

"Can I take a look at the tholos?" I say.

"Of course!" he says, "I forget you haven't seen it. Yes, let's do that later on. I'll get someone to sort out a ladder. I'll leave you to it now. Have a think about what you're going to be doing and how you'll approach it."

"I'll start by walking across the site and around it," I say.

"Let me know at lunch how you get on."

My first feeling is that I'm lost. There seems to be nothing much to pick up in a drawing. I've done survey drawings before, but always of standing buildings that give you a lot more to go on. I'd be happiest if I could start by drawing up the accommodation block, but that's the one thing I don't need to do. It seems crazy to have put it on the site like that. You'd think there must have been a risk of doing real damage to the archaeology. It's aligned with the site's grid, so it's quite useful as a reference point, but this grid's a bit of a worry. It seems to have taken over as having more significance than the things they're finding. The walls they've uncovered are fragmentary, and their worked surfaces aren't always evident, so it's not always clear which is the exposed face of a wall – are we looking at the inside or outside? And maybe they were making terraces, shaping the ground, so there'd have been only one exposed face. It is clear that the walls didn't run in straight lines. I can fix a point on the ground and work out where that ought to go on the plan, but that's just a point. For it to mean anything, it has to be more than just a point. If it's one in a series of points that I can join together, then I get a line, which feels like a start – but where are the lines? I have a chat with Toby, who tries to be helpful, but he's not been looking for lines. He's trying to make sure that his team of diggers doesn't go through an archaeological layer without noticing it. There's a plane of stratification, somehow – it means nothing to me – but it's easily dug through, and if it's lost, then it's lost forever in that spot – we can pick it up on either side. There's samples to take, above and below that stratum, to put in what look like ice cream tubs – plastic containers with lids. A label goes on on-site, and then they have to go to Athens for analysis in the lab.

"Wouldn't it make sense to bring the lab equipment here?" I say.

"In our dreams," he says, "but we don't have our own lab. I hand these samples over, and the microscope people can do the analysis when it suits them through the rest of the year – or some other year if it comes to that. Then Charles can work out what to do with the results."

"You don't interpret them?" I say.

"When I'm more senior, I will," he says.

"So your job is just to put the earth in tubs?" I say.

Toby laughs.

"Well, I don't quite do that. I supervise someone else putting the earth in tubs," he says, standing on his dignity, "We have to sample at regular intervals and at the right levels, so it's quite exacting in its way, but if you want to put it like that, yes. It's hardly Indiana Jones, is it?"

"Don't you get bored?" I say,

"Good god, yes," he says, "but we don't talk about that. Sometimes, we find things, and then we get excited."

"Thank heavens for that," I say, "What have you found?"

His diggers are within earshot, but they don't say anything, and they keep their heads down. Their hats have wide brims to keep their necks and shoulders well-shaded, even when they're outside the tent. They all wear navy-blue carpenters' aprons with a broad pocket across the front, so they seem to be wearing a uniform, even though behind the apron, they're wearing their own clothes – arms and legs covered against the sun.

"We keep finding these small discs," he says, "and we don't know what to make of them. They look like coins, but if the settlement's as old as we think it is, they can't be coins unless they're the oldest coins anywhere. We sent one to the lab for analysis, and they told us it was iron, so Charles had a fit. This dates as a Bronze Age site, so we want Bronze Age finds. The iron must have been brought here later, so we need a story to make sense of that."

"Places can be re-settled," I say, "You often get different layers of inhabitation on the same site."

"Of course," he says, "but these discs are actually in the old walls. They don't look like they were put there later, but maybe they were. Charles doesn't like them because it makes the wall look a thousand years newer than he wants them to be."

"What happens to them? I say.

"They're all in the ephoreia," he says, "except for the ones up at the top. I'll show you later. This season's haul."

"Can I read up about them?" I say.

"Charles isn't ready to mention them in print," he says, "In fact, I think he prefers it if we don't mention them at all."

38

Back at the photographer's, we wait again on chairs, looking past the table to the mirror where we see ourselves against the big photo of the forest. The mirror doesn't go all the way to the wall. When Mr Galanakis makes his entrance, he comes out from behind it, like walking on a stage. It's like a conjuring trick. He steps out of thin air. He looks unassuming and intelligent, quite elderly but alert.

"What did you have in mind?" he asks.

I let Loukas do the talking, translating for him.

"A portrait," says Loukas, "I'm impressed by what I see in the window."

"Thank you," says Galanakis, "One portrait? or two?"

"One portrait of two people," says Loukas.

"Very good," says Galanakis, "I work in black and white. If you want color, I can't control the process. It has to be sent away. I can put a color film in the camera if you want color; some people do, but even if you like it, I'll be disappointed with the results."

"Definitely black and white," says Loukas, "I want it done as you think it should be done."

"You've just had your hair cut," says Galanakis with a quizzical smile. His eyes flash. There's intensity in his gaze when you catch it, but if you're not paying attention, you might think he was half asleep.

"What makes you say that?" says Loukas.

"I can see your skin change color where your hairline used to be," says Galanakis, "It's pale where your hair was covering it. It hasn't seen the sun. If I get the exposure right, I'll see it in the photo. You might not. Maybe you'd prefer to come back in a few days when the line has gone. The sun will even it out."

"I bet he can smell the cologne," I say to Loukas in English. He half-winks at me in acknowledgement, but he responds to Galanakis.

"No," he says, "We'll do it right away. We're based on the other side of Chania. If we don't catch the moment, it will never happen."

"The decisive moment," says Galanakis, smiling to himself, "Come through to the studio," says Galanakis, and he leads the way behind the mirror into an airy room that's bright with light that streams from overhead, but it's bounced around by blinds and screens, so there's no direct sunlight in here. It's a much bigger space than you'd guess from the street, but rough, like a warehouse or a barn. We look at his backdrops, which hang like pages of a book, on arms that pivot as we turn each one away. Some are very old-fashioned – stagey paintings of urns and trees – which have a certain charm, as though we're in a palace garden, but obviously fooling no one. Loukas chooses a plain grey background. "That's a good one," says Galanakis, "It comes out darker than the bright parts, paler than the dark parts. You'll show up well against that. I have some props here if you want something to hold. Sometimes, people come in with a guitar or a bunch of flowers. Maybe you'd like to hold a book, or … what have we … an antique helmet? Or maybe one of you would sit." It's like a junk shop: chairs that don't match – some of them imposing – a classical statue without head or hands or feet, lying on its side – a piano – a candlestick that stands on the floor.

"I like your plainest portraits best," says Loukas, "We'll stand here just as we are."

"As you like," says Galanakis, "It's all the same to me. Stand close together. It's best if I can't see light between you. Overlap a bit. You're taller," he says to me, "so stay behind him so we can see you both."

He keeps us standing for a long time while he seems to be interested in other things. He's absorbed in looking at his light meter. He moves a blind across by pulling cords. The camera's shutter clicks from time to time, at odd moments, usually when he seems to be looking elsewhere. His control is on a cable, so he's not close to the camera, and sometimes he's talking to us when the shutter does its thing. It's like it didn't happen, as if he's trying to keep us guessing. He moves behind the camera. "Right, look this way," he says, the camera clicks, "and smile." It clicks again, and that's it finished. "They'll be ready by the end of the morning."

"It's a busy day tomorrow," says Loukas, "We'll come back the day after if that works."

"OK," says Galanakis, "It's just the contact sheets at this stage, on flimsy paper, then when you've chosen, I can print something larger on a better base. Something for framing, if that's what you want."

"We live the other side of Chania," says Loukas, "It will be a while before we can get back here. I trust your judgment. Do a good large print of the best one so we can take it back. I'll pay now if you like. We will return in the future, but for this visit now, that's what I need. We'll look at the others, of course, and maybe order more for later, but let's have one good print to take away with us the day after tomorrow."

Galanakis is charmed completely.

Loukas looks no less distinguished for the peasant shirt he's wearing. He makes it look more expensive than the one I'm now wearing. I suppose it's in the posture or the confidence of manner: the way he can appear to be so sure that these little things will turn out as he wants them, and that puts much bigger things almost within his reach.

On the way back to the hotel, we stop at an optician's, and after some polite questions, we come out with two pairs of sunglasses with good frames, one for Loukas and one for me. With them on, I feel confident. The reflections in shop windows have never been more fascinating. I keep looking for myself, and I don't look familiar. With the dark glasses and the haircut, I'm a fine young man-about-town who sometimes chooses to wear peasant clothes because they suit his mood, but the shirt I'm wearing today has a label in it, I'd like you to know. Loukas and I are looking more alike as if we're in the same team. I know it's just pretend, but I feel taller than before, feel that I've escaped the hold of the village, feel that I can pass as someone who belongs in a town.

39

In the midst of the tallest trees, the ladder's been put in place for me. There's hard-hats to wear, with lamps on the front of them like miners used to wear.

"Be careful," says Chris, who's leading the way, "It's a long way down."

The air's much cooler below ground. The lights flatten everything out – you're always looking along the beam of light, so the shadows don't come from the side at all – and the space is quite confined. I can see that it follows the general shape of the beehive tomb I saw a couple of weeks ago at Mycenae, but it's not nearly as large as that, and it doesn't have the large ceremonial-looking doorway that that tomb has. I look around for a lintel and find it. If this was the original floor level, then the entry point would have been low – you'd have had to crouch to bring the bodies in here. It was blocked up with stones that were properly finished on the inside, so they cared about making a good impression on the dead.

"Fantastic," I say.

"There are the three slabs here," says Chris, "and there were skeletons laid out on them, undisturbed, when Charles found the tomb. If they had gold masks like at Mycenae, they were robbed in ancient times. Look: you can see where the robbers dislodged some stones from the vault – they broke in from up there, almost the same way we came down."

"Fascinating," I say, and it feels like quite an adventure, seeing something like this that isn't accessible to the public. It's not absolutely the most spectacular tomb, but it's quite something. If there's other masonry around the site of a similar quality, then there'll be something to draw, but it hasn't yet come to the surface.

Everyone packs up and goes away at midday when the sun is too hot to expect anyone to continue. I don't have much to show for the first day's work, but I've worked out how to make a start.

"We go down to the beach now," says Jem, "then have a sleep. Then we'll eat later. Join in or avoid us as you like." She's relaxed in her dealings with me, as are the others. She takes it for granted that I'll like her, and I do. I go to the beach with them, taking a book, my sunglasses, and my Panama hat, which feels absurdly smart for the beach when the others are all wearing baseball caps. I'll look like the adult in charge of them. It's not a sandy beach. They all have flip-flops to wear to get over the pebbles. I don't, and the pebbles are hot and hurt my feet as I hobble over them. They'll sell flip-flops somewhere nearby, and I'll invest in them as soon as I can. Without my glasses, I can't see any detail, but the featureless sky looks just the same, and the water's a surprisingly comfortable temperature.

"We should have an evening in Chania," says Phoebe, "There must be a disco there."

"How would we get there?" says Chris.

"Oh yes," says Phoebe, "What about Gerani? We could walk there."

"There's some big hotels there," says Chris, "with swimming pools. I expect there's people there who'd want to dance."

40

When we go back to see Galanakis, I wear the sunglasses, feeling self-conscious but knowing I'd like him to see me wearing them. He's pleased to see us. The photos have come out well.

"Here's the contact sheet. There's a magnifying glass if you want it. Take the sheet with you. I keep the negatives here, and if you decide you want any more pictures printed, then let me know. You can just send me a note or telephone. They're all numbered on the contact sheet you'll see."

There's dozens of little images. At this size, I don't at first see much to choose between them. There's one where we're smiling. I think that's the one I'd choose. There one's where I'm looking at Loukas, and I look like I own him. There's one where Loukas is looking at me, and I'm looking straight at the camera. Somehow, he looks too adoring altogether. These images go wrong in unexpected ways. I hadn't noticed before how straight and emphatic my eyebrows are. I look determined. Loukas looks wistful. I'm only slightly taller than he is, but I stood slightly behind him when we were close together, with no light between us as instructed. We're touching, and we make a unified image. You couldn't cut me out of the picture without it looking wrong.

"I went with this one," says Galanakis, opening a cardboard folder with the large print in it. I can see that he's watching us to see our reaction.

I'm entranced by the picture. I've never seen myself looking this good before. Normally in photos, I seem to have blinked at the moment the picture was taken, or my smile looks forced, I'm standing awkwardly, or with my face screwed up from looking at the sun. Here, we both look serious, like equal partners, going about some worthwhile business. We're cropped, so it's only the head and shoulders. I'm pleased I was wearing Loukas's shirt at that moment, pleased that our haircuts match, pleased my peasant trousers don't show.

"Brilliant," says Loukas, "Yes, you've chosen well, sir. Alekos: you'll be able to make a frame, won't you?"

"Of course," I say, "It deserves something special."

We don't hurry back to the borrowed car, and once we're on the road, we stop along the way in some ordinary little villages that Loukas finds charming. We have coffee and a drink of water. It's hot in the car, and the breeze as we go along is hot, too. We don't say very much. My thoughts keep going back to our final hours in the hotel. I woke up when Loukas opened the shutter on the balcony to let the morning breeze in and fill the room with light. It was all so different from being in the house, where it's dark until we're presentable. Waking up naked and aroused in a room that's over-lit so everything's on show, especially both our bodies. At home, our bodies meet in darkness, so it's all about the touch and feeling that we're close to one another – pressed together, clinging, knowing that in that time, the whole world is just what we can feel. In the bright hotel room, there was the touch of the cool morning air and everything I could see, so I felt more naked there, more exposed, but not vulnerable and far too excited to even think of being ashamed. We tried to excite one another as much as possible – by touch, by look, by backing off, by laughing, playing. All inhibitions shed. What we were doing before in the dark felt like love-making – saying I love you, I want to be so close to you we merge together. This is something different altogether, something wild unleashed from deep within, with a thrill and intensity to it that leaves me feeling changed – even more than that first time, when in the village everyone could see it in my face, though they didn't know that that's what they were seeing. I know that something's happened to me that I can't begin to describe. All I know is that we have to do it again, and we won't be able to do it like that at home. We can love each other silently in the darkness and fumble our way through to quiet domestic ecstasy, but this other thing jumps the tracks. It's a catastrophe – a destruction of all the things I thought I knew – and it's gone. It couldn't last, but it can be repeated. As I'm driving, I'm wondering how we can arrange our lives to make it happen. Of course,

we can go back to the hotel and no doubt we will. We must.
While I'm thinking about it, I'm lingering in the afterglow
of that glorious moment, lost in Loukas and the world that
he makes around him.

41

Back at the stoa after the swim, I don't really sleep through the afternoon, but I go to my room because it's expected, and then I come out to look at the cupboard with survey tools in it. I've brought pens and pencils with me, masking tape, compasses, tracing paper and notebooks, an adjustable set-square, and a T-square. There is a good tape measure in the cupboard, and that's all I really need for now. I put it out on the table. I tape some paper to the table and use the T-square against the table edge to draw a pencil line. I realize it's not quite a secure alignment. I draw a second line, and it's not exactly parallel with the first. This won't do. I go to the end of the table and crouch down so my eye's close to the corner of the tabletop, and I can see that it's not quite a straight line. It wanders. I look beneath the table, and I'm amazed. It's supported by a central line of legs that are part of the building. It's like an engineering structure that cantilevers out to the edges without needing any table legs around the edge, so you can put chairs wherever you like. It's very elegant and very stable. It would be impossible to move it, but there's no need. It's effectively floating in just the right place for everyone to meet up as they go about doing whatever it is they do. Its grain is very fine and straight, and it's been followed meticulously at the edges. That's why they're not quite straight. It's all been made from a single piece of timber, but goodness knows how it was brought here. If it was by crane, it must have been put here before the roof went on. I start to pay attention to the building and realize how carefully it's been put together. The floorboards are much wider than usual and seem to go on forever – the whole length of the building – which isn't possible, but they've been made with invisible joints.

When Winchester comes along, I say, "I've been admiring your building. It's beautifully done. Really extraordinary."

He looks quite taken aback.

"Thank you," he says, "How are you doing with your thoughts about the survey?"

"I've realized I'll need an assistant," I say, "Not for anything demanding, but I'll need to take measurements, and there'll have to be someone to hold the other end of the tape measure."

"We can arrange that," he says, "Is that all?"

"Well," I say, "I've realized I'll need some sort of drawing board. I thought the table would do, but it's not quite right for what I need. I'll be OK, to begin with – I can begin with using compasses and a straight edge to set out the triangulated measurements, but when it comes to putting things together on the grid – at that stage, I'll need something different."

"If you can work out what it needs to be," he says, "we'll sort something out."

He catches me looking at the photo on the back wall.

"Haha!" he says, "Have you worked out who that is?"

"I haven't," I say, "I suppose if it's someone, I might guess that one of them must be Luke Zimbrean as a schoolboy."

"You are correct," says Winchester, "Zimmers."

And then it dawns on me that the other guy must be Winchester himself, a long, long time ago. Which one is which?

"You were blond," I say.

"Correct," he says, with a chuckle, "Wasn't I beautiful then? My mother took the photo when Luke came to visit one summer."

It's overexposed, and it's been blown up too big, so it looks very grainy, but it's part of Winchester's claim to authority and legitimacy as head of the project here.

"You look much more distinguished now," I say, now that he has age to give him gravitas, and the hair is grey, but there is still the same wariness about the eyes. Zimbrean, by contrast, looks open and unguarded. Between them, the leaves of a potted palm make an emphatic pattern. It makes me think of those Annunciation paintings where the angel and the virgin are kept apart in their own spaces by a central column or a plant. There's space between them, and they're in different worlds despite their almost-matching tweeds.

42

"Panagia," says Mum, "What have you done to your hair? You look lovely – both of you– but Alexakis, you've never before had your hair cut without me nagging you to let me do it. Never."

I laugh. Loukas smiles.

"You see," he says, "I'm a good influence on you."

43

One of the diggers is assigned to help me. I expected it was going to be awkward because of my lack of Greek, but he turns out to speak impeccable Australian-accented English. He's Australian with Greek parents, and he comes to the island every summer to see his grandparents, who are now very old. He stays in Ziros during the week and with them at weekends. He loves the island, loves his grandparents and the work on the site pays for his fare. He does building work when he's in Australia. He hasn't said a word in front of the English people at the stoa, and they have no idea that he can understand them. That amuses him. Somehow, I'm not put in the same category, and I'm pleased about that. Although he doesn't actually ask me in so many words, I understand that I'll have let him down if I let on. His name's Menelaos, but it's the done thing to call him Len.

I settle into a routine of taking measurements during the morning while the diggers are on the site. They all go away round about noon when the sun makes it too hot to go on, and they don't come back until the next morning. Our little group at the stoa, as often as not, goes down to the beach for a swim. It's a short walk – ten minutes each way – but there's long enough to settle in the sun with a book and take a dip in the sea when you start overheating, then come back, take a shower, and try to plot the day's measurements on the plan. It works well as a routine, and it means I keep up with things

142

and can keep track of the information I'm gathering. It's a bit like seeing constellations in the stars. After a while, you start to see patterns emerging, and with increasing confidence, I can literally join the dots, so I'm getting a picture of curving lines. It doesn't help that the excavation's all being done following the lines of a grid, one square at a time, and often random squares that aren't next to one another. That doesn't help me at all.

44

A bit too hot. I'm more than half asleep in citrus shade beside the house. The sun is glaring, blistering, bleaching – purifying stuff to reddish dust. Sun hardens earth and drains the tint from paint, rots fabrics, cooks a person lobster-like – so I'm in deepest shadow, drowsy, close to dreaming – but awake enough to keep control – to hold at bay my demons – I won't let them in. Lemon's in the air, fresh, brighter leaves are coming through, and piny resin's there – an earthy incense. The soil is breathing with me, and I know it's there, familiar in its mustiness – it's always there. Always has been. I know I'm home. It's all in place around me, like the orange of my eyelids that I'm seeing from inside, and reassuring sounds – my breathing and the pulse of blood behind my ears cicadas, of course, noisy like tinnitus – ignore them – but beyond them (can you hear it?) quieter but unfamiliar: a murmuring of voices – real – I'm not imagining. They're not local voices – they sound gentle, almost secretive, and not so far away, they're coming close – but they're not stopping here, just going past, so I don't have to stir, and they won't see me here if I don't move, and if they do they'll think that I'm asleep. They must be just the other side of our fence that's rusting on its wall. A dazzle of azalea picked out by sun holds my eye, but I don't see strangers. It's not like an intrusion. There's no worry with them – no threat – they're self-absorbed – but something's up. Who's out in the sun? I just-about see through the veil of my eyelashes – it's bright out there beyond the tree – I'll hurt my eyes – a fleeting glimpse: two hats – pale hats – fine straw hats – interlopers' hats – bobbing up and down from right to left, incompletely in my view. Smudged spots in motion. Hats that know no better.

I'm out of the intensest heat. Matthias leans over, looks me in the eye, and gently smiles – I'm his age now, maybe older. He's still in his uniform – my monster – trouble – and yet there's something good about him when he smiles. There's mischief there, and everything seems fine, but I know that I can't trust him, know he'll lose his temper – throw a tantrum – maybe not today, but I feel wary.

"I'm your true and faithful friend," says Matthias.

"I know," I say, and I smile.

"Don't never forget," he says.

"There's no danger of that," I say, and with a jolt, I wake. He's gone. It's not quite so hot. No butterflies. No hats. No voices now. No sleep, not now, but still, it's early to be moving. The sun's still here, and I don't want to move.

45

I show Charles the lines I'm beginning to sketch as an overlay on tracing paper.

"Snakes," he says, "It's snakes, isn't it!"

"It could be," I say, "It seems to curve this way, then that. A serpentine line. The line of beauty, William Hogarth called it."

"That's as may be," says Charles, "but snakes make sense round here. There's definitely snake-worship on the island, so if we have snake walls, that's suggesting something different from the bulls at Knossos. There's the labyrinth there – confusing but rectilinear. Here, we have snake walls, so it would be snake-worship – pythonism."

"They have that snake-priestess statue," I say.

"They do," he says, "but supposing they came here to worship. Maybe this was the center of the cult. I bet Paleoziros was based around snake-worship, and that's what they've taken up with the serpentine walls. This is a breakthrough. I knew it was a good idea to bring you here!"

I explain the idea to Len the following day.

"Come with us for lunch," he says.

"Sure," I say, "Why not."

So when the diggers pack up and go, I go with them to the village. It's not far – ten or fifteen minutes. It's a light sociable lunch. There's loud conversation that often sounds like argument. There's bread and salads that circulate on small plates and bowls – pungent tzatziki, the typical salad, smoky aubergine paste – all very traditional, all good, and a delight to eat compared with the daily misjudgments up at the stoa. There's wine and water, and I'm treated as part of the group and not expected to pay. Nobody pays here. It's part of the deal. It's touchingly companionable and unstuffy. It's just a snack to take the edge off hunger after the morning's work – yakka – the main meal in the evening.

"You're all Australian, aren't you?" I say.

"Fuck me dead," says Len, "I wondered when you'd twig. Just don't tell those dags up the hill."

"How come they've never noticed?" I say.

"Perhaps we didn't want them to notice," says Len.

"And they none of them know about this place," I say.

"That's the way we like it," he says. He has a warm manner and a friendly smile, and it amazes me that the archaeologists haven't properly made contact. We're in a place they call the megaron, opposite the church. There don't seem to be any shops in the village, but this place is like a village hall, and we're well looked after here. Compared with the other villages around here, things seem to be well made – properly done. Elsewhere, everything seems bodged or unfinished or falling apart. Here, there are bougainvillea flowering in hot cascades of red and pink growing over the buildings around the square and a feeling that it's all rather well looked after. The megaron's linked with the excavation. There's a plaque to Luke Zimbrean, with a low-relief bull, or a buffalo perhaps, and below it, an old-fashioned photo of two young men who look very dashing. One of them presumably – I'd guess the smaller one, on the right – must be Luke, maybe ten years older than in the photo with Winchester and dressed as a peasant here, in looser clothes. They both look very serious and idealistic, with very good haircuts and plain off-white shirts. The guy on the left has a more penetrating gaze and more emphatic eyebrows. He's wearing similar but smarter clothes. Maybe they're brothers, but one takes after the father, the other the mother. Up above, high on the wall, there are three Venetian carnival masks – leather, with light gilding. What are they doing there? They remind me of bucrania – the ox skulls that sometimes figure in classical decoration – associated with the altars where oxen were sacrificed – obviously that's not happening here – it's a modern building – and they're not actually skull-like – one of them has a very long nose.

"I'd better go back," I say, "The others will be at the beach by now. Don't you go to the beach?"

"Not that one," says Len, "There's plenty of beaches here."

I take my leave and go back to the site. I go to my room and sleep without meeting anyone there, and then I set up with my measurements and compasses at the end of the table.

Jem comes to start preparing the meal. We talk a little about this and that, but I don't mention lunch or the village.

46

Every morning, I go up to the roof to pump water. The pump clanks about a bit, so I leave it until everyone's up and about, and sometimes, like today, it's mid-morning before I go up. Stasia's there, sitting with Mum, both intently looking at their laps. They're sitting on chairs put right at the end of the roof where it's level, and they're behaving as though it's a respectable terrace. There was some rain in the night, and that's good at this time of year.

"Hello," I say, mainly so they're not startled when I start with the pump. They look up.

"Hello," says Stasia, and she smiles. There must be something about my hesitation that seems to ask a question.

"Embroidery," says Mum, "I'm teaching Stasia."

I wonder how long this has been going on. I wonder why I didn't notice. Loukas has been the center of my attention, and I haven't been noticing what Mum's done with the room upstairs. The door's open, and I can see inside. The room's gone all womanly. She's hung bed sheets on the walls to hide the cracked and crumbled plasterwork, and they drape beautifully in a regular rhythm along the walls and across the window. There are little sprays of blue flowers embroidered here and there. It looks like being in a tent. There's something comfortable and happy about the way it feels — fresher than downstairs with its accumulation of things that have come to rest there over the years, and a feeling of inertia and neglect has settled into place. I must repaint, at least. We need something new to refresh us. But downstairs, we have Loukas. Up here, there's an independent life going on.

"I saw your napkins," says Stasia, "and thought they were beautiful. I'd like to be able to do that sort of thing. Hanna said she'd teach me."

"Lovely," I say. I'd never thought of Mum embroidering them, "Did you sew them? I thought they were from a grandmother."

"Yes, they were a present from my grandmother to my mother. I didn't do them, but I was taught how. It's my Phrygian heritage."

"I didn't know you were Phrygian," says Stasia.

"Oh, it's just fanciful," says Mum, "My grandmother liked to tell me stories about growing up in the mountains. I thought her mother invented embroidery, but it's an ancient tradition that embroidery came from there, and the grandmothers felt it was their duty to teach it. The mothers were too busy doing other things."

And then, as I'm walking home, I can feel Matthias beside me. He's not saying anything. Sulking.

"You're looking tired," he says.

"It's been a long day. Our guest has arrived," I say, "I borrowed Costas' van and had to drive to Kissamou to meet the boat."

"Yes, I know," he says, "You eat with him tonight with just your mother, then you bring him to eat with others at Maria's tomorrow. I know everything you know. You must tell me everything. I live through you. You bring me all the joy I know."

"And then," I say, "I had to give Costas the van and find my way back here by other means."

"You had a lift," he says.

"Not all the way," I say.

"He has dark eyes," he says, "Not German."

"Romanian, he says," I say.

"I know," he says, "but there's a way you look at him. You never look at me that way. You're going to forget me."

"There's no danger of that," I say, and I think I only wish I could.

"You wish you could," says Matthias.

48

The next day, when I'm in the field with Len, he says, "The boss wondered who you were. I told him you're an architect and now he wants to meet you. Can you come to the megaron for the evening meal with the mayor?"

"In principle, yes, I'd love to," I say, "but I'll have to let the others know what I'm doing, or there'll be questions. They'll worry. Is that OK?"

Len shrugs. He says, "I should've thought of that. Just don't make them feel that they're invited too."

I go to the beach with the students. It's the same every day, sometimes windier than other times, but always the perfect sky and the sun always in the same part of it.

"The mayor of Ziros has summoned me to dinner," I say.

"Wonderful," says Jem, "An assignation!"

"Hardly," I say, "Have you met him?"

"No," she says, "but I think Charles used to know him somehow."

I go down to the yard. Loukas said he was going to read about farming, but he's at the gas ring in the kitchen making coffee. He's always making coffee.

"How's the farming?" I say.

"If we organized water, we could get the trees to give much more fruit," he says, "Do you think I could get hold of the land by farming it first and then excavate it once it's mine?"

"That sounds too devious," I say, "Ask mother. Don't try to deceive anyone in the village. They'll feel bad when they find out. You're better telling them that you're looking for buried treasure, so long as you promise them you won't run off with it. You can sell it on the black market and make them all rich, and they'll be happy. Or give it to the museum, and they'll be happy. So long as the museum's in Chania and not Athens. If you trick the authorities, you'll be admired, but you mustn't trick your neighbors. They'd find out."

I'm working on my drawings when Charles comes out for his aperitif.

"I've been invited to meet the mayor this evening," I say.

"I used to know him quite well at one stage," he says, "He made this table for us and the chairs. In fact, he designed the stoa here."

"Oh," I say, "He must be good."

"He used to make himself useful here," says Charles, "but he got taken up by an Italian furniture company and now he doesn't have time for us any more. I haven't seen him in years."

"He must be very good," I say.

Winchester doesn't smile or give me a greeting to pass on.

And then I feel that I've had a sleepless night, but that can't be right because when I'm lying there thinking I haven't slept, I find Loukas lying beside me on the bed. He's asleep and close to me. It's a bed that's too narrow for two people, so we're very close together. I don't know what to make of it. I lie there for a while without moving, but it's later than it usually is when I get up, and although the room's fairly dark, I can see the glare of sunlight on the step outside the door – just a fine line of dazzle against the dark of the door. I try to move silently, but Loukas wakes up the moment I move.

"You were shouting," he says, "I thought I could calm you down. You were shouting in German."

"I don't speak German," I say.

"Werde ich nicht. You were refusing," he says.

"It must have been Matthias," I think, but out loud, I say, "Maybe it's time for a coffee."

"If you like," says Loukas.

When I reach the megaron, I look around for Len. I don't see him, but there's a man with a thick grey mustache smiling at me. He seems to know me, and his face looks familiar.

"Good evening," he says, "Thank you for coming. I'm Xander. I saw you here yesterday, but I don't think you saw me. They tell me you're an architect."

"Ian Bell," I say, "I have been an architect. I'm an academic now. I'm working with the archaeologists at Paleoziros." I know he knows this already, but it's something to say. "Do I know you from somewhere? Your face …"

"That's me in the photo," he says, "You were looking at it yesterday."

"Oh yes! Of course," I say, "It's a fine photo."

The passing years have changed him from the strikingly handsome young man in the photo to someone who is arresting in quite a different way. He has authority. His hair is much longer, and it's no longer dark. His face is broader, jowly, and the eyebrows no longer have such prominence now that they're paler and they've lost their definition. But it's a pleasant face, and he's inclined to smile.

"The photographer should be famous," he says, "Galanakis. He was a good man. He would be famous if he'd taken photos like this in New York and made friends with journalists. The work's good enough. Look: we'll eat here with the others, but first, let me show you my ergastirio. It's here on the plateia."

It looks very smart. The workshop has a vault that runs back from the street, and the end of it is glazed-in with plate glass and a glass door in the middle. The front is treated as a showroom, with two things on display.

"This is my Cretan Hound Chair," he says, "they make it in Milan now. I have the original prototype upstairs. And this is my Daedalus Stool. It folds." He demonstrates how the seat separates into four square pieces that rotate on the diagonal and move in a graceful and unexpected way. He folds it back again and invites me to sit on it to show that it will take a person's weight. It's a beautiful thing.

"Architects always like my things," he says, "That's why I invited you. There's a workshop here, as you see. I like to call it my laboratory."

"And you have a drawing board," I say, my attention caught by a parallel motion apparatus on a cast-iron base.

"I have indeed," he says, "You say that as someone with an interest. Would it be useful? Come and use it if you like."

"I'm managing with the long table up at the stoa, for the moment," I say, "but – of course – you know – the edge isn't perfectly straight – it follows the grain."

"Bravo," he says, "No one has mentioned that before."

"When I'm piecing things together and relating them to the grid," I say, "it would help enormously. It's just what I need for that."

"Whenever you like," he says, "I'm not using it at the moment."

"These are intriguing," I say, pointing to some sinuously sculptural shapes made of wood.

"Forcole," he says. "They're to support the oar on a gondola. Venice."

"Ah. Venice," I say, "So, the masks in the megaron are your doing?"

"A souvenir of my honeymoon," he says, "They seem at home there somehow. That was my first visit. I've brought a forcola back each time since."

"How does someone from here have furniture manufactured in Milan?" I say.

"By chance," he says, "Isn't it always by chance? We met an architect when we were on our honeymoon. I had photos with me. He liked my chair. He liked my photos. He designed a shop that had a gallery, and when it opened, there was an exhibition of my chair in the window downstairs and some photos of my joinery in the gallery upstairs. It changed my life. I took the photos here. The good man Galanakis printed them for me, and I framed them. In fact, the photos were of the frames before they were assembled. They're special Chinese joints that slide together like magic.

Everyone who came said, 'What a beautiful chair, how much does it cost?' and there was only one, and it was made with a branch that naturally grew in the shape of a Cretan hound's back leg. I made it for Loukas Zimbrean, and he paid me for it, so it wasn't mine to sell. It couldn't be made again. It was a one-off. The Cini Foundation bought the whole set of photographs and their frames. The architect said I must talk to the people in Milan, and he sent me there with an introduction. They did this version of the chair. You see, it still has the dog-leg shape, but now it's made by steaming it into shape. It's still a very light chair. We carve the dog's paws before the steaming. They charge a fortune for them. I've never sold one from the shop here. No one would pay that sort of money round here, but there are people who buy them, and we do very well out of it."

"The village certainly seems prosperous," I say, and it does. There's a feeling of well-being here.

"Come upstairs. There's a gallery." We go up outdoor steps to an open terrace that looks back over the square, and you can see the sea. There's a door into a room. The prototype chair's there, and a set of uniformly framed photographs. A picture of the exhibit in Venice. Close-ups of timber joints. An arresting mask in the form of an octopus.

"Is that from Venice?" I say.

"No," he says. He looks at me. "It's from Hawaii. It's now at the Smithsonian in Washington."

"Amazing. Do you know anything about it? Why is it here?"

"I just found it charming," he says, looking at the picture, "exciting. What's the word?"

"I'd say 'arresting'," I say. I'm drinking it in, but I can see Xander's looking at me very carefully. Is he expecting me to recognize it? I look at him again, and he's looking out of the window into the courtyard below.

"There's Dmitri," he says, "My assistant. He lives down there. Let's go and find him." He locks the door when we leave the upper room.

53

And then Matthias says, "You know your mother's telling Loukas he has to fall in love with the village. What she really means is that the village has to fall in love with him." He looks me in the eye – a monster, trouble. Oh god, what's he doing here? He's in the shadows, and I know the others can't see him. He's beyond the reach of the table's candlelight, and he's speaking German, and I know in one part of my mind that I can't understand German, but I can understand his every word. He comes and says things to me when my defenses are down – when I'm over-tired, and even when I'm fast asleep. Maybe I've already fallen asleep in part of my mind, but I can still see the others talking, and I can see Matthias in his smart uniform with his good haircut. I give him a hard stare to tell him to go away, but he ignores my message. I'm older than him now. He always stays the same, and he enjoys the power he has over me, but I don't know where it comes from. I know that he's not real, but sometimes I forget it. "Oh, look at his puppy-dog eyes." I can't see Matthias's eyes. They're in the shadow. I can't speak. The others will hear me. My mother catches my eye.

"You need to sleep," she says.

"I know," I say, and she knows, so I don't have to say that I'm also afraid to sleep. It's better that I'm only half asleep so I can keep Matthias under control. When he gets out of control, he tells me to kill myself, and I argue back, but even as I shout and cry, I know he has the better side of the argument. There's something about his beauty that gives him authority even though I know his uniform is discredited and I was never in his army, and he has no power over me if I don't give it to him – we've been through this a thousand times. I feel like I'm half asleep most of the time now, and my dreams seep into my waking life. There's Dinos, too – the old man with his old-fashioned Cretan waistcoat and his crooked stick. He visits sometimes, but he's not here this evening. He doesn't wish me harm. He looks after me in his way.

The megaron is lively again, with the tables set for action.

"This is all very impressive," I say, "I expected the village would have a little grocery at most, but there's a fine gallery and a very exclusive furniture shop. There's something special about this village."

"It's down to the Zimbreans," he says, "without them, we wouldn't have the excavation, and we wouldn't have the diggers. There isn't a grocery as such, but if you need anything, just come and ask here at the megaron. There won't be a charge. They have the things you'd expect anyone to need."

"How does that work?" I say.

"It's how we run the place," he says, "We like to share our prosperity. It's hospitality. Good will."

"Why don't the archaeologists ever come down here?" I say.

He shrugs and says, "You'd better ask Mr Winchester about that."

And then I wanted to be dead. I still feel guilt and shame because deep down, I know I should be dead, and the only reason I'm not is because I ran away. Nobody blames me, except, of course, for Matthias, and deep down, I know he's right. Nobody hears him. Nobody has talked about it. Why was I not caught? Luck. Luck and cowardice. I could survive, and I did. Let's call it cunning. It's more to be admired than cowardice. Alexakis poneiros cunning like Odysseus. I ran. I hid among the cypresses, my sentinels, and listened to their whispered comforts as they bade me bide my time.

At the back of the showroom, there's another plate glass wall and a small square courtyard with Dmitri's room on the other side of it, shutters closed. Dmitri himself is in the workshop part of the space. Xander goes over to him.

"Ian," says Xander, putting an arm around Dmitri's shoulders, "meet Dmitri."

"Hi," says Dmitri, giving me a smile that might be conspiratorial or guarded. He narrows his eyes. He has questions to ask.

"It feels like there's a party starting up in the megaron," I say, "Is it like this every evening?"

"During the dig season, yes it is," says Xander. "It doesn't go on late. They have to work in the morning."

"You're the mayor," I say, "so I suppose you decide."

He laughs.

"I'm not the mayor," he says, "the nearest mayor's at Gerani. They call me the mayor because they don't want to call me the boss. I'm not the boss."

"You are the boss," says Dmitri.

"Well, for you, yes," says Xander, "but I'm talking about the village."

The sound of an accordion drifts in from across the plateia.

"Come on," says Xander, "Let's see what's up."

"There's Len," I say. It turns into a relaxed and convivial evening. Dmitri's English isn't good, but he's friendly. Len has plenty to say about Australia, but he likes the sea here better. I like Xander's obsession with the details of joinery and might have expected that. He seems very contended and settled here. He's lived here all his life, with some visits to Italy and Turkey. He doesn't trust anything to do with Athens or Istanbul, but he likes Venice.

It gets quite late.

"Hang on a minute," says Xander. He comes back with a flashlight. "You'll need this. There's no lights on the track."

"Thank you," I say, "I'll make sure to bring it back before I go."

"Come here again," he says, "tomorrow if you like. See how it goes. No. Come tomorrow afternoon with your drawings. Use the drawing board. Stay for dinner with the family."

And then I'll head back to the house, and it's as I'm thinking about Loukas and the fields that I notice I'm not alone. It's Matthias, walking along beside me, muttering. I want to ignore him, but he's not having it.

"You've got to send him away," he says, "he's not good for you."

"He'll make up his own mind," I say, "He might well go, but I'm not going to talk him into it. You know we need the money, so there's no way I can send him away. Mum would be upset about it."

"You'll forget me," says Matthias, "I might have to kill him. Well, you might have to kill him for me."

"I will not." I'm shocked. I stop and turn to look him in the eye. He looks hurt and furious.

"We're supposed to be on the same side. I'd do the same for you. You say you love me." He sounds as if he means it, growling. There's no point in reasoning with him when he's like this. I walk on. He stays where he is. He can't do anything. Sometimes, he can talk me into doing things, but today, he's not being persuasive. He can take me by surprise, but he can't force my hand. At least it makes a change from him saying I ought to kill myself. "At least you have to send him away."

I'm glad of the torch. Without it, there's no way to see anything – no sense of the direction or where your feet are landing. With it, the path looks unfamiliar, but at least you can tell it's there. There's a light at the entrance to the compound and some lights within. Some people will have gone to bed, but not everyone, by the look of it. To my surprise, it's Winchester who's sitting at the table. He's usually the first to go. He's waited up for me.

"How was your evening?" he says. He's been drinking.

"It was good," I say, "Xander was good company, and I met some other people."

"I met him the first time I ever visited this place," he says, "So long ago. I was very young then. We both were. We all were."

"When was that?" I say.

"Back in 1950," he says, "I was traveling round Greece with Luke, and it was such a different world then. We had Pausanias with us and took the bus or boats or walked – we walked a lot. We'd both done National Service and weren't put off by a bit of walking. There were lots of places that weren't known, but we read Pausanias – he was writing for Roman tourists – he tells you enough to be able to find places – in relation to a harbor or the hills – and we had a high-old-time imagining our eyes were the first modern eyes to see some classical sites. I'm sure we were right, at least some of the time. Luke really thought he'd got a knack for spotting things that couldn't be seen. The eye of faith. We came here hoping to find a big settlement in the west of the island to rival Knossos. He was convinced he'd found it here. At least, that's what he said later. I'm not sure what it was, really. I think it was that man you met this evening."

"Xander, the mayor?" I say.

"Yes," he says, "He used to call himself Alekos. There was something crazy about him. Seriously, I'm sure he was mad. He was very good-looking, and I'm sure he turned Luke's head. Luke was queer, you know. He came here and never looked back. It was an absolute fluke that there was an archaeological site here at all. At first, he was dead-set on coming here to farm the land."

"What happened to him? He'd be the same age as you." I say.

"There was an accident," he says, "It was never properly explained. They never got to the bottom of it. He fell into the Samaria Gorge. It doesn't make sense. It never made sense. And then there was this story about getting married to a woman. That never made sense, either. There was this boy, Alekos, bewitching him."

He pours himself another drink. It's the Metaxa. He gestures to me to help myself, and I pour a little into a tumbler that's there on the table, mainly to encourage him to go on talking. I get a sense of the emptiness he feels in his life. There's the loss of his friend, Luke, but also the feeling that he wishes he could have turned Luke's head the way Xander, as a young man, evidently did. He lost the closeness of that friendship when the romance started if romance is quite the word. But then, how come he's ended up here now?

"What happened to put you in charge here?" I say.

"Oh, that was Luke's mother," he says, "She knew that Luke and I were close friends, and she liked me. I was the only person she knew who'd ever been here. She saw it as the natural thing to put the archaeology in my hands, but I know that I don't have any real talent for it. I've thrown away my life on it. Looking back, maybe I should have stayed as a school teacher. I'd be a headmaster by now. My wife would have been happier if she'd been able to bring up our children with her mother somewhere nearby. She insists on spending the summers back in Gloucestershire. The kids do their own things these days. I wouldn't have wasted all this time scraping away at ground that doesn't have much in it."

"It's a lovely part of the world," I say, "There must be plenty of people who envy you."

"That's some sort of consolation, I suppose.." he says, "But Alekos – Xander – he's had a charmed life. He married the girl. His furniture business is doing really well. He did a lot to help us set up here, but I fell out with him a few years back."

"Why? What happened?" I say.

"Oh! Maybe I should have accepted it was the way of the world," he says, "I felt I couldn't trust him anymore. I found he'd been taking us for a ride with the bills. Of course, I should have thought to pay him something for his trouble, but I wasn't being paid, and I thought he'd want to be treated as a friend rather than an employee. I bet Luke had been giving him money. I should have thought of him as a rent boy. Then I'd have got it right. He was inflating the cost of the building works and everything and quietly taking a commission for himself without mentioning it to me. It must have been going on all along – for twenty years – and when I challenged him about it, he just laughed and said, 'You don't need me now' and walked away."

"Shouldn't you sue him then?" I say.

"That's not the way it works," he says.

He looks defeated – as if the important things in life have passed him by. He's lived a life that someone else might have enjoyed – might have left them feeling fulfilled – but it's done him no good. He's taken on a barren site that might have been someone else's passion, but it's not his. Even his big discovery – the tomb – wasn't his, except in his version of the story. It was that woman Dan told me about. It's too late for him to change his life for another one. He has to make the best of it.

"I've avoided him since then," he says, "It's easily done. I haven't had to put much effort into it. We kind of need the village on side for the site's security, but we're all set up now with the diggers and everything. I can organize anything that needs doing by going through them. We can't afford to alienate the village, but I feel pretty sick about the way I've been treated."

"Maybe you need to get some rest," I say. He's only going to get more maudlin. The things he's telling me about should make him depressed, so it's no wonder he's getting that way. How do I change the subject?

"And he's there in the megaron. He's in that photo. It's the two of them. It should have been me. I was the one who was with Luke when he first came here. It should have been me." There's some real deep-seated bitterness there, but I don't get the feeling that Charles is going to lash out against Xander. He seems to be turning it all in on himself. What didn't he see? The importance of the site? The importance of his friendship with Luke? He blames himself for the loss.

"I think you shouldn't drink any more this evening," I say and move my chair back.

"You're quite right, dear child," he says and looks desolate.

"Can I help?" I say.

"No. Don't worry. I'll be OK." He looks a little unsteady as he goes to his rooms, but he'll manage. He'll be OK.

The thing is, Xander is obviously bright, and he's good company. Of course, I want to see him again. His life has turned out better than he could have expected, and there's an underlying buoyancy in his manner. He can't be all that different in age from Winchester if you think about it, but he behaves like a much younger man. He's not weighed down by his problems – if he has problems – and life doesn't seem to be a burden to him. He has a sense of mischief in his smile, and he seems interested in all sorts of things. That stool is amazing – the mechanism is something very special – the way the stool seems to turn itself inside out as it moves – I'm going to have to get one at some point, but it'll be too expensive for me now.

And what am I hoping for from my involvement here? I don't know that I want to come back again. It's quite interesting being here once, and the weather's great. I'll contribute to some publications, and that will help my career along – that's the main thing. The young people here are all hoping one day to get the kind of job that I already have, so it doesn't feel like I'm setting my sights high enough, but on the other hand, the fact that they're rather impressed that I'm a lecturer makes me feel like I'm some kind of success. When I talk to my architect friends, they seem to think I'm on a career break and I must be wanting to go back into designing buildings and managing building projects, but that's not how I feel – I've found my own path that's taking me somewhere different, but I don't know quite where that will be. For now, I can dream about serpentine lines snaking across my drawings. A place dominated by a snake cult – pythonism – so much that they make their streets meander in rhythmic waves. I must think about how a snake moves. It does its slithering twisting thing but then moves on the diagonal – it's not like running forward along the line of its body but sidewinding. I wonder where I can see a film of it. It makes me think of the folding mechanism on the stool again – you move it in one direction, but it doesn't slide along that line – it deflects the movements sideways, along the diagonal, and it twists as it goes. How would a society think if it based its values on snakes? Shedding skins, renewals, rebirths. Don't I remember something about them being kept in ancient houses to stop mice from getting the upper hand? Winchester will know lots of things about snakes. He's excited about the idea. I should try to get him thinking about how the snake thing might tell us something about the place. It will need a new name. Snaketown. Serpentville. Pythonopolis.

59

We're eating with the neighbors at Maria's table.

"When you're learning the patterns, it's better to use the strong colors," my mother says, "so there's a contrast. You can see more clearly what's going on. The traditional designs always use strong colors, but it looks more sophisticated if the colors are subtle. At its most refined, you don't notice at first that there's embroidery there at all."

"What a shame! To do all that work and then not notice it," says Maria.

"Well," says Mum, "You notice a general richness of effect. The trick when you're wearing it is to think of it as someone else's work so you don't care too much about it. Then you look like a princess. Inside, you can feel proud of the work, but from the outside, that pride must seem to be beneath you."

"No one should be ashamed of having done work," says Maria, but Eleni and Stasia are paying attention. This is something from Mum's past in Constantinople – the grand life she didn't in the end lead. It's a world away from Dad's straightforward pride in his work – but also his work could be self-effacing. He could make a fine table that he'd never be invited to use once it was delivered. Of course, no one wanted to order new furniture once the war started. People just wanted repairs and utility jobs. If your world's going to go up in flames, you're not so worried about your dining room looking smart. But then again, if your world's going to go up in flames, you can't believe it's going to happen. The day before it happens, everything seems normal, and your plans for the future are still intact. Dad was planning to move his business into Chania and was doing some sort of deal with Costas so he could expand, and I'd have been there to help. Then he was dead.

Stasia certainly is very pretty. She's taken to wearing makeup around her eyes and lips. It makes her look older and more sophisticated. Her embroidery lessons seem to bring her around quite often. Apparently, she's making progress and wants to come and show my mother what she's done or to ask about a problem detail here and there. Loukas smiles at her, and she smiles back.

"She'll look like Maria in 20 years," I say in English quietly, "You know that Cretan girls turn into their mothers, don't you?"

"Bitch," says Loukas, quietly, laughing, "Maria's not her mother. Eleni's quite presentable. Don't worry. You've nothing to worry about."

"How was Heraklion," says Stasia, in Greek.

"It was good," I say. I'm still translating for Loukas, but he's getting better.

"We found the library and had a look around Knossos. Have you been there?" says Loukas.

"I went a long time ago, with school," says Stasia, "I'd like to go again one day. I'd understand it better now."

"We'll be going there again soon. Join us if you like," says Loukas.

I give him a look.

"I'll ask my mother," says Stasia.

"What are you thinking? I say later when we're alone.

"Your mother's been explaining," says Loukas, "The surest way to get the land is to show that I'm committed to staying here, and the best way to do that is to get married and do up a house. She and Eleni are sorting it out with Stasia."

"What?" I say.

"I think you heard," he says.

"I can't believe what I heard," I say.

He shrugs.

"Where does that leave me?" I say.

"What do you mean?" he says, "It doesn't change anything. I still love you just the same."

"It changes everything," I say, "How could you?"

"Hang on there," says Loukas, in a tone of voice that's intended to soothe and comfort. "Of course, I'm going to stay. I'm going to need a house. I love being with you, and you can live in the house if you want to, but of course, it's obvious I'll need a wife, and if it's going to help things along, I might as well marry Stasia. She's not going to make trouble. We'll have to work it out after the wedding just how it's going to be arranged and just what it's appropriate for her to know. But maybe you'll want a wife too, and we'll see each other when we can. I don't know how it works here."

"How would it work in England?" I say.

"Oh, with a bit of hypocrisy and discretion," he says, "People who live in big houses have a lot of scope for doing what they like. They show the world a respectable face. There has to be a wife, and she can have affairs – it doesn't do for children to be born illegitimate – but no one worries who the father is: the man who owns the house pays to bring up his wife's children, and everybody's happy. There are scandals from time to time – when someone with middle-class manners is involved – and divorces happen, but on the whole, they don't. People find a way to get along."

"Are you sure that's how it works?" I say.

I'm shocked, but don't want to show it. I feel very naïve.

"I think we live much closer together here in the village," I say, "Everyone knows what's going on. I don't think it could work here, not like that."

"Do you think your mother knows what we've been doing?" he says.

This startles me. It hasn't occurred to me that she might.

"Well, she's living with us," he says, "and if she doesn't know, then that shows there's room for a few secrets in the village. I'm going to have to encourage Stasia. It can't do any harm. You have to be grown-up about it."

I mutter something even I can't hear. Stasia's being groomed. That's what these embroidery lessons are all about. Is she going to expect a wonderful romantic marriage? Or maybe she'll be thrilled with the financial security and quietly accept the arrangements Loukas has in mind. Will she start to hate me? Will I hate her? I'll envy her position or resent it. It's all closed in around me like I've walked into a trap. What was I expecting? I hadn't thought. I suppose I just want things as they are to stretch out ahead of us to the horizon, but that's not the way things are. Enjoy it while it lasts, and come down lightly. I'm upset, and I mustn't show it. When Loukas says it, it doesn't sound so bad, but around here – it's not going to work like that. There's no adultery within the village, no divorce, just curses, death, and excommunication – exile for the few people who can't follow the codes. It's not to do with the law or what the priest says. It's just the way the village works. Maybe I'm naïve, and the adults know something different.

60

I am at the drawing board in the afternoon. It makes a world of difference. I can draw a horizontal line and know it's parallel with the other horizontal lines, which is what you want when you're trying to plot the position of points on a surveyor's grid.

"How are you doing?" says Xander.

"It's going well," I say, "It's a real help. But I'm ready to stop."

"Good," said Xander, "Would you like a shower before we eat?"

"That sounds like a good idea," I say.

"Come through here," said Xander. He opened the door onto the courtyard and led the way across it to Dmitri's room. It's set up like a hotel room with the facilities to make it self-contained. There is a hint of a kitchen, even, with a gas ring in the corner.

"Is Dmitri away?" I say.

"I've sent him to Athens," says Xander, "You'll find everything you need. The bed's been made up clean. I assume you'd rather stay the night than find your way back in the dark. You can decide later. But look – have a clean shirt – my mother will appreciate it. Come on up when you're ready. We'll be on the terrace."

There's a freshly pressed white shirt with a collar neatly laid on the bed, alongside a large and small towel, some pajamas, and a toothbrush. There are beams and floorboards here – different from the vault at the front of the building. How would it feel to be an apprentice here? There'd be no escaping the supervision of the boss. Dmitri hasn't personalized the room. There's a cupboard with some clothes in it that must be his. The soap smells of lemons and the shirt of lavender, so I'm feeling refreshed and perfectly clean when I go up the outdoor stairs to the terrace. Xander's there lost in thought, but then he notices me.

"Come on," he says and gestures for me to turn and look at the view.

"Wow," I say, "I forget how close we are to the sea."

From the ground, you can't see it, but from up here, you see over the flat roof of Maria's house, next to the megaron, which is taller and blocks the view of the horizon.

"You can see the cypresses over there," says Xander, looking into the sun's low glare.

"Oh yes," I say, "but not the stoa. The others will be starting to cook. They're not good at it. The food's much better here."

"They can always come here if they want to," says Xander.

"Len said it was best if they didn't," I say.

"He's a good judge of these things," he says.

"You know some of the people here," said Xander, leading the way around the corner.

There is a round table on a broad paved terrace. Four people are sitting at it. They stop talking and turn. Three of them stand up.

"Len," I say.

"Ian," says Len, who is smarter than I've ever seen him before, dressed in a shirt exactly like the one I've been given.

"This is Alice Cyprian," says Xander.

"How do you do," says Alice Cyprian. She's wearing a dust-coloured dress in a fine fabric and has a gleaming line of gold around her neck and gold seahorses dangling below her ears. Her eyes, too, are gold.

"My mother, Jael," says Xander.

"Excuse me for not standing up," says Jael, who looks old, her long white hair tied back in a bun and leathery but well-oiled skin.

"I wouldn't expect it," I say, "How do you do."

"And my wife, Anastasia," says Xander.

"Please, Stasia," says Xander's wife.

"Please," says Xander, gesturing to an empty chair.

"Are you enjoying the island?" says Jael.

"What little I've seen of it," I say.

"How is Charles?" says Alice.

"Winchester?" says Ian, "He's fine. Maybe a bit depressed."

"Don't mention that you met me here," says Alice, "It would make him unhappy if he thought I'd come here without paying him a visit."

"You're welcome to come to the site," I say, "Did you know Luke?"

"I did meet him," said Alice, "Why do you ask?"

"It's just that Charles seems to have problems with people who knew him," I say, "In his past."

Where would this marriage leave me? In the shadows. I'll melt away and won't be in the photos. I'll be around, out of shot, a specter at the feast, a hanger-on, anomalous, without acknowledgment. There's no accepted role for somebody like me. I'll have Loukas, of course, at least for now, and if as years go on we drift apart, the world won't know it, will be none-the-wiser – it won't show: no need for explanations, divorce, nothing on the surface. It's just a quiet shift behind the mask. Maybe that's the way it should be. Maybe that's the best. Maybe this is a phase I'll grow out of, and I'll want to move on. The less there is apparent, the less we face embarrassment, and the less there is to explain if things go wrong further down the line. I won't need Loukas's money because my business will grow, and I'll have the house we're in now when my mother dies, and I daresay my wife will be living there long before that. Who can say? That's all for the future. For now, I have things as they are – and as they might stay for a while – to make my life worthwhile for as long as this blissful moment lasts – and not just for those moments, but for memories of them that might have to sustain me for a lifetime. I'd know at least that I'd been happy once, the way I'm happy now. Or up till now.

The food is already prepared and waiting on a long side table. Every so often, Stasia and Xander bring something from it to pass around. Fried cheese, small cubes of spanakopita, meatballs, spinach, tomatoes, salad, broad beans, chicken, and yogurt. The light fades from the sky, and Xander brings a tray of small, already-lit candles in white glasses for the table.

"We're supposed to be going to Heraklion for a team visit the day after tomorrow," I say.

"Make sure you don't go round the museum with Charles," says Alice, "He'll bore you to death."

"That's where we met," says Xander, "In the museum."

"Was it you?" says Alice, "or was it Luke? who was looking at the octopus vase."

"I think we both were," says Xander, "I remember being entranced by it. I could hear the wash of water in my ears, and it was looking at me with its soulful eyes. It seemed to make a world around itself and drew me into it."

"I'll look out for it," I say.

"Everything else is fake," says Len.

"You exaggerate," says Alice, "but there's a lot of imaginative restoration. You'll see. You have an eye for it."

"Do I?" I say.

"Oh yes," says Alice.

An easy rapport falls across the table as the meal works its magic. Everyone speaks quietly, and no one tries to show off. We all seem to feel comfortable together, and the evening feels like a success.

"You will stay over, won't you," says Xander, "There'll be breakfast here in the morning. Come up when you're ready. The kitchen door will be open if we're not up, but we probably will be."

It feels like the most natural thing to do. The room is ready and waiting.

"Let me show you where things are," says Xander.

"I'm OK," I say, "I think I know."

"Let me show you," says Xander.

We go down from the terrace and through the workshop and the courtyard, and Xander hugs me and kisses me on the forehead and says goodnight. I wonder if he's expecting me to invite him to stay, but I don't find out. I go to sleep so soundly I wonder if I've been drugged, but there's nothing untoward except in dreams that I don't quite remember. They involve swimming underwater. There's the underside of the surface of the sea, like a sheet of rippling cellophane, and great golden chandeliers of seaweed, and other people around, also swimming underwater. It comes back to me again when I'm swimming in the sea in the afternoon.

63

When we go to Heraklion again, it's in a hired car that was made in Yugoslavia and has an engine like a sewing machine's. Eleni's in the front with me, coming as the chaperone. The love birds are in the back seat. We check in at the Hotel Megaron. Loukas and I have a room on the top floor with a balcony overlooking the harbor. The women are on the other side of the block on the first floor. We meet for a volta, strolling around the city walls, admiring the views. Eleni and I end up together while the others go on ahead and seem to be engrossed in conversation.

"Oh, isn't this lovely," says Eleni, "You can see the mountains and the sea."

You can see mountains and sea at Ziros, I think, but I'm being polite, so I murmur some appreciation. In fact, she's hardly looking at the scenery. She's watching Loukas and how he's treating her daughter. He's being very polite.

Back at the hotel, when I'm in bed with Loukas, I want more than ever to make him writhe with pleasure. I want him to know that he'll never find this with Stasia. She'll just lie there and expect him to do everything. I know where to press, where to slide, where to squeeze, where to suck, and how to keep it all going, how to make him helpless, how to make him beg for just a moment more. How to make him late for breakfast.

"My God," I think, "I'm thinking like a whore." And I blame it on Stasia, which I know isn't fair, but what else can I do? I think in the future, she's going to look daggers at me, so I'm starting to resent her in advance.

I rehearse my excuses, thinking I'll have to explain myself when I meet the students at the beach, but they don't ask any questions, and I don't have to explain anything at all. I wonder if they can read in my face that I've had some sort of adventure, and they're too tactful to ask. But perhaps they just don't notice. In the water, my body seems to have been transforming and is singing about being there, fully immersed. I seem to be merging with the water. I'm not a fast swimmer, but I'm secure in the water, and I can relax and let it heave about, and I go with it, my nose barely out of the water, and I can see. I have goggles with prescription lenses in them, which do a surprisingly good job. The water's in me as well as around me. It's in my veins. I'm sixty percent water. My lungs are over eighty percent water. Fifty pounds of water and four ounces of flesh. No. That's not me. That's a jellyfish, but the thought's lodged in my mind. The water's completely comfortable, at just the right temperature, so I don't feel it at all, only its resistance when I push at it. My internal organs feel like oysters and sponges, swimming about in the salty bloody sea inside me, tethered by the tubing of veins but ready to float apart and lead quite independent lives. My bones are deposited like coral. My muscles all relax. I'm buoyant in the saline solution of the Aegean, and I move like seaweed with the bobbing waves. My pores open up, and I taste the salt, sensing the wavering light refracting through the water in the brilliant glare. I can feel something leaving me through my skin – a scent – a hormone – an ecstasy-like sunburn cooking my flesh, but coolly underwater. The sky-blue sky is flawlessly blue. My body blurs with the sea, breathing but not breathing. I've been turned inside out, and my skin's like the skin that's inside the mouth – intensely receptive and delicate and overwhelmed by salt and iodine. My hearing is internalized and then muffled. A pulse throbs through my head, which has disappeared. It's a pulse in the body, perhaps as sound at first, but more like pressure in the veins. I'm spreading out in all directions, becoming layers of filtering membranes – skin – blood vessels – lungs – letting in the chemicals I need – oxygen – iron – calcium carbonate.

"You're not drowning, are you?" says Toby, splashing about.

"Just meditating," I say.

"Cool," says Toby, and splashes around some more.

65

At the museum and at Knossos, Loukas acts as the guide and says none of the heretical things that brought Alice out of the woodwork. He tells the stories just as Sir Arthur Evans would have wanted. He's being a good boy today. No mischief in public. There is no hint of anything unsafe about him.

On the way back to the hotel, Loukas excuses himself, and the rest of us keep stopping to look in dress-shop windows.

"I call it 'taste formation,'" says Eleni. The idea is to see what the fashions are and then do something like them at home. There's not much embroidery in evidence. "These days, it's all in the cut. It's such a shame."

Stasia says less, but she's paying attention to where the dresses hug the body and where they hang free. I don't feel inclined to be drawn into the discussion. It's not expected of me. I know that Stasia is brilliant at cutting cloth to make the right shapes. A waist is a good thing to have, apparently. Some women have them, and some don't.

"I used to have a waist," says Eleni, "when I was a bit older than Stasia. Your hips are still developing. You need to eat more at your age. When I was a girl, the smart women in town used to wear corsets. They made people the right shape even when they weren't. You are the right shape. If you cut the dress right, you'll look as if you have a waist, even now. Look – like this one. It's close-fitting down to here. Then it goes fuller."

"It's nicely done," says Stasia, "There's no seam there going across. It's all tapered in. There must be seams where the tapering happens, but you can't see them."

"It works because of the fabrics," says Eleni, "They couldn't do it with a stripy fabric. If it were something plain, you could do it, but it would have to be absolutely exact. These flowers make your eye jump about a bit, and you don't notice."

"If I did it plain," says Stasia, "and then embroidered flowers over the seams, they'd disappear completely."

"You could," says Eleni, "It would be more work. It might look even better."

We walk past Galanakis's studio. I linger to look in the window, and I notice among the wedding photos and portraits that he's introduced a small print of the picture of Loukas and me. It was a glorious moment, and it's there, preserved. We look like film stars. The others don't notice, and I don't draw it to their attention. I'll tell Loukas about it later.

When we're quite close to the hotel, Loukas catches up with us. The women go quiet about the clothes and ask him what he's been doing.

"I was looking for some books about very old coins," he says, and his answer meets with a murmur of approval.

66

"On the drawings, I'm piecing together the fragments of wall," I say to Alice, who's having lunch at the megaron today, "and I'm finding these serpentine lines. Winchester connected them with snake-worship, so we imagine it as maybe a religious center for pythonism. He's thinking we could rename the settlement. Obviously, Paleoziros is a modern name – it's only about thirty years old – so he's thinking he could publish it under the name Pythonopolis, which would really literally put it on the map."

Alice laughs as if she can't help herself doing it.

"Charles is such a scream," she says, "He gets it so wrong every time it's almost brilliant."

"Why?" I say, "What's the problem?"

"There's no problem for me," she says, "Let him do it. I just know that he's wrong and couldn't be more wrong."

"How do you know?" I say.

She hesitates.

"I can tell you, but then if you tell anyone else, I'll have to kill you," she says, and she laughs again. I have the feeling it's not a joke, but I laugh along to keep alive the possibility that it is.

"Perhaps it's best that I don't tell you how I know," she says seriously, "but he's seriously wrong with the 'snakes' idea. The Snake People were in the east of the island. Forget snakes. Think octopus."

"But there's no evidence to support that," I say.

"There's plenty of evidence," she says, "if you know how to see it. It's obvious to me that your serpentine walls aren't snakes; they're octopus tentacles. That's evidence – big evidence – if you read it right."

"I'm not going to be able to persuade Winchester if that's all we've got," I say, "It could go either way, and he's dead set on snakes."

"Yes," she says, "that's fine. I don't care what he thinks or what he publishes, but we feel differently about you. You have the capacity to understand. Charles never did. Now that you're staying in the village, the old village that we're learning to call Neaziros, you're surrounded by our people. Have you noticed that you're having different thoughts or different dreams?"

"Well." I say, "I've noticed thoughts entering my head. I'm dreaming about water more often than I used to. I thought it was just something to do with being on the island, close to the sea."

"Yes," says Alice, "It's probably just that." But she looks unaccountably pleased with herself.

"Are you saying it's some sort of telepathy?" I say.

"We don't say 'telepathy'," she says, "We think it's normal. We say that people who don't do it are 'blocked'. Charles is blocked, it won't surprise you to learn. Len noticed you weren't."

67

And then I've reached the cypresses, my sanctuary. The soil with Dinos's blood and who-knows-what underground. I'm feeling fragile but still quite determined – holding on, but I need comfort. My mother has betrayed me, all unknowing, and I can't complain to her. Persuading Loukas that the way for his plans to succeed is for him to marry Stasia. And he's going along with it. He seems to think it doesn't change things between us. But it does. It's no longer him and me against the world if Stasia's in there, too. Maybe we become a team, so it's the three of us against the world, but that's not going to be what she has in mind when she says yes to Loukas. Loukas is not the rock I'd hoped he'd be. I'm safe here in the stani – in the middle of the ring of tallest trees. I lie down on my back and look up to the sky. The sky-blue sky. The Cretan sky. The ends of branches move wavily, like seaweed underwater, as a current washes by. I practise my slow breathing and tune into the atmosphere, the seething and the sighing of the breezes up above. The air thickens – that golden moment– I could be breathing water. My breaths are so shallow and take such a long time I might altogether stop needing to breathe – just take in the honeyed air through the pores of my skin. I keep very still, flat on the ground, pressing into it. It has a body's warmth. I can feel it breathe with me like Loukas was here, and he is – I can see him – he's come to the wall, but he's not stepping in. He hasn't seen me. He's looking across, but I keep still and silent. I close my eyes. The sounds could be the sea. Maybe there is some distant sea sound in there beyond the wind – if I stood up, I'd be able to see the sea from here; if it weren't for the olive trees – there must be some sea sound to hear. I'm melting into the ground as I melt into Loukas when we embrace – the boundaries between us go away, and I feel safe as if nothing can go wrong so long as we stay that way. It's the earth here now that's doing that, and it's never going to let me down.

"I'll never let you down," says Matthias.

I say nothing. He's looking at me with his piercing eyes, gas-jet blue. I'm mesmerized, and he knows it. I know he's not real, but he looks real and sounds real.

"You started to forget me," he says, "but I'll always be here. You know that."

"I want to be with Loukas," I say.

"He'll disappoint you," says Matthias, "He has disappointed you. He'll destroy you."

"I'll get over it," I say, but I know I don't believe it. Matthias smiles slightly, and the golden light catches him. I'm transfixed – held in weird suspension while the light fades, goes ungolden, and breaks this subtle and insidious spell. I've pulled myself together by the time we eat. You wouldn't know that anything at all had changed. Nothing has changed except that everything's changed. I'm a little less naïve. It's no big deal for the others that my world has come crashing down around me because, so far as everyone else is concerned, it's all still in place. So far as they're concerned, this is another day for me like yesterday, but I know now that although my mother isn't out to thwart me, I want something she won't let me have – or rather, I want something that won't happen because of what she's doing. Loukas still wants to be with me, indulge me, and learn from me all the abrupt idioms that give him access to my world – or Stasia's world, if mother's plot works out. In Loukas's mind, these plots aren't incompatible – mother's and mine – they wrap around each other, hugging like a Chinese joint. One piece has this shape. The other fits around it, so it's solid where the other has a gap. They're cut so when you look, you just see squares, but internally, you can't figure out what's happening: they slide together on the diagonal, which takes you by surprise, and if you try to take it apart without knowing that, it seems impossible, bonded by magic.

68

"It's decided," says my mother, "Loukas will make his speech to the women at the Thesmophoria. Then there will be a decision about the land, and everyone will be a witness to it, so it will have good standing."

"It sounds daunting," says Loukas, "How many women? And who are they?"

"Not too many," she says, "but enough. About thirty. You'll know some of them. They're from local villages. In principle, it's the women who've had children."

"There's something like that in England," he says, "It's called the Women's Institute."

"Then you'll know what to expect," she says. She turns to me.

"Alexakis, she says, "There's a chestnut festival at Elos that same day. You should go there with Stasia. Have a nice time,"

"Why would we want to do that?" I say.

"It will be strange in the village that day," she says.

Elos feels like a foreign country. I'm not sure that we belong. There are tables and chairs everywhere around the plateia, and the whitewashed tree trunks look like café walls, a poster here and there. Colorful rags are strung overhead across the streets and among the leaves that look tired as if they can hardly wait to drop. Children are running around, some of them in traditional costumes. Older people are sitting with their little cups of coffee that last all day and the tumblers of water that need regular refilling. There are some market stalls. You can buy chestnuts, of course, if you want some to take away with you after the day's done. There's olive oil, tins of honey, and jars of fruit preserved in honey syrup. Stasia is alert today, and she seems interested in everything, not just the stalls.

"Look at the houses," she says, "I think we've got used to living in ruins."

"Loukas is doing up the house," I say.

"Yes," says Stasia, "But everywhere here looks well-kept. It feels good. Imagine living here."

I grunt a reply. They have more money here and more men to do the money-making work. Ziros is all women. Elos is all men.

"There's hardly any women here," I say.

"There's plenty of children," says Stasia, "The mothers will be back after the Thesmophoria."

"We should have a coffee," I say.

"You order," says Stasia, "I'll be there in a minute."

I sit at a table under a tree. It's crudely made, and it wobbles. The chairs are ordinary but sturdy and look as if they've been around for decades.

"Yassas," says a man about my age. I'm thinner than him. His work must need him to lift things. He didn't shave today, and maybe not yesterday, but he has a very good haircut.

"Two coffees," I say, "Sweet."

"Where are you from?" he says and sits down at the table.

"Ziros," I say, and when he looks blank, I say, "It's near Gerani."

"Ah! A fellow West-Cretan!" he says.

"I am," I say.

"Tassos," he says.

"Alekos," I say.

"Don't pay for anything, Alekos," he says, "You're our guest. The prices are for the tourists."

"Oh," I say, "Are there tourists? I feel like I'm a tourist here."

He shrugs in a lugubrious way.

"You're a guest. It's different." he says, "I hope we have some Italians here at least. We want them to feel like guests. Then they spend their money. Two coffees," he says to the bearded man who's shown up now, "Sweet. Did you want anything else?" he says to me.

I make a dismissive gesture with my hand.

"We don't have tourists in Ziros," I say.

"We're working on it here," he said, "We're not by the beach, so we're trying to make chestnuts a thing. Before we started the festival, the only visitors were communist guerrillas, and they weren't welcome."

"That business in the gorge?" I say.

"That put an end to it," he says.

"You're in the hills here," I say, "We had a visit from Nazis, but nothing since."

I could tell him about Loukas, of course, but he's not a visitor. He's an immigrant, and it's too complicated to explain what went on without saying too much. I'm not going to tell him about Matthias either. He's included in the visit from Nazis, so I'm not lying. He visited and changed more than anyone knows, and it's impossible to explain.

"You're lucky," he says, "Those communists were trouble."

"We were not lucky," I say, "We really weren't."

We were devastated and haven't yet recovered, but I don't want to talk about it here. Tassos would have heard something about us at the time, but he doesn't know the village name, and he hasn't made the connection. Something now seems to stir in his memory. He looks abashed and looks at the ground apologetically.

"What a time to start a civil war, eh?" he says.

"That hardly touched us," I say, "But there weren't any men left by then, and the women don't go in for politics."

"Oh, they do round here," he says, widening his eyes.

The server comes with the coffee.

"He's our guest," says Tassos, "I'll bring you some chestnuts unless you want honey."

"I definitely want to take some chestnuts home to my mother," I say. I want a token to prove that we've come here.

"I won't be long," he says.

"You see," says Matthias, "you're going to be bored with Loukas. You're better off with me."

"It's not as if I have to choose," I say, "You live in different worlds."

"We meet in you," says Matthias, "and someday he's going to realize it."

And then Loukas says, "You're shouting," and I wake up. Matthias has been here. I can feel it. What havoc has he wrought? Loukas holds me, "Relax, you're OK," he says. There's plenty of light in the hotel room, but it's coming in through a narrow slot where the shutters don't at the moment meet. The sun outside is glaring harsh and brilliant, but the balcony's in the shade as we'd want it to be. I don't want to go back to sleep again.

"I met Feni," says Stasia, "She's living in Kefali now."

"I remember her wedding," I say.

That was in Ziros, and the women hoped that the couple would stay there, so they set about charming the husband-to-be with smiles and gifts of little cakes, but his family's income was from a café with a view, and this young man was expected to take it on, so Feni left, and we never saw her again. Her mother went too.

"How's she doing?" I say.

"She's having another baby," says Stasia, "Her mother's looking after the other one today. She makes the father lose his temper, so he stays in the café as much as he can."

"I hope they're happy," I say.

"She seems to be," says Stasia, "She didn't say it out loud, but she knew I didn't have any children yet, and she wanted me to know that she was ahead of me. Winning the game of life."

I wonder whether Stasia will have children. Loukas doesn't seem to think he's going to stop sleeping with me. I'll have the downstairs room that connects with Loukas's study through a trapdoor and a retractable ladder that I've already installed in the house. Stasia is smiling a secret smile to herself, knowing that once she's married, she'll be better off than Feni ever will be. We'll see how it works out for her. I'm smiling a secret smile, too, knowing what I know.

71

And then Loukas says, "You're tense," when he wraps himself naked around me, "You smell lovely. What is it? It's like you're wearing a cologne."

"I'm not. It's just me."

"It's you, but you've been smoked, and there's some sage there – or something – oregano – and you, of course. I could breathe you in." I grunt something sleepily. The desolation dissipates into the night, with Loukas holding me, but something lingers, so I'm feeling – what? – cautious when I used to feel I could let go – guarded when I didn't used to feel there was anything to guard against – not with him.

At first, when my mother and Loukas hatched the plot for him to marry as a way to show he was serious about settling here, it seemed like a joke. Then, when they fixed on Stasia, I didn't like it. Loukas didn't like me shouting at him – I think because he knew my mother would wonder what the problem was. He told me not to worry that things wouldn't change that much.

"Be patient," he said, "Keep calm."

"I feel used," I said, "You just did what you did to win my trust."

"I love you," he said, "Nothing's going to change that."

"I used to believe you when you said that," I said.

"Come here," he said, and he held me, and all my misgivings melted away. They came back again when he wasn't there, but when we were together, everything seemed to be OK again. Maybe that's what my life's going to be like – vague unease most of the time that disappears when we get together.

72

"Your Chestnuts," says Tassos. His eyes are piercing. For a moment, I feel lost, as if I've been taken to a different place. I hear Stasia clearing her throat, but Tassos has my eyes.

"Let me introduce my neighbor, Anastasia," I say without looking at her.

"Fascinated," says Tassos, without looking away, "Fascinated."

"This is Tassos," I say, "He's brought us some chestnuts."

"That's very kind," says Stasia,

"I go through Gerani on the way to Chania," says Tassos.

"You would," I say.

"You might meet at the market in Chania," says Stasia.

"It's possible," I say. Tassos smiles broadly.

"I'll see you in Chania then," he says and takes his leave.

Stasia goes quiet for a while and seems to be in her own little world.

And I'm in another world again, with Matthias. He had the bluest eyes I've ever seen, and they held me, moth-like. We looked at one another, and the world went away. It was a feeling of absolute purity. I could feel our souls leaving our bodies and meeting in the air between us. The air was singing. It's a pivotal moment in my life, and I'm back in that moment.

"He's Stasia's now," says Matthias.

"That's what she thinks," I say.

"What was that?" says Stasia.

I don't say anything. Matthias looks insolent and smirks.

Someone's strumming a guitar, and there's an accordion.

"Let's see what's happening," I say.

It's schoolchildren doing a well-rehearsed dance. It's charming in its way.

Later, there's a man who shows how it should be done. He stretches his arms out in a graceful curve, the palms turned up, trailing a handkerchief in his right hand, striking a very deliberate pose and somehow taking charge of the whole square. There are other men and women, too, grouped in a circle that's not too precise. The man with the handkerchief takes the lead, but the others all know what to do. The music's from an accordion and a guitar. They start slow and very grave. There's a look of inward intensity on the leader's face as he twists on one foot, turns his hands, moves along the line of the circle, holds out his foot, following a sequence that he might be making up as he goes, but the others, watchful, are all doing the same. The guitar's doing most of the work, rapid strumming now, and the dancers are jumping about – light little jumps and skips –

happy movements – nothing spectacular, but quite energetic. The thrilling thing is that they all know what they're doing, and they're doing it together. The square is filled with joy. It's rapturous. It goes on longer than you'd think it could. It's delightful. We don't do this in Ziros. We used to, when there were men there. I remember seeing people dancing when I was younger, but I never learnt the moves myself. It wasn't this dance. We can't join in here. I'm smiling, and I'm clapping along, and you'd think I'm having a good time in an uncomplicated way. My body knows from the dancing, even though it's the dancing of others, that I'm having a good time. But this sort of good time has gone from our village. The tradition's been broken. If it comes back, we'll have to learn it in an artificial way, but here it's real. We have to do something about Ziros. Its colors faded. Red earth. Yellow earth. The doors and shutters always used to be dark green. Everybody knew that the dark green pigment is the one that lasts best. That was the one to use. Now, along the coast, everybody uses blue. It's the nationalist thing. The blue and white of the flag becomes the blue and white of the villages. That didn't used to be an issue, but somehow, the civil war made everyone into nationalists. It always used to be Cretan independence. Then, it switched to being free Greece against the internationalists. I'm smiling, remember. I'm having a good time. I envy the good fortune of Elos and its people, who've survived in a way we haven't. I'm an outsider here, whatever Tassos says. I can witness their good fortune and their ability to conjure up a party from a few baskets of chestnuts and scraps of colorful paper made into flowers that have been strung up between the trees. There's a buzz of happiness in the play of the music, the rhythms of the dance, the feeling of not being hungry, the feeling of having enough.

Back at home, it's different. I go and lie on Loukas's bed, but he's not there. Sleep is not going to come to me. My mind is racing but going nowhere. I'm alert, but there's nothing in my head. I'm not even bored. I'm listening and hearing nothing but my blood. My eyes are open, but it's completely dark. I'm not feeling hot or cold. I'm feeling panic, but it's directionless. I do not want to run. I've gone a long way inside myself, but everything's completely awake to the outside. It's just that there's nothing there. Nothing outside. Nothing inside. Blank. Blank. Blank. Empty. I'm empty. The world is empty. Everything's gone.

It's the last week of this summer's dig, and Alice has joined Len and me over lunch at the megaron overseen by the Galanakis portrait, the Zimbrean bison, and the Venetian masks. It's not her habit. She normally stays out of sight, but then again, she's no stranger here. There are lively Australian conversations going on at the two long tables, and she doesn't join in with the everyday banter. She's a generation older than the diggers, disguises her grey hair with blonde streaks, and hardly touches the food.

"Has Xander ever taken you to the old house?" she says.

"What do you mean?" I say, "The house he did up? Where he lives." I know she can't mean that, because I've eaten with her there. She must know I use the drawing board there every day and I often sleep there as I nearly always eat either at the megaron or the house these days. The stoa with the archaeologists in it still has a room for me, and I'm often there during the course of the day, but this year, they don't expect me to be there for meals.

"No," she says, "his old house, where his mother lives."

"No," I say, "I haven't been there."

"There's something I'd like to show you," she says, "I'd like to know what you make of it. There's no hurry. When you're ready."

We walk to the edge of the village, where dark-leaved citrus trees crowd around a house that has a whitewashed wall and a green door onto the street. We go through the door, and we're in a yard with the house down one side of it and outbuildings at the end. On the side opposite the house, there's a low wall with iron railings, and a view out among the trees. The house wall has a step running all the way along it that makes a bench, but as it's in full sun at the moment, you wouldn't want to sit there. There's a small round table like you might find in a café in the shade of the trees and four chairs with rush seats against the railings.

"Mrs Ziros is probably asleep," says Alice, "so no loud noises. This way."

The door is already open. We're in a fairly large room with a made-up bed in the corner. There are two quite large windows, one on the street and the other on the yard, but they are both shuttered, so the only light is coming in through the door. There's some dusty-looking shelves with old jars on them and a few books, and a large table that has red cartridge paper laid on it, and on that, there are small objects at regular intervals. At first, I think they're coins, but some of them look more like pebbles.

"Have a seat," says Alice, gesturing to a chair at the table, "This is the one I'd like you to take a look at. What do you think it is?"

It's tiny. A stone the size of a coin. Not a stone – earthenware – but it's been pressed by a stone. It's like a seal stone but convex.

"It was made by a seal stone," I say, "but it's ceramic." I take my glasses off, and hold the clay pebble five centimetres from my eye.

"Very good," says Alice, "Instead of using wax for this seal, they used clay, and then there was a fire, and it's been baked hard. If there were wax seals near it, they all melted, and there's no sign of them, but this one was made more permanent. Before I say anything about the image, just tell me what you see when you look at it. Take your time, but don't overthink it. Just say random things as they come into your head. Don't worry about making sense. I want your honest reaction. Don't tell me what you think I want to hear."

"Well," I say, "There's a man standing on a roof. He's quite fluid and bendy, and he's holding a staff that drops down quite straight. Maybe he's a statue. There's things around that look like buildings. But if they're buildings, the man's a colossal statue. And it's not the pose of a statue. A statue would have to be more like a column if it was going to stand up – if it was, how big – if those are buildings, are they three storeys high? He's three or four times life-size. You couldn't build a statue that size with that posture. Not with bronze-age technology? No. So, are they buildings? Are they miniature buildings? Like tombs or something. And what's that in the foreground? Is it the sea? It seems to have a geometric grid in it. It doesn't look like the sea. It's more like paving. And just above it – I thought they were rocks or something, but there's some symmetry in it – you know: that reminds me of the lions at Mycenae – the lion gate – a column with a lion on each side of it – you can't really make them out as lions, but the shape reminds me of it – the RIBA uses it as its insignia, it's a thing I recognize. Maybe I shouldn't."

"Thank you," says Alice.

"How did I do?" I say.

"Magnificently," she says.

"How come?" I say.

"I want to know what might be there without someone from the museum misdirecting me," she says.

"What did you see when you looked at it?" I say.

"I saw it as a city dominated by a colossal statue," she says, "I wondered if it might be Palaeoziros seen from the sea – so I'm interested in your impression that the foreground might be sea. I'm finding my own first impression less convincing now that I've heard yours. I don't see your lions at all. But what you say about the figure is good. You're right. It doesn't look like a statue. But if it isn't colossal, then those are not regular-sized buildings."

"It's making me think of the way in old paintings they used to put in figures at different sizes," I say. "You get unimportant people shown half the size of the important ones. Maybe it's something like that. It's not a colossal statue, just an important person. A hero."

"Most of the other seals are either figures or animals," says Alice, "There's a few buildings, but not many. It's tantalising. These tiny images are the only ones we have that are intact. There's limited detail, but they're complete, so they give a better general impression – if only we can work out what it's an impression of. You wouldn't want to imagine the site with a colossal statue towering over it?"

"Not if this is the only evidence," I say, "It's a lively figure. He looks like he moves about. And that staff – what is that? Is it something to do with authority? Is it going to turn into a snake?"

"You're right," says Alice. "It doesn't look static enough to be a statue. Especially a Bronze Age statue."

"What did they make statues out of then?" I say, "It would be big for a timber statue, and you couldn't do that posture in stone. You surely couldn't have cast bronze on that scale back then."

"It would probably have been timber," says Alice, "with some sort of framework and maybe draped with cloth to hide some parts of it. Is that his house he's standing on – a palace – or is it a city? Is it a necropolis? Are they tombs? Is he a priest? Is he a living god, looking after the city, presiding over it? Are those pinnacles on the roofs, or is the whole site in flames?"

"They're too regular for that," I say, "If they were flames, they wouldn't just be at the corners of the buildings. Or maybe flames are difficult to do, and they didn't come out quite right. It's impossibly small, and the sculptor just had a few scratches to do the modeling. It's intriguing. Where was it found?"

"Here at Paleoziros," says Alice, "last week."

And then, really, I've come for the flat horizon, for a sense of the future. The sea always hides its past and wipes it clean. There's nothing to see. There may be shipwrecks and sunken cities somewhere nearby, but on the surface, every day starts clear, with nothing lingering from the day before, the year before, or the century before. On land, everything gets cluttered. The Venetian fort isn't useful anymore, but it's still here to look at just because it hasn't fallen down. Under the fields, the Minoan palaces are still there, even though no one has cared about them for aeons, and maybe they're under the sea too, but the sea lets you start again. You don't have to take your past with you. The light makes the water sparkle a long way out. You can see the darker water where the currents run fast, and from here, you see a complicated web of them, telling you there's something running deep, going on below, but it's the surface I want: the sea is the place to be, where the water meets the air and makes this unfathomable layer – so thin – so delicate, but never broken – like tinfoil only finer and more mobile – plastic – filmy. I can feel my arms waving like tentacles, but I don't actually move. I'm just lost in the moment, lost to the sea, lost to the light, lost to myself – letting myself change shape in the current, in the dancing wavelets. The water's reflecting sunlight flickering across my face and lighting up the hulls of boats with dancing lines. Everything can change.

Everything can dance. Everything can flicker. Everything can disappear in spots of light.

"We'll be all right," says Matthias, "but you have to trust me." The light's dancing across him, too, and he looks less solid than he usually does.

"I thought it was all going to work out with Loukas," I say, "I thought I'd forget you."

"That's what I was afraid would happen," says Matthias, "but it won't. I won't let it."

"You can't trust him," says Matthias, "You have to kill him. You can't trust your mother either."

He shrugs and lets me draw my own conclusion.

"I'm not going to kill him. I don't have to listen to you," I say, "and I'm certainly not going to kill her."

"Oh," he says, with a sly smile and a twinkle in his eye, "but you know I'm right."

75

Unblindfolded, Luke looks around a forest clearing – a crowd unfocused, women chat in small groups.

"What do we do now?" says Luke.

"Now," says Jael, "We wait."

It's a clear sunny day in late October, still early enough in the day to feel cool, but everyone knows it will be hot later. Maria, dressed as an official in a long pale grey dress, comes over to explain.

"Your speech is after we've eaten," she says, "Relax for now and join in with the feast."

Luke stands with Jael, apart from the crowd.

There's Ariadne, leading Grylla forward. The priestess, if that's what she is, swings a huge mallet like a sledgehammer, hitting Grylla on the head. Grylla staggers and lies down on her side, and someone's there already with the knife at her throat and a beaten copper bowl to catch the blood. Grylla's confused and looks at Ariadne, trusting, and Ariadne looks right back, locked in the gaze. They've taken Grylla's foreleg and moved it up and down, pumping it like bellows to keep the flow of blood going, filling first this bowl and then another.

Luke turns away. He's reeling. They might have warned him. But they're all behaving as if this is normal. It's just what people do. They get on with it, solemn but matter-of-fact. When he turns back, the pig's strung up by the hind legs looking like a crucifixion, supported on two poles, bleeding in a bucket.

"You're looking pale," says Jael, "we should have left the blindfold on."

"When does the meal start?" says Luke.

"Oh," says Jael, "not for a while. There's quite a bit of preparation to do. They've taken the intestines. They have to be washed and turned into the sausage for the first course."

"Jesus Christ," says Luke.

"Iero gourouni," says Jael, "This year, we're doing her for the feast of Saint Anastasia the Roman."

"Is that Stasia's name day?" says Luke.

"No," says Jael, "That's in March. A different Anastasia."

"There's so much to learn," says Luke. His speech is rehearsed in Greek, and he will be able to do it reasonably well, with a proper Cretan accent mixed with his Englishness, but his Greek isn't up to following the ebb and flow of a conversation with multiple voices when the women are speaking to one another.

"You should have a drink," says Jael, "Even if you don't drink it, you will look more relaxed if you have a glass in your hand."

All the conversations sound passionate and as if they might come to blows.

"What are they talking about?" says Luke.

"The price of fish," says Jael.

As the only man there, Luke feels self-conscious, but he is not the center of attention. He hangs around on the edge of conversations and fails to join in with them. When people sit down at long trestle tables to eat, his stomach turns at the smell of the plate that's put in from of him. There are dishes of vegetables and salad circulating, and they're mainly what he eats. There's more. An interlude with some singing from a woman with a good voice and then some hymns that everyone joins in. Everyone except Luke, of course. Then there's the main course, which is slices of Grylla, very nicely cooked. It's delicate meat and easy to eat, except that it's Grylla, and Luke is hesitant. There's wine circulating, and the glasses are never empty.

"Let sacred silence prevail!" says a voice, "Let sacred silence prevail!"

The priestess dressed in red steps forward and declaims in a voice that does not carry too well:

"The Mother and the Virgin, Queen of Heaven, who makes the earth teem with life:

We salute you.

For you, the ocean levels laugh, and birds and greening meadows,

Bring forth their goodness.

We celebrate the harvest and dedicate ourselves to producing and nurturing,

Perpetuating with the cycle of the seasons,

Life: survival and renewal.

Amen."

"Amen," says everybody else.

A hymn that everybody knows save Luke, who makes out just a few words. "Pepsi" takes him by surprise, "metamorphosi" easier to catch, and "soma" and "pneuma" more to be expected. The pitch is approximate, and the sound ethereal – thin and reedy – dispersed in the clearing, not held in by a building.

It's time for Luke's speech, which he delivers well enough, with Jael as his supporter to help with answering the questions so they can endorse him as a worthy villager. He has already started the renovation of a village house. He'll farm some land, arrange its improved irrigation, and bring piped water to the households of the village. He will also bring in proper electricity for everyone at Ziros who wants it. In return, he wants to marry Anastasia, Eleni's daughter, and to start an excavation of nearby land. If any treasure's found, it will belong to the whole village. He believes there's something there and wants to find it, but he's not in it for the riches. He hopes he'll build a reputation. That's what inspires him. His reputation will be the reputation of the village, which will prosper collectively through this dream.

The questions begin quietly and sound technical. He comes here unknown, with no supporter from his early life, no relative who can affirm his character. What does he want from us? A guarantee so he can raise the money from his father. What guarantee can he bring us? What do we know of him? What do we know of you, Mrs Ziros? Is your name Hanna or Jael? Have we ever heard your real name? Eleni: how long have you known this man? We understand you like him, but it's our duty to remind you to be circumspect. What do you know of him? Is he really what he seems? He's washed up on our shore with no credentials we can trust. There's money, yes, and that turns people's heads, but what's the source of that? Does he look German? Hanna-the-belly-dancer's son alone was spared by the Germans. Is she in league with them? They don't trust him, and now they don't trust Jael either. They won't be taken for fools. There's cunning everywhere, but Loukas poneiros has overreached. Loukas koutoponeiros. They're not falling for it. He's overreached, and his cunning is nothing but stupidity. The do-gooding pretending to do the actions of the state with private money – he's obviously a communist. He's trying to turn us into communists when we fought them in the civil war and defeated them. The communists are coming back in disguise in him. The women draw in closer to each other, and the bonds between them strengthen. The mood has shifted and unified: the crowd becomes a pack.

Luke doesn't understand what's happening. He's patiently thinking that there's a discussion going on that will reach its predicted conclusion, but in their minds, he's become a communist and the cause of slaughter. Everyone whose lad got shot in this war or that is up in arms against him. It took a moment's turn from murmurings to make a tight-knit pack of Maenads out to get him – tear him limb from limb. Luke saw it in their eyes. Dozens of blazing eyes all fixed on his – and you can't say he was wrong to run.

Instincts kick in. When the prey runs, you run too. God knows what the women thought. It wasn't really that they were thinking, just acting on an instinct that would have been resisted had they not been together in a pack. In that moment no one questioned it. They all knew what had to be done and they all knew they acted as one. Luke by running marked himself as prey and right away sensed madness and peril hunting him. He ran among the trees headlong. His legs gave way as he outran them, stumbled but went on. Seeing light ahead, he felt sunlight would save him. He flung himself into the brightness, not seeing till too late the precipice that fell away before his feet.

He hurtled in the gorge, too startled to let out a cry. The others stopped themselves in time, saw the loose ground, and held on to wiry bushes, and some at least felt triumph for a moment, but then, as sanity returned, they felt remorse but cloaked it in denial. If you ask, you'll find it never happened. No man has ever been seen at the Thesmophoria, and anyway, there never was a Thesmophoria. We were all at home, doing the things we sensible mothers do every day. We were washing, looking after children, cooking, or – as you saw – dancing for the chestnuts.

76

I don't have my glasses on, so I can't see Alice clearly, but she'll be watching to see how I react, and I've already reacted. I close my mouth and put my glasses on.

"I'm guessing that Winchester doesn't know about this," I say.

"You'd be guessing correctly," says Alice.

"What about these other things?" I say, looking at the coin-sized pebbles and discs on the cartridge paper.

Alice shrugs.

"They're waiting to be photographed, "she says, "We thought we'd let Charles have the one you're holding. It's good if he finds something remarkable each season. Otherwise, people will get discouraged. We take photos of everything, and everything's well documented, so we know what's what. Your eyes, by the way, are amazingly good. Xander's sorting out special lenses for the camera. I can't see anything there without a magnifying glass, but Xander works wonders with his special lenses. He says he's trying to see like an octopus. Do you think it could be a view of Paleoziros?"

"Well," I say, "I suppose it could be. But there's nothing here that corresponds with the curving walls we're uncovering, and this is showing something that looks much closer to the sea. It's a very portable object, but obviously, it's from Crete. And it's not a photo. It might be something that the engraver invented, not a view of anything real."

"It's all there is," says Alice, "so we want to take it as seriously as we can. Charles will mess up the interpretation – he's bound to. Has he been thinking about the iron discs, do you know?"

"He hasn't mentioned them to me," I say.

"We keep finding them," says Alice, "Look, there's some of them here. They have no market value, so we let Charles have them, but he just hides them at the ephoria. He doesn't know what to do with them."

"What should he do with them?" I say.

"He should tell the world about them," says Alice, "and get people thinking. They're iron discs at a Bronze Age site, so they're remarkable. Charles is worried that people will say he's got his dating wrong, so they stay in the store room. If he got them out into the world convincingly, they could tell you that the people who were living here had worked out how to smelt iron way back in the Bronze Age, and they were really special people, way ahead of their time, but Charles doesn't like explanations that confuse his categories. We could sell them for a spectacular price if people knew what they were, but we can't let on where they came from, so we can't sell them. They're an even greater treasure than the seal stones if Charles only knew it. The next great advance in technology was rehearsed here, hundreds of years before it became mainstream."

"Shouldn't you tell him?" I say.

Alice laughs.

"As if he'd listen!" she says, "He has all the facts. He just can't see what he has to do with them. He's not good at creative thinking. He can remember what he's been taught, so people have found him an apt pupil, but he's not a researcher. You won't have heard of Alcuin Cowie, I don't suppose."

"I've come across his name at the Lantern," I say, unable to remember anything beyond the name.

"He had the measure of him," says Alice, "I remember when I tried with Charles to air the idea that people might have lived in timber huts, and that's why we don't have any sign of settlements from some periods – they rotted away and didn't leave a trace."

"The Dark Age?" I say.

"That's what they call it," says Alice, "Charles wouldn't entertain the idea for a moment. Somehow, he knows that every Dark Age house was a stone house. It's exasperating. You know, he says that even when he has Knossos using great fat timber columns and beams – even if they've been modeled in concrete. And even he himself is living in a timber stoa, built with local timber, grown on Crete. OK, there's no actual evidence of timber building 3500 years later, but you have to admit it's a possibility."

"I know in Egypt they used mud brick," I say, "for everyday buildings, and they had tent structures. The stone was only used for the monuments. They're what's survived, so we know far more about ancient Egyptian religion and burials than we do about everyday life."

"You see," says Alice, "It's common sense. Why wouldn't the Cretans – who were in touch with Egypt, by the way – do the same? Away from the palaces – if they were palaces – the agricultural workers must have lived in houses they could build themselves, and there's no trace of them. Charles wants to say that everyone lived in the palaces. I think very few people lived there. Suppose it was mainly for the dead, with just some live-in guards to keep the place secure."

"So where would people have lived?" I say.

"Exactly," says Alice, "They're not even asking. I gave up on Charles long ago."

"He has no idea you're here," I say.

"It's best that way," says Alice, "Don't tell him."

"How do the things find their way here?" I say, "The work on site's being supervised."

"It's very straightforward," says Alice, "Charles is too lazy to notice what's going on. We supply the diggers. It's convenient for him just to pay for them through the Lantern. We find them and train them with some basic conjuring. The diggers control where the attention goes as a conjuror does. The kids are naive, and they don't suspect that there's anything going on. You aren't blocked. You'd have picked it up. The objects are all small enough to palm. If there's anything bigger, Charles gets it. He gets a reasonable amount. The diggers' aprons all have double pockets: one for show, so you can see it's empty, and one just in behind it where the things get put."

"You shouldn't be telling me this," I say, but I'm very pleased to know.

"We know we can trust you," says Alice, and she's right. I'm more interested in knowing what's going on than I am in protecting Winchester's interests. I know where I'll have the more interesting time.

I stay at Xander's overnight and sleep soundly with peaceful dreams about drifting underwater. Breathing underwater. The water's flowing through me without that being a problem, and I'm making no effort to move, just drifting with the current, stretching a limb here and there, horripilating in waves as dappled light passes over me.

77

A policeman comes to the house. Somebody's been found. They wonder if it's our missing person, Zimbrean. Can I identify him? I've come to Chania to a shady morgue with no refrigeration, smelling of formaldehyde and methane. There's Loukas with no life in him. Nothing charming anymore. No feeling that we're in it together. He's here, but he's gone. I think I'm going to vomit, but I don't. I think I'm going to faint, but I don't. I think I can't go on. I don't have to.

"You shouldn't drive, sir," says the policeman, "Sit in a café for a while."

I'll go and find Costas. I can't take it in. I can't believe it. It isn't true. In some parts of my mind, of course, I know it is true, but my body denies it. At first, I blame Matthias. He's indignant.

"I'm Prussian nobility," he says, "I don't go round pushing civilians off cliffs. I'd have shot him. We'd have had a duel."

"You can't shoot him," I say, "You wanted him dead."

"I don't dispute that," he says, "I'm just saying it wasn't me that did it."

"Did you make me do it?" I say, "You know I don't trust a word you say."

He shrugs.

"There's nothing I can do about that," he says.

I'm numbed. Nothing works anymore. Nothing makes sense. My dreams feel more real than my life when I'm awake. I'm not sure that I can always tell the difference. A darkness settles behind my eyes that takes the sparkle even out of bright sunlight. I can see it's sunny, but as though through sunglasses. Everything's like that, night and day. I think everyone in the village is shocked. There are questions from the police. They make sense of things in their own way.

"There's some figures here I think you should look at," said young Winchester.

"Oh," said Sir Alcuin, "Are they interesting?"

"They're troubling, sir," said Winchester, "I'll leave them with you."

"What's the problem?" said Sir Alcuin.

"I'm not sure we can trust the accountant," said Winchester, "There seems to be a big gap between the money we've paid out and the money we actually owed to people. I wonder if some of the money is going into the accountant's pocket."

"Are you sure?" said Sir Alcuin.

"I'm not sure," said Winchester, "What do you think?"

"Leave it with me," said Sir Alcuin.

At the market in Chania, there's a woman with home-sewn sackcloth bags holding salt that she's scraped off the rocks by the sea. You wonder how she keeps herself going, scratching along so close to the edge. If we want salt, we go and get our own, dissolved. We always fill a bottle with water for cooking when we're by the sea. People in town buy from people like her the way they'd give money to somebody begging and hardly notice what they've bought. In town, everything turns into money, and the money runs away.

There's no room in Costas's shop. It's stuffed. It's full of things that have a useful look about them. He's found space for my chairs – there they are – three of them turned upside down on the other three, surrounded by things that will rust if they stay here too long: olive oil cans, nails, lamps, bowls, and pans – some of them big enough to do a village feast – there's also electrical flexes wound round drums, coils of ropes and a lingering tang of tar. There are lots of knives, too, with long curved blades, some of them jagged. They don't look useful, really, just murderous.

"What are these knives for?" I said once.

"They make good presents," said Costas. I looked sceptical. Everyone knows you're not supposed to give knives as presents, but Costas, ever the salesman, continued as if I was looking for a present, "Then perhaps I can interest you in one of these?"

"What is it?" I said.

"It tells you how hot it is," said Costas, "Look – you need to get the angle right – can you see there's a line of silver? At the top of it, you read off the temperature on the ruler at the side. It's saying 19 degrees."

"Is that good?" I said.

"It's what it is," he said.

"So what can I do with that?" I said.

"You can say 'it's 19 degrees'," he said.

"How does that help?" I said, "If I'm feeling too hot or too cold, I already know it. I don't need to have a number for it."

"They're selling well," he said, as if I'd said something that was obviously wrong, "Everyone wants to know the temperature."

Costas turns it into a running joke. He now tries to sell a thermometer to anyone who comes into the shop while I'm there. He hasn't succeeded yet in my presence. I start to wonder if he's ever actually sold a single one.

Aris looks in to see if anyone's going for a coffee. He looks as if he lives outside. His face has deep crevices in it, and his whiskers look very pale against his skin.

"Have you given thought to the temperature?" says Costas, "It would be good to know when you're leaving the quay whether you have the right clothes for the day." He has a thermometer in his hand, and he looks at it as if it's a wonder to behold. Then he looks to Aris.

Aris gives him a look right back. He knows well enough what to wear, and he doesn't have money to throw away. He makes a sound deep in his throat that isn't a word. He might be preparing to spit.

"You know where a vet would put that," he says, "don't you."

It's not as though young Winchester knew what he was doing as deputy director. He had an idea that if he was going to be serious, then he would need to look at the accounts. He noticed how easy it would be to pick up the pen that the accountant used and copy his way of writing the number 1. If you put an extra 1, such a simple stroke, at the beginning of a number, you multiply it by ten. There was an idea of making things add up, so if you add 1 here, it makes the number at the end go up, and he wasn't going to try to do 2s and 3s, so he put in a few random 1s in further down the column, and a final extra 11 in the total and left it at that. Nobody was going to notice. It wouldn't affect what was in the bank or anything.

Aris is teaching me how to use his boat. I have oars in my own little dinghy on the beach below Ziros, but they're no good for going anywhere. That boat must have been built for someone who did something useful with it, I suppose, but I'm the only person who uses it now, except occasionally when the archaeologists borrow it to play with when they swim. Aris's boat's good. The motor takes a bit of starting, with a pull-cord to turn it over until it fires. Aris makes me do it. "There's a bit of a knack to it," says Aris. His dog's excited by the motor's noise and barks at it. There's hardly any change of level between the harbor and the water. The dog climbs into the boat without help – just a bit of encouragement.

It's a small boat but very solidly built from timber planks that have been steamed and curved into place. It's bigger than my dinghy – big enough to carry a few sacks. It's had so many coats of varnish that when you touch it it feels more like plastic than wood. Aris's world's not the same as mine. I see the joinery in the boat. He sees the mobility and the fishing it makes possible. I can't steer it. "Not so much. You're over-steering," he says, "Keep it still. Just gentle touches." Once I've realized how slight the adjustments are, it's straightforward enough. "OK," he says, "the open sea!" I look him in the eye, and he looks past the Venetian fort to the water beyond it, and I realize he means it. "You need to be careful of currents," he says, "They won't take you under – not round here – but they can take you a long way away, and then you'll run out of fuel before you get back."

"What happens then?" I say.

"Don't let it happen," he says, "You can see them currents at a distance show up dark, but then they disappear when you're close to them. If you're pulled away, get into the shore as soon as you can and deal with it from there. You won't do it a second time."

"Has it happened to you?" I say.

"Aye. Just once, when I was about your age," he looks at me, "No, I was younger, but I had more experience with boats, so I was confident. I was cocky. I had to get the bus back from Rethymno. It was humiliating. I'm lucky it wasn't worse."

I'm not feeling remotely cocky. I'm feeling anxious. The waves outside the harbor are disconcerting. I want to go back, but I'm not going to say that.

"I went back with a can of fuel," he says, "and a spare, and I brought the boat back, keeping close to the coast – never far from the rocks – the next day. It took all day. There's a spare can of fuel under that seat you're on. I always take a reserve."

"I'll learn from your experience," I say, "It's not an experience I want to have for myself."

"Oh, you don't never forget lessons you learn like that,"
he says, "One misjudgment and before you know it, you're
dried out and heat-struck. And that's that."

He's trying to frighten me, to make me remember, but it
looks as if he's learnt a few lessons that way. His left hand
is missing one and a half fingers, and the third finger on his
right hand is oddly bent.

"You can always tell a fisherman from his hands," he
says when he catches me looking at them.

We're out beyond the fort. An unfamiliar view. We're
close to the water – almost in it ourselves. It's thrilling. It's
like we're here without anyone's permission, and we can go
wherever we like. I really belong here. I'm bonded with the
sea. I can feel that I have a right to be here that I've not felt
before. Maybe this is where cockiness begins.

"We'd better go back now," says Aris.

I want to contradict him, but after a fraction of a second's
hesitation, I know that he has the authority here, and I'd
better obey. But the effect of being in the boat, being in
control of it, is instantaneous. The boat on the beach is fun.
The boat in the harbor is different, more businesslike. The
boat outside the harbor is freedom. With the motor and
everything, this isn't play. I want to be familiar with it.

"Can we take this boat out again next week?" I say, "I'd
like it to feel familiar. I'll pay."

"Buy my drinks," he says, "I want you to be good with boats. It's part of your heritage as a Cretan. Your father would have taught you."

He reminds me of Dinos, and it dawns on me that I haven't been seeing my demons very much of late. I expect that's a good thing. Galanakis is my new Mentor, and Loukas is my new demon, and they're healthier influences. They don't keep telling me to kill myself. I wonder if Aris has a wife. I only know about one part of his life, in the harbor, where he seems so completely part of the scene that it's hard to think there might be another side to him. There's bars around the harbor where visiting sailors go drinking. He doesn't seem to join them. They're younger, and they go in for serious solitary dancing. I've tried taking photos without getting in the way of them. I don't want the sailors to be self-conscious, posing for the camera. The lighting levels are low, and I need to use a long exposure, so the dancer is always going to be blurred. It's worth a try, though.

I do need more money, Charles thought, now that there's a baby and Charlotte's decided to spend so much time with her parents. The parents will look after the school fees when they're needed, but even the cost of Charlotte's travel is a strain on my meagre allowance here. She could come to the site, and her living expenses would be claimable from the excavation, but she hates it there and wants little Perry to grow up knowing England as well as Greece. I want it too, of course, but I have to be here for the project. The project is my passport to glory. If it goes well, maybe in twenty years, I'll be director of the school and get a knighthood like Sir Alcuin. Meanwhile, if I show that I'm serious, I can show I deserve a pay rise. I'll draw Alcuin's attention to that page in the accounts where there's something wrong. That will show him that I've been looking at them and keeping an eye on things. He'll be impressed. He'll give me a rise.

"Look at this," says Costas, "I had an accident with a thermometer." He shows me a matchbox that has a globule of mercury that runs about in it. It's like a pet beetle, this shiny drop, bigger than it should be. It breaks apart into several and then reunites to make a perfect little mirrored ball. It's wonderful and mesmerising, and you'd think it was alive.

One of my clients comes in. It's Mr Phe, who ordered the chairs.

"Good day, Mr. Phe," says Costas, "Can I interest you in a thermometer? This box has arrived. You could be the first person to have one."

Mr Phe's looking neat and scrubbed and out-of-place here, wearing a proper jacket and tie. His hair is cropped close and receding, and his whole head looks polished and rather sleek.

"Young Mr Ziros here has your chairs," says Costas.

"I already have a thermometer, thank you," says Mr Phe, "I'm pleased to see the chairs at last. Delighted! Hello, Alexandros."

"Good day, Mr. Phe," I say. I wonder what level of formality he's expecting. He's addressed me not as Mr Ziros but as Alexandros, which sounds friendly, but it's more formal than I've heard in ages – my full first name. But I know that I have to address him as Mr. Phe because I have no idea what his other name might be, "I'm sorry the chairs took a while. I've worked out a new way to make the joints, so they'll last longer without needing to be reglued."

He takes us for coffee: the smart place I don't normally go to by the covered market. There are tables outside, but we go indoors. We're in an unfamiliar world of shiny surfaces, formica, and chrome. The waiters don't look like the kind of people I know. Their hair is different. Their skin is different. Their clothes look new and precise, bought from shops.

"For three?" says the waiter, "Certainly, sir. I'll bring the menu."

"Just coffees, and a plate of small cakes," says Phe. The waiter doesn't even look to see if I have anything to say. Phe's tie looks correct here. This is part of his world. I feel like a scruffy child. Costas smiles, and his teeth show, their jagged yellow framed by his black beard. He looks predatory. We sit on chairs with taut racquet-like seats – stretched fibers of cane. They're not made locally. I'd love to be able to do work like this. The timber is so fine – bent into shape – steamed, so the curves don't cut across sideways the grain of the wood. Come to think of it, a tennis racquet has the same construction. They're incredibly light and made from just a few pieces, with no skill at all in the joints: a neat fix, but anyone could do it. They leave the screws showing. I'm glad Phe didn't think of them when his thoughts turned to furniture. Still, this is my competition: chairs made in factories, with machines that steam the timber so it bends, and something to bend it round. I can't set up a thing like that – you need a factory – but once it's in place, they can turn out their chairs by the thousand – hundreds of thousands. They'll sell for a price I can't match.

One fine afternoon in 1939, four hundred gliders skimmed the air and arrived over western Crete, silent and at first unnoticed in the glaring sky. When some of them were shot at, they showed they had machine guns, and their eerie stealth gave way to dry mechanical snarls. Then, higher in the sky, waves of dully grumbling planes arrived in tight formation, and ten thousand people with parachutes jumped out of them – to drift like jellyfish – delicate silk buoyed by air into a dome – half a kilogram of silk and half a tonne of air. There was noise from the ground, where clumsy anti-aircraft guns did what they could, and people went out to dispatch whoever landed, but there were so many they couldn't all be tracked.

The day Loukas's parents come to visit the lawyer and Ziros village, I look in at Costas's shop and Ty's there. He often hangs around the shop. He's my age, but he grew up in Chania and is streetwise like they are in the town.

"Can I interest you in a thermometer?" says Costas, his patter prompted by my arrival – his running joke. Ty isn't in on it. "This box has arrived. You could be the first person to have one."

"Why would anyone want a fucking thermometer?" says Ty.

"So they know how warm it is," says Costas.

"Sure, but you already know whether you're warm or not," says Ty.

A thought enters my head. I could take one home and break it so I could drain the mercury from it and watch it run about.

"I'd like one," I say.

"There you go," says Costas, "A customer."

Ty looks at me in disbelief. Everything I say these days seems to have that effect on him.

"Some buggers have more money than sense," he says, "I suppose it's Lulu's doing."

I wish he didn't call Loukas Lulu, but it's become a habit, and he doesn't see it even as a joke anymore.

"His parents are coming here today," I say.

"Oh right," says Ty, "That's why you're dressed up like a ponce."

"When are you going to see them?" says Costas.

"In an hour at the lawyer's office," I say.

"Let's have a coffee," says Costas. He hands me the matchbox that has the mercury in it, "You can have a thermometer if you want, but I know you. You'd rather have this. Keep it flat."

"Thank you," I say, "You can read my mind. Save it for now. I'll be with the visitors this afternoon."

"Of course," says Costas.

We have coffee overlooking the harbor. The water slops onto the paving. It's almost winter, but it's still comfortable outside.

"They say tourism's going to make us all damn rich," says Ty.

"It's going to make the rich bastards richer," says Costas, "You're not going to get rich as a bloody waiter."

"I just need enough to get to New York," says Ty.

"Good luck with that," says Costas.

"I guess Lulu's left you rich," says Ty.

"He won't have left me anything," I say, "It's up to his parents what happens now."

"He wasn't expecting to die," says Costas, "I don't suppose he'd have made a will at his age."

"He didn't have any money of his own," I say, "He just got his parents to pay for things."

"You should come to New York with me," says Ty, "If you want to get rich."

"I have the business here," I say, and he's obviously out of his mind if he thinks he's going to be able to make a fortune in America.

"You'll be stuck here in this shithole for the rest of your fucking life," says Ty, "I've got to get out. Have you no bloody ambition?

"What would I do in New York?" I say, "I couldn't afford it."

"Everybody's rich in New York," says Ty.

"You know you'd end up as a waiter," says Costas.

"I might start as a waiter," says Ty, "Waiters become millionaires there. I'll catch me a rich bitch."

That's not going to be as easy there as fishing for your tourist sprats here in the summer," says Costas.

"That's good practice for me," says Ty, "I'm a fucking charmer, me, when I turn it on."

Costas smiles smugly, contented here in middle age, with his wife and child above the shop and business ticking over without too much effort. In the village, we can accept a life without money, but it's better to have some, and while Loukas was paying us rent, we were better off than we'd ever been. The rent's come to a full stop, but we're OK for now. Costas and Ty's world should be my world, but somehow it isn't. I've had glimpses of a further horizon, and even if I stay here, I inhabit a wider world.

"Alekos mate," says Ty, "You've got to get out of that village. See the world before you're stuck here."

"It's not a bad place to be," I say, "Ask the people who come here for their holidays. Anyway, it's not the right time. Not for me."

"Bloody Lulu," says Ty, "He's really shook you up."

"It's not that," I say, but I know it is. I don't want adventure just now. I want to curl up at home. I want to cry. The water in the harbor is reaching out for me. It's lapping over the edges. It wants to draw me in. Maybe I want to curl up in the water, let it envelop me, see if I can breathe it. I want to sleep in the water, floating or sinking, in a boat or in the sea. I don't really care.

86

The room here has lost Loukas now. I look at his things. They're tidy now. That tidying removed him. Until two days ago, it was as if he had just left the room – there then was still a trace – an absence that was to a nicety an absence just of him – but that has gone. Pitiful, these things now, without the quickening mind that made sense of them, sprang them into action. A few clothes. A steady-growing number of books, now in neat piles by the wall. Some notebooks and loose papers. Photos. Nothing that much matters. Evidence of learning Greek, as much as anything, and he was just beginning his great project, so no developed thoughts to uncover leafing through, just random things that had caught his attention.

I am carried over hidden reefs.

Alcman was a household slave of Agesidas, but since he was talented, he was set free, and he turned out to be a poet.

I know the songs of all birds.

He did pencil rubbings over some of the coins in my jar and went over them with some ink lines to clarify the markings. He was going to look them up at some point and identify them properly.

Desire has shaken my mind.

Grief makes me weak at the knees. Grief makes me crumple on the floor. Grief makes me cry in my bed – just one of the mattresses we shared. I wallow in the grief now that I can. It feels like luxury – a surfeit of a sentiment. I can indulge in this excess only when I'm by myself. It can't go on forever, but I want to know it while it's here – let it develop. It matters to me now, and I want to remember it – I want it to pass through my body, convulse me and make me tremble in my bowels, prickle on my skin, make my hair bristle, make my eyes and nose stream and my mouth – I want to bellow from my diaphragm like an incoherent sybil without the shaping words but echoing a pain that resonates through livestock, recognizing loss. But I do it quietly, even now knowing the masonry around me has its limits and my mother must not know must never know the depth of my despair.

87

"You'd best be thinking about Vardas," says Costas, and I have no idea what he means, so I give him a blank look. "Your friends will be at the lawyer's," he says, and he looks as if he's worried about me.

"Of course," I say, and I get up to go. Of course, I know that Vardas is the lawyer. Nothing feels quite real. I'm numb in some way. I can find my way around. My feet touch the ground, but not at the moment I expect it. I'm convinced I could cross the road without looking for traffic. Nothing can hurt me.

Mr Vardas's office is familiar enough. There's something frigid about its perfect walls and its clean surfaces. It feels like it's challenging me but also telling me I'll never be up to it. I'd never be able to afford Vardas's fees. I only ever came here with Loukas, but he isn't with me this time, and I don't have to translate. Mr. and Mrs Zimbrean look at home here in their perfect clothes, and they have brought a bilingual lawyer from Athens with them to check on Vardas, who's fidgety today. The other lawyer looks much sleeker than Vardas and makes an actor's gestures with his hands when he speaks. Charles Winchester's here, too. I met him when Loukas first came to the village a lifetime ago. Less than three years, but time plays tricks. He's put on some weight but still looks much the same. His face is pink and freckled. In the future, he could start to look like a pig. When Odysseus met Circe she turned his sailors into pigs. Then she changed them back again, so Odysseus could go. One of the sailors, Gryllus, didn't want to be changed back. Winchester would be Gryllus. He looks complacent and a bit bored, but he's listening. Mrs Zimbrean dressed as if for a funeral: all black with a broad-brimmed hat. She has a string of black pearls round her neck and looks distinctly unimpressed.

88

I take up again that thing we did: to see the field at setting sun, to see the shades stretch out across the slopes. And when I'm there and tuning-in, Loukas stands beside me. He stays just half a step beyond the edge of what I see. He is a comfort. I know I can reach out and hold his hand. I know it so clearly there's no need to put it to the test – no need to reach out for real. Everything is like it used to be when things were right, before the thought of getting wed put a term to it. – an end to how it should have been – to standing silent, breathing slowly, holding breath when I've breathed in, holding breath when I've breathed out, slowing-down my body so I can see the shadows move, picking up the curving lines of something underground like muscles under skin, slowing-down my heartbeat, slowing-down myself, right down so I can see the heavens' shift as movement, not just a difference from when I last looked up, but moving: a shifting thing going on before my eyes, like when clouds' shadows scud across a hill in windy weather. I do this now at daybreak. Shadows fall the other way. I get up in the dark and make my way in twilight before dawn. It's there. The sunrise seems so quickly to be over. The shadows scamper in a chase, making line-on-line of fleeting presences that vanish within moments like echoes of something that isn't quite a sound – trembling on the point of being there – a dark mist clearing with the morning – and gone as light takes over, clamoring – another day in paradise, bleaching all the stuff that's delicate. The shadows go. You'd never know they'd been. I live for those ten minutes in the mornings. That's where my mourning goes to find a salve, to meet with Loukas and the mist-like shadows.

Costas knows someone with a camera I can borrow. A good camera with a good lens, a tripod, and a switch that works like a brake cable on a bicycle that means you can press the button without joggling the camera on its stand. So I can take a series of photos from exactly the same place over the course of an hour, pick up the shadows in different positions, and layer them over one another. With the right equipment, it's easy enough to do. I do it three times over, one day after the next, and run off a whole reel of film.

89

"Have you actually found anything here?" asks Charles at the site of the excavation before it's been fenced in, "anything archaeological, I mean."

"No, not yet," I say, "but I'm not an archaeologist. Loukas was convinced he could see the lines of something under the fields. We dug out a sample here just to see how deep the topsoil layer is."

Charles doesn't seem very impressed, and I'd quite like him not to be too keen on the place. It's Loukas's place and mine, not his – except in law. Now, it's his to direct. Now, the trustees say it's up to him. I half want to persuade him to think the place is a hopeless delusion and to give up on it right away, but something's got hold of him.

He can't make a start right away, of course. He's a teacher now in England, so he can't just come and go. There are things that will need preparation, some permissions, and he won't be here to do it. It will have to work in with the school holidays. He'll need help. He'll try to set things up to get moving next summer. He'll come back then with a team to make a start.

"Can I stay in your house, where Luke was staying?" he says.

I can't very well say no, "Leave his books," said Charles, "I'll be able to use them. I'll move them once we have something more permanent set up."

Charles knows nothing, but he thinks he knows enough. He knows nothing about the house on the plateia, and I'm not going to tell him about it. He's not going to take it over. Let's see how he behaves once Loukas's parents have gone away. Maybe he'll come to trust me. If he does trust me, maybe I'll feel that I'm fooling him. His instincts are less devious than Loukas's were. Loukas had a feel for cunning – ponirós. He had me thinking he was on my side, but what did he feel for me? Was it what I thought it was? or was he letting me feel loved as a way to find his way to what he needed from the village? He wouldn't have got his land without seducing me. He wouldn't have got his land without seducing Stasia. He made her fall in love with him by saying things to her that I know he didn't believe. Did he mean the things he said to me? I think he did, but maybe I'm just credulous. If he said the same things to Stasia, why would I think he was fooling her and not fooling me? He meant the things he said at the moment when he said them, but he might have set them aside when his attention was on other things. Who knows what the future might have held as he settled in and found the village more limited than the world he knew? He'd have broadened our horizons, but we'd have limited his. As it is, I have some memories to treasure. They can't be tarnished by betrayals, by loyalties divided between me and Stasia. In the house, everything would look proper, and it would have made us hypocrites. It was no perfect future shaping up.

I take the negatives to Mr Galanakis in Heraklion. He can tell I'm serious about something, even though I might not be a good photographer and I don't know the proper words for camera-things. He's patient. He's quite old, but not bored with his work. He cares about it gives it the time it needs. He has a craftsman's values treats me with respect. He develops the negatives and looks at them.

"They're all the same," he says, "Is that what you're expecting?"

"They're all looking at the same view, but the sun's moving. The shadows move. What I want to do is to pick up the shape that the shadows are making – the whole shape – you just get part of it each time."

"I see what you're getting at," he says.

"I thought maybe if you could do the prints on transparent paper, I could put them on top of one another, layer them up, and when you see the set, you'd see the shadow as a whole."

"Right. Printing on acetate. I can do that, but I'd have to send away for special things. It would be like a giant transparency. They can be done. I haven't done them recently myself, but it's possible."

He breaks off and thinks.

"I can do something quicker that I think would give you what you want," he says.

We spend the late afternoon in the darkroom as he carefully registers each image and makes a multiple exposures, which altogether bleaches out the brighter parts and leaves a shadow-image that gets paler every time. The first time through, it's completely over-exposed, and the fields are just white, with the dark band of trees in the distance. He's disappointed, not dismayed. He starts again, unhurried. The second time there's enough of a trace to show that there's something there if we get it right. The third time, it's clear – still pale, but definitely there: wavy lines are showing up. They go across the field in an irregular way that at first looks uncontrolled, but once you see it, it's unmistakable. The wavy lines converge on the cypresses. My mind lights up. There's singing going on somewhere. Loud singing. I can't be sure whether it's inside or outside my head. I want to jump around the room and bounce off the walls. I'm standing still, in fact, but my face is wet with water, and I'm struggling to breathe – a trembling shallow breath – I won't go into spasm – control, control. Breathe slower. Breathe deeper.

"Is that what you're after?" says Galanakis.

"Perfect," I say, very quietly, as a gasp. I want to hug him, but I hold back the torrent of my gratitude. For him, it's been a technical thing about getting the light right. For me, it's a glimpse of heaven. I can see a whole new world – a pattern of convergence. Something clicks into place. I don't know what it's going to be, but obviously, the stani holds the answer. I'm not coherent as I leave, but he can tell I'm very grateful, and I do my best to be polite. I neglect to offer money. I must go back there when I'm calm again. For now, it's high excitement. If I'd been with Loukas, he'd be paying. We might have stayed in Heraklion rather than driving back this late in the day, in this state of mind. It's not good for my driving. I know, but I don't care. I'm running on adrenaline, and I feel I'll never sleep again. I drive back right away. I get back late. There's light blazing inside me. I'm possessed. My mother looks worried.

"We have to do it right away!" I say, "If we wait, we'll be too late. Winchester will come. He'll take control, and everything will go."

"Calm down," she says, "Calm down. You're not making sense. Have some water."

She pours some in a tumbler from a jug that's by the sink.

"We have to dig," I say, "We have to dig the stani. There's something there. We have to dig. There really might be the tombs of kings. That's what Dinos says. That's what he said all along. We have to get to them before Winchester does. For Loukas's sake. For Stasia's sake. You saw how they treated her! We're nothing to them. We must dig the sheepfold before they take it all away."

"You need to rest.," she says, "You can't do anything tonight. It will make sense better in the morning."

But it's a sleepless night that just continues into morning – clear enough, I think, in my delirium – everything's plain for me to see, but how do I explain to others? How many others? I'll need help. Lots of help. It's all or none. We can't keep this a secret.

"There's definitely something there," I say, "It's evident. There has to be. We have to get there first. If we hesitate, we leave it for Winchester to discover. It will go to Athens with his name on it. If we get there first, it's ours. Then we decide. It belongs to the village. If it's something good, it will be taken off us, but at least we'll have the village name on it. If we all agree to keep quiet about it, we can sell it. Then there's a windfall for the village. We all prosper. We deserve it after all we've been through."

"Maybe there's nothing there," says my mother, "Maybe it's going to be a disappointment."

"If it's nothing too special, we'll be allowed to keep it, and it can go on display in the village," I say. I shrug. "We've got to do it, even if it turns up nothing. Then, at least, we know. The only problem is that legally, the land now belongs to the foundation, so we should not be digging there. It can't be strictly legal. So we can't go to the ephor with it. It mustn't go to Athens. But we can't let Winchester get it! It's Loukas's vision, not his, that brought us here."

"It's your vision, in fact," says my mother.

"Loukas knew that there was something there. He went with that feeling. That's what made me look. Now I know for sure there's something there. There has to be. If we act fast we can rescue it, hide it, take as much time as we need to decide what to do. It's going to be hard work. There's digging to be done – heavy work. We'll need everyone to help, and we'll need everyone to be implicated. Everybody has to keep the secret."

"The village can do that. You need to think it through carefully. Present the case. Inspire the crowd. You won't get a second chance, but you're of the village, one of them. They will give you that one chance."

And then I'm still there looking towards the Cypresses, but I'm looking at the place from a long way away, with Matthias beside me, speaking softly in my ear. I turn to look at him directly, and he smiles broadly. "Come on," he says, "we've things to do."

"No!" I say, in a harsh whisper, "I can't leave."

Alekos speaks – becomes a hollow body with a rush of air produced from deep within to make a voice that thunders in the plateia.

"Twelve years ago, four hundred gliders skimmed the air and turned into a thunderbolt that killed. We live with what was left. Lost voices echo in our thoughts. They visit in our sleep and even waking. Guns crack in our minds when things are still. We get by without the help we would have had. We don't ask for much. It's best for us to stay below the radar, somewhat unknown. We didn't ask for it: to be caught up in business far beyond ourselves, way beyond the village. Big things to do with states and empires somehow found their way to us – parachuted in, then gone for ever – left us changed. We were brought together. We help one another. Now, there's a new thing. A new thunderbolt. A stranger came – a catalyst. He changed things here. He helped us past despair to see a future. To see a past we didn't know before. He brought ambition, money, and attention. Very soon, there'll be water on the way and electricity because of him. Our trees will grow more fruit, and we'll meet more often in the megaron. That's not the end of it. We can prosper if we take control. Under the ground, our ancestors lie buried. There's treasure there, for sure. If we leave it to the outsiders to find it, we'll be robbed. The treasure will go to Athens and be gone from us. If we get there first then we can sell it. It will be gone, just the same, but we'll be rich. Not very rich because there's lots of us involved here, but we'll prosper. After all we've lost, we need some balm. We would not have made the sacrifice of our fathers, husbands, brothers, but that's been done. This is how we make the best of it – make the best of our lives shattered by thunderbolts. The best way to deal with what we've got. We must all work together with Thesmophoric secrecy. Death will come to anyone who breaks the silence; be sure of that. You will know who it is, and you know there'll be no escape from your anger. We owe it to the slain."

There's silence. Then Alekos makes a sound so primitive it's like an animal in pain. It's coming inside him, and he's not in control of it at all. It shakes his entrails and seems unmodified by tongue or his wide-open mouth – a kind of growl or bellowing. It takes all the breath from his body in a great rush, and he falls to the ground.

"You can leave the next part to us," says his mother as he's coming to, "Try to sleep. They can see you're haggard, short-of-sleep and thin. They know how Stasia had a future – a secure and enviable future – snatched away for nothing in its place. Any trailing fiber of a hope was snapped by Loukas's parents. They know that they're not free from blame – the women from the Thesmophoria. They want to help."

93

This time, visiting Athens, I feel like an old hand. I have my drawings with me, but I haven't looked at them since I was at Paleoziros last year. There have been plenty of other things to think about. In my room at the Lantern of Demosthenes, I open the portfolio. Immediately, in a rush, I have a sense that feels more visceral than memory of intense sunlight and heat, of drawing these lines in blinding light. The information is all there and accurately transferred to the plans, but it seems very slight – some tentative wavy lines that might smudge away if I don't ink them in. I must get a clearer sense of the general outlines somehow. I can make the lines thicker, but they seem drained of information. There's so much careful plotting of the points, and then, at the end, there is just a line that feels much too precise compared with the ruggedness of the stones and crumbling dry earth. My aim for this season must be to find a way to flesh them out so they feel properly hesitant and properly substantial. I've said that I'll arrive there in a week's time and tune in with the dig for three weeks. I know Winchester will be there. I know Xander will be there. And I know they won't meet. I hope I'll be able to work with Len again. He knows what to do now.

94

The women establish a routine. Patient dig and pass, dig and pass, dig and pass small buckets of earth back along a chain of hands – a dozen women at a time – each doing her bit like a cog in a machine, working rhythmically. They keep the rhythm going with a song.

Across two great connected seas

Kanaloa reached the shingle

Because he's mighty – mighty Kanaloa,

Cephalopod, cephalopod, cephalopod –

He eats everything he meets along the way.

Ranking first among the nobles,

All the way to the horizon, firstborn of the firstborn.

Kanaloa's back to water-heaven,

Anointed of the Lord of the Horizon.

He overcame vertebrae and spine.

He took the hearts out of the gods.

Kanaloa's majesty will not be taken from him.

95

"You should take a look at Piet de Jong's work," says Winchester, as we sit with glasses of ouzo on the terrace of his apartment, "I met him in the 1950s. Marvellous fellow. He worked with Gilliéron, who worked with Schliemann, then with Evans, so there's a direct line going through the restorations."

"Oh yes," I say, "You mentioned him before. His illustrations are in all the guidebooks. I've been warned not to trust them."

"Whoever's been saying that?" says Winchester, "Nonsense. They're brilliant."

"Don't people say that Gilliéron and Schliemann cooked up forgeries together?" I say.

"People will say all sorts of things," says Winchester, "but you mustn't be taken in. They're the most authoritative reconstructions there are. Gilliéron made reconstructions and then made brilliant copies of them to sell to museums. They're not forgeries."

I know that the reconstructions were made on the basis of scant evidence, and I expect the reproductions were fantastic because Gilliéron was reproducing his own work. He did the statuette of the snake priestess with bare pushed-up breasts, which is a sensational exhibit in the Heraklion museum, but I can't tell what about it is archaeology and what's from Gilliéron's imagination. Plainly, Winchester isn't going to want to hear me say that, so I don't say it. And I mustn't say that Gilliéron's murals remind me of Klimt. Winchester wants me to produce some images that make it look as if Paleoziros was part of the same Art-Nouveau culture as Knossos.

96

It's February when we reach the rock. After months of forcing sharp-edged spades through earth that's full of fibers – roots that knit it together, so it resists – the spade's scrape is unmistakeable. It's bedrock. We've come to the end and drawn a blank. There'll be nothing here, and we can't go any further. We can't pretend we were looking to dig a well. Water's brought in buckets, and we wash it down and re-fill the buckets with muddy water. There's nowhere for it to drain away. The women find a rough hole – a sort of indentation – that's filled up with earth. They scrape it out, pour water in, and wipe the mud away. They need some rags to mop up. It's only when things are a bit drier that my heart misses a beat. That rock isn't natural. It's been made. Roughly made, but that's not a natural surface. This surface is all broken – chipped away. I'm crouching on worked stone. It's been moved into this position. Maybe the hole was made at the quarry to give a lever something to push or pull to move the stone on to a cart. It's a big stone, that's for sure. We're not going to be able to move it. Let's find the edge. The thunderstorm is in my head again. It's the first time I've really known that what we're dealing with is real. It's not just a hope or something we know must be there because everything points to it. It's real and solid. We've had to pretend for ages that it's mainly a practical problem, but despite my faith in Loukas, I've always had to be prepared for disappointment. He let me down by deciding to marry Stasia. He let me down by dying. He could have been wrong again about this, but he wasn't wrong. It's real. It's here.

"We need to change direction," I say to the women back up at the top, "We need to go sideways, just on one side. We need to find an edge and go beyond it. We don't need to go down any deeper. We've arrived." It will be a different group of women tomorrow, but they'll know what I've said. I'm murmuring, saying the words but hardly saying them aloud. The women all know things at once, immediately and invisibly, the news goes rippling through the group. If one knows, they all know. They adjust. I'm still in a fogged cotton-wool grief-world where the edge is deadened, and anything that's not to do with Loukas doesn't matter. I'm listless when there are other things to do. I forget them. Stasia's the same. She's been hit hard. She doesn't come around so often to the house, but when we meet, we find we end up crying and hugging each other. I feel better for it, but now crying feels like self-indulgence. I just have to think of Loukas, and the tears start to flow. I go out to the fields to meet him every day. I haven't made progress with the chair I'm making for him. The branch is in the workshop, stripped of its bark and planed down a bit, so it's looking more like a timber block, but it's still obviously a branch. I need to set it up in a secure vice-hold so I can make a long saw-cut down its entire length to make the two matching pieces. If I do that when the timber's not properly dried, the grain will open up in a few years, and there'll be shakes. It needs time. The grief will pass with time or at least be more manageable. I've heard it all before, mainly second-hand. People expected my mother to feel grief when my father was killed. Somehow they didn't expect it of me. They just expected me to be damaged. They think I've done alright. They don't know the half of it with Loukas, and they don't know about my monsters. The dig is the one thing that must not be delayed. We have some time, but not much. It must be done before the idiot Winchester comes back here. Everything about it feels like hallucination. The mood, the dulled senses, the feeling that it must be done: there's so much else I could be doing but that I don't want to know. It crowds out everything.

"Piet was a genius," says Winchester, "You could give him a fragment of a pot, and he'd go into a trance and then do a drawing showing it complete and in a room with people. He had such a feel for things."

Winchester's obviously describing a con-man at work. There doesn't seem to be any rigorous method there, just something more like a séance, but he's looking old and dreamy, and it would feel cruel to push my point, so I stay silent and let him tell me how inspiring Piet was, and how he would know how to make my serpentine walls come alive as a temple for snake-worship. Obviously, he's going to be disappointed with me if I stick to my facts. My thin lines look very pedantic and flat-footed.

We start to dig sideways, and the earth falls away quite easily. It's the usual hard work going sideways at first, but then the earth from around and above falls down without much trouble. It makes a natural vault, so if we don't have to go too far, we won't need to prop it. We go along a piki and reach the edge by mid-morning, and I can't bear to break off then, but there's no alternative. Then it's Saturday and the market at Chania, but I'll give it a miss. We must find out what's beyond the edge of the stone.

"You must go and see Costas," says my mother, "If he worries about you, he'll come here to see how you're doing."

"I'm not doing well," I say, "He'll see that if I go."

"He'll think it's grief," she says, "He'll want you to talk about it. Have something ready to say. Keep your routines with the outside world. The more normal things look, the better. We don't want questions."

99

I wonder if he's already had other architects on the project before me. People who've disappointed him and not come back. There'll be someone I can ask about that. Who's been here a while? No one I can think of. Everyone seems to be a recent arrival. The students never stay for very long. They all have a home institution to return to, which will actually award the degree. They have meetings and seminars with visiting scholars, but they're just visiting. The permanent staff here are just Winchester and Dan and the people who work in the office – two secretaries and, from time to time, an accountant. The younger secretary, Natalie, is outgoing and chatty. She wears emphatic eye makeup and bright floral print dresses. The older one, Doreen, doesn't say much, but she's quite friendly. She's just a person who prefers to be quiet and fade into the background. She's more likely to know, but she's also likely to feel that she should be discreet. I'll drop by the office.

It takes a week to sort it out. It's a colossal stone, almost a piki deep, so goodness knows how they got it into place. We'd need a crane. There's a flat top, a vertical surface dropping down, and then it's held up by smaller stones, neatly jointed. This is fantastic! It's definitely a building, a round building. The huge stone's its capstone – the top of its vault. It's underground now, of course, but it was always supposed to be underground. This outer surface isn't finished, and any craftsman from any time would have done a better job if it was going to be seen. We need to dig out of the earth enough space to make it possible to get to work on these smaller stones. There's no point trying to move the big one. There might be a door somewhere, but to find it, we'd have to dig far more. Let's just smash our way in. What do we need? A sledgehammer? We need to dig out enough space to get a good swing.

"They were jumping off the balcony into the swimming pool," says Natalie, "then running up the stairs and jumping off again."

"Oh, yes," says Doreen, plainly pleased she hadn't been there to see it.

"I don't know what they'd taking, "says Natalie, "but they were off their heads. It was an amazing night. We drank sooo much. Hello Mr Architect."

"Hello," I say, "Sounds like you had a good time."

"It was amazing. What can we do for you?"

"Oh, nothing urgent," I say, "I was just thinking I ought to visit Delphi, and I wondered if you have any advice."

"We don't have anyone with a project there," says Natalie, "You're best just doing one of those tourist visits. They're quite efficient – take you there and back again. You don't want to be trying public transport for that one. It takes days. Of course, you could hire a car if you don't mind driving."

"I'm not going to drive in Athens," I say.

"I don't blame you," says Natalie.

"You could ask at the French School," says Doreen, "They might have someone going up there. You never know. I'll phone and ask if you like. They'll let you use their library if you need to know about the excavations."

"Thank you very much," I say, "I think I'm going as a tourist, really. I'll take some photos for lectures, but I'll be out of my depth trying to talk to a French archaeologist." I want to go because it's a famous site and because it's one of the places where, before Apollo, snakes were worshipped. I might get some ideas there. I'm only asking now because I want to talk to Doreen so I can ask her questions in the future.

102

It's dead of night. I'm thinking about the stones. They'll be wedge-shaped. If we slam a hammer against the wedge, it will force it more firmly into place. The thing to do would be to pull it out. It's dead of night. I'm thinking about the rubber-bulbed syringe. It's one of the household treasures, but I never think about it. It's never figured in my dreams, but it has some ancestral authority to bestow on things, like a sceptre. It's absolutely dark. I can't tell whether my eyes are open except by knowing they're open. The room's too dark to see the syringe, but I know it's here with me. It's dead of night. I can see the image of a baby goat being roasted over charcoal flames. Xylanthrakas. Basted with olive oil from the syringe. There's no light in the room, but it's inside of me, the flicker of charcoal flames. I can hear a high-pitched fizzing in my ears and see a crackle of little dots. I'm fidgeting and trembling. I'm lying on the bed, but I might as well be pacing up and down around the room. My face is twitching. It makes no difference if I open or close my eyes. I'll wait until some light begins to show beneath the door. I won't move till then.

103

"That's a very good idea," says Winchester when I tell him I'm going on the tourist bus, "Let me know how you get on. It's one of those places that was taken over by the Hellenes. They had the pythoness doing prophecies there, and when they brought in the worship of the new god, Apollo, they didn't see any need to antagonize anyone by giving up on the old practices. They instituted the Pythian Games – which worked like the Olympics, bringing everyone together. There were four games, which ran in rotation … NPIO: Nemean, Pythian, Isthmian, and Olympian. There, I can still do it! That's why the Olympics were every four years."

"Thank you," I say, and I'm patient listening to him, but I've read this stuff already. That's why I thought I'd better go to Delphi in the first place. Winchester really isn't a researcher. He thinks like an undergraduate and thinks that knowing stuff from other people's books is as far as it goes.

"The day after tomorrow," he says, "there's a cocktail party on the terrace. You should come to it. There'll be some trustees, some donors, and some embassy types. They like to see a few pleasant young faces around." I smile. Now that I'm in my thirties, I like it when I'm taken for young.

"I'll be there," I say.

I book a ticket: Delphi the day after tomorrow. I'll be back in time for the party.

104

I go through Loukas's empty room to the kitchen. I splash some water on my face. I strike a match for the gas flame, which shows up bright. I set a pan of water on it. It will take an age to boil, so I go to the workshop, where I look at the scissor hooks that lift stones. Are they any good to me? What else is there here? A crowbar might be good if it could find a way in. I'd really like something powerful like road builders use. A jack-hammer. Those noisy things that will break the surface of a road. A powerful drill would be good. There are drill-bits here that I've used for fixing shelves to walls. They're not up to it. There are other bits in the range, much bigger, that I've never seen in use. There's the drill they go in. Just a cranked handle. You push against the flattish wooden knob on top and turn the handle around. It would very slowly score a line and eventually a hole. It would be a way to make a start. But working on the stone? It's like geology. It would take a thousand years or more to smooth a pebble. Set someone going working for a lifetime, for a hundred generations. We don't have that time. Back to the kitchen before that pan boils dry.

It's quite a bag of things I take with me. A bottle of olive oil and a sledgehammer, just in case, as well as things from the forge and the syringe. Some water, too, but that's for me. I slide and scramble down the slope and look at the exposed stones. There was no mortar between them that could be chipped away to get in there. They were made to fit without it. They're packed close. They're not all aligned on this side, though. On the inside, there'll be a good smooth finish, I expect, but here on the outside, some stones stick out a little more than others. Here's one that's a finger's breadth further out than the ones on either side. That gives me a place to start. I use the syringe to spread some oil along the crevices. If it's drawn in it will help the stone to slide. There isn't room to use the scissor-hooks. They might have just enough room to get a grip. We must excavate more earth to make some space. The oil seems to go. It must be going in. It's best along the upper ledge, but every little will help. It has a way of working its way secretly through things you wouldn't think it could – climbs out of bottles, even when you try to stop it. I squirt some more. I hear movement, not from the stones, but from someone arriving on the site.

"Yassas," I call.

"Yassou," says Varvara. I tell her what I've been doing, and she giggles, familiar with the syringe. She has one at her house, too, she says. She looks at the scissor hooks as I explain how they work and how we need more space. "What if we don't use them like that," she says, "If we put them this way, flat against the stones, and pull enough for them to take a grip, then maybe we could use it as a lever. It wouldn't move it much, but it could be a start."

"Varvara, you're a genius! Let's keep going with the oil until someone else arrives. Then they can tug the rope to give the grip, and we can hold the thing in place and try to push the handles as a lever."

Feni's next to arrive. She's less strong than Varvara, so She comes down to hold the spikes in place. I thread the rope through the handles and give the ends to Varvara. She pulls them tight. I put a crowbar across to make a fulcrum and started to push the handles back.

"Keep it tight," I say, "Really hard now." I give a forceful push. The points slip off the stone.

"Ow," says Feni. Up on the ground, Varvara staggers backward. I step back as the tool whizzes past my face. There's danger here. More than I anticipated.

"Are you OK?" I ask.

"Let's try again," says Varvara, and that's what we do.

It's the same again, but this time, I take care to keep out of the way of the tool as it loses its grip and is pulled up past me.

"Let's try again," says Varvara. And we try again.

"I think it moved," says Feni, "I heard something."

"Heard what?" I say.

"A grating sound," says Feni, "just for a moment."
We can't be sure.

"Let's try again," says Varvara.

"I think it moved," says Feni, "It did. I can see the marks. It's moved a bit."

"Let's try again," says Varvara.

"It's definitely working," says Feni. You can see at the sides the joints are there now. You couldn't see them before."

"Let's have a think. Is there a better tool to use now?"

"We could do this a few more times," says Varvara, "Then there'll be more space at the side. Maybe we could put a crowbar there. Would that help?"

"We need to pull away. The best thing would be to have more space," I say.

"A week of excavating or a week of these little moves," says Feni.

"How's your patience?" I say.

"Let's try again," says Varvara.

"Feni. Could you put some more oil there," I say. There're several more tiny moves. Then, it looks as if the crowbar might fit in the gap. It's bent to a right angle at one end, with a notch taken out so it makes a claw. That's the end I put in, then rotate it so the angle hooks on the back of the stone. It won't move.

"What about a sledgehammer hit to the side?"

"Give it a go." There's enough projecting now for there to be something to hit. I feel like hitting something. It shifts the stone to the side and wedges the crowbar solidly in place.

"Now hit the crowbar." It's a slow business, but each move takes us ever-so-slightly in the right direction. We're teaching the stone the idea of moving about. Maybe it will start to find it easier once it gets the idea. It's going to take more than one day. We flood the joints with oil where we can to leave it overnight. Or until later in the day. Now, we've reached this point where we've got to finish. I can't bear to go away. We're so nearly there. It's not a one-person job, though. I can't do anything by myself alone. The women go to start their day. To do their normal things. I can't let it rest. I'm back again later in the afternoon, sluicing it again with oil. It can't do any harm. We've got the measure of the block's depth from the crowbar's hook. It's about the length of my forearm. I have an idea. I could bring a vice from the workshop. If I could fix the stone to it somehow, I could turn it, and its screw mechanism would give a stronger pull than we could do by hand, even with the lever. I can remove the vice from the workbench and bring it here, but how do I attach the thing to pull? I look around the workshop among the blacksmith tools. A crowbar with an angle at each end, if it's the right length, would do it. The jack from the van! That's a screw mechanism. A person, without straining, can lift up the van with it. That might be better. It's certainly easier to take it there. Now. Is there something like a crowbar with an angle at each end? It will have to be as long as my arm so it can reach the back of the stone and hook over the jack. There is such a thing. It's a cramp for holding furniture together while the glue sets. It fits across a chair or something. One part slides into place in an approximate way, and then it kind of locks into place. If I slide the moveable part off its track and put it on back to front – then I'm away. I can do this. I can do it by myself. I can do it now.

The cramp slides in. I turn it sideways so the fixed end is at the back of the stone. The other part is here now with the jack fully depressed. Now, I turn the crank handle to get it to open up. It takes the pressure. Everything gets stressed. Now, it's hard to turn, but not impossible. Every turn of the handle brings the stone along half a millimetre each time. I can hear it scraping. I can't stop now until it's done.

I'm absolutely drained but thrilled. The stone is out. It's not enough. I can't go in alone. I'd better wait until there's someone here. The opening isn't yet big enough, but it's going to be quick work after this. Two more – three will be enough.

"What on earth have you done to your face?" says my mother.

"I've opened up the tomb!"

"That's wonderful. Take a look at yourself in the mirror. You'll need to clean yourself up before we go to Maria's."

My face is smeared with soot, and I've wiped sweat off it with my hand. I must shower, but it's too cold to stay under the shower. I let the water fall past me and scoop what I need from the air as it passes me. The volta's done not sauntering as usual but with a skip and jump in my step, with palpitations and murmurings in my heart, and flashes of insanity in my darting eyes and smiles. My mother takes me for the walk as she might walk a dog. Cajoling and instructing me, making signals to steer me towards normality.

I get back to Athens after the cocktail party has begun. The olive trees in their painted boxes have been moved around. They've been pushed into a group so that more people can stand and see the view of the Acropolis. It's a very sleek crowd. The people I know are involved with talking to other people who look important. Everyone here looks kind of important, certainly well-heeled. The trick to wearing formal-looking jackets when the weather's as warm as this is to have one that's made of very thin fabric. The women are mostly of an age where they prefer to keep their arms covered, and they have gauzy jacket-blouses through which you can see they're wearing shoulderless dresses. The men's jackets have the appearance of being a bit more substantial – linen or seersucker – but unlined, so where someone's wearing a dark shirt, you can see where the jacket's layers of fabric double up. My wardrobe doesn't include such a jacket, but if I'm going to be making a habit of this, it should. I have put on a tie, as has Winchester, but few other people are wearing them. It's the women who seem to have the conversations. The men listen or pretend to listen, and drink or look at the view of the Acropolis. The women are interested in what the Lantern does, or at least feel that it's a good thing. The men make money and give their wives the wherewithal for their social standing. It's very clear to me, and I'm sure to them, just from the way I look, that I'm part of the scholarly community, not the patron class. The cocktails aren't serious. It's a watery Pimm's-like concoction with cucumber and strawberries in the jug and a few mint leaves.

"It's the house special," says Winchester, "It was invented by Lord Ambleside when he stopped here on his way to Troy. The recipe is a closely guarded secret."

"Is there any alcohol in it?" asks the chiffon-clad matron standing next to him.

"Just enough," says Winchester, smiling.

"Should I be helping with that?" I say.

"By all means. Pick up a jug from Doreen there and circulate with it."

I prefer this role as a waiter. It gives me a reason to move around and have conversations with people and a reason to move on. The students seem to be sticking together. One of them, a good-looking young man they call Trigger, has a hip flask from which he's stiffening his friends' drinks. I offer him a top-up from the jug.

"No thanks. It'll dilute it too much," says Trigger.

"What have you got in that flask?" I say. I want to say something to him, "Vodka?"

"Polish spirit," he says, "Vodka's for kids."

"You shouldn't all be huddled together like this," I say, "Disperse a bit. Charm the guests." Trigger fixes me with a look in the eye and grins broadly.

"I'll see what I can do," he says. I smile back hesitantly and move on.

"I can't believe they're still serving this," says a woman who clearly doesn't blame it on me personally. She's wearing pale linen, which appears to be miraculously uncreased, and gold seahorse earrings.

"You've known the school a long time?" I say.

"On and off," she says, and I recognize her but can't place her, "Mainly off. I studied here before it was in this building – it's a great improvement. What a fabulous view. I noticed Doreen. She was there in the old building. I suppose she's still making the drinks."

"She is," I say, and I know where I've seen her before.

"What are you doing here in Greece?" she says.

"I'm working at Palaeoziros," I say, "I'll be there in a few weeks. We met there last summer."

"Of course we did," says Alice, "You look different here. Your city clothes, I suppose."

"You look different too," I say, "Today I went to Delphi."

"Oh, how beautiful," she says, "It's ages since I've been there. It's too far inland. I'm boat-based these days."

"It sounds idyllic," I say, "sailing around the Aegean."

A policeman catches my eye. I'm not sure why he'd be here. Maybe we have an ambassador or two in our midst. He's standing at the edge of things, close to some of the olive trees that are away from the view. He's looking a bit bored, but who knows when he might be called upon to spring into action. He's armed, wearing a navy blue short-sleeved shirt.

"In some ways, it is," she says, "What prompted the visit to Delphi?"

"Well, it's one of those places everyone should see, isn't it," I say, "And then I wanted to see the omphalos and the Python place."

"There's not so much to see," she says, "You'd get more insight by reading up about Voodoo. Voodoo's your best way into Delphi."

"Thank you," I say, "I don't suppose the libraries here aren't going to have books about Voodoo in them. That might have to wait."

"There should be some in the library here," she says, "unless Charles has thrown them out. Alcuin bought them when we were at the old place. I imagine they were brought here."

"I was picking up serpentine lines on the site at Palaeoziros," I say, "Winchester thinks it might be a snake-cult place to balance the bull-cult at Knossos."

"Snakes," she says, and she laughs, "Oh Charles!"

"He's just across over there," I say, "if you want a word."

"Don't mention that I was here," she says, "It might unsettle him."

Somehow, everyone's chatting and keeping one eye on the Erechtheion. I turn away from the view. Trigger's talking to the policeman. I feel a pang of jealousy. I feel that I'm missing out on something. Trigger hands the policeman a drink.

Alice has gone. I must have been looking away too long. I wonder who that is that Winchester is talking to. Winchester's trying to look important. I move in his general direction, holding the half-empty jug. I stand within earshot with my back to him and pour some drinks.

"Oh, thank you," says a man in a pale linen suit with some small red wine spots on the sleeve that haven't altogether washed out. I can hear Winchester name-dropping shamelessly. Melina Mercouri, Enoch Powell, Telly Savalas, Mary Renault, Bernard Levin. They've all been here, if not on the terrace, then in the city or something, and he gives the impression that they spoke with him somewhere or other, but it might have been many years ago, and I start to think they might have been things he read in a newspaper. For a moment, I thought he was claiming to have known Aristotle, but that turns out to be a living person by that name.

"No, we're Demosthenes. You're thinking of Diogenes," says Charles, "He did have a lantern. He went through the streets in broad daylight, carrying a lantern, saying that he was looking for an honest man. He didn't find one."

"Don't I know it," says the blowsy woman with thinning henna'd hair, "'Twas ever thus."

"Ah, Ian," says Charles, "Can I introduce the United States Ambassador's wife?"

"No," she says, "that's not me. Call me Maisie."

"How do you do," I say, "Have you tried the Ambleside cocktail?"

"I have," she says and gives a disapproving look, "Do you think we can get a Martini?"

"I don't know," I say. "I can ask. What about a shot of Polish spirit in the cocktail?"

"That might do the trick," she says, "You're a doll."

Practical things: before anything is moved, I must take photographs. The borrowed camera at the house. We can put the masks in sacks and take them up one at a time by rope. We should leave the rest – whatever's there – dusty shapes there to explore. When Winchester's team gets here, if they find something, they won't ask too many questions about what's gone or start on over-careful forensics. If there's nothing at all for them, then they'll scrape the more and might find clues that put them on our trail. They like coins. Let's give them coins to help them. I empty the coins out of my jar – already sorted with the Turkish taken out. I take some photos with a flash within the chamber, with the masks in place, and then we move them. I'm the only person in there. Not too many footprints. I rub them out with my hands where I can. The masks go up. I go up and, as a parting gesture, throw my coins behind me, making dull thuds too quiet to hear as they reach the dusty ground. The tomb is open just one day and closed up before night. Some field-stones block the hole – the dislodged blocks stay where they fell. We've touched almost nothing. The earth can be re-filled quite quickly, over the next few days, with lighter steps and singing that's less dirge-like and mysterious than before. The earth's less densely packed, so there is some left over to scatter. This time, the women's voices make sounds more like the folk songs people sing in cafés.

I'm now a hero in the most-tried way. I've robbed a tomb, and that makes me at least a prince, if not a god who has overcome death and knows the secrets of the tomb. The only thing is: no one can know, no one beyond the village, and even in the village, no one says. But now I take my hero-name: Xander. I decree it, and the decree's obeyed. Little Alexakis has come of age at last. Everything has to carry on as before, in others' eyes, but for me, everything has changed. I'm miraculated by my inner lightning, radiant like Apollo, glorious as the dawn. I must be just. I must be benevolent. I must carry on as if nothing has happened. The less outward evidence, the better, but Radiant Xander blesses the world in which he walks because, benevolently, he knows it's his.

I go inside, thinking I'll see what's there, and if not, I'll see if there's anything left in that flask. Trigger suddenly comes into view from behind the olive trees, moving quickly, holding a napkin to his mouth. He looks like he's going to vomit. So much for that Polish spirit. Doreen and Natalie are inside at the trestle table with the glass jugs, most of them empty now.

"Any chance of a Martini," I say, "for Maisie, who says she's not the US ambassador's wife?"

"There's a chance," says Doreen, "but she'll have to have it in the same sort of glass as everyone else, or they'll see she's got something different, and they'll all want one."

"She's a character," says Natalie, "I'll take it to her."

"There was someone here before who was asking after you," I say, "She said she was here when you were in the old building."

"That's a long time ago," she says, "Who was it?"

"Alice Cyprian," I say, "She seems to have slipped away. She seemed to know Winchester quite well. She decided to avoid him."

"Oh yes," says Doreen, "She used to work with him, but there was a falling-out."

Dan appears, holding an empty jug.

"I get the feeling that they've had enough of this," he says, "With luck, they'll be heading off to eat soon."

I look outside. The big sliding glass windows give a clear view across the terrace. Maisie's hooting with laughter already, delighted to see Natalie or the Martini. The policeman's standing by the olive trees looking flustered – he's glancing around. He shifts his weight from foot to foot, but he has to stay in place.

"It's a terrible drink," I say.

"Don't say that out loud," says Dan, "It's what people expect. Cheap local alcohol with plenty of water and sugar and enough fruit to disguise the taste so we can pretend it's an English custom."

"Who's Lord Ambleside?" I say.

"I've no idea," says Dan.

"There never was a Lord Ambleside," says Doreen, "That was one of Sir Alcuin's little jokes."

"Winchester seemed to believe it," I say.

"Charles might have believed him," says Doreen.

"I think he does," says Dan, "We don't want the drink to be too good. We don't want to look like we've got money to throw around. Charles will be begging later – in a few weeks, before they've forgotten. This evening's just to make them feel like we're their friends."

The light's beginning to fade, but it's picking out the north porch of the Erechtheion very crisply. The pale leaves of the olive trees are catching the evening breeze and fluttering delicately. Natalie reappears, fizzing with suppressed energy. She's dying to tell us something. She looks around the room to check who's there.

"You see that dishy policeman?" she says, "The students are saying that Trigger just noshed him."

"I didn't hear that," says Doreen, her gaze drifting off to the Acropolis.

"Did what?" I say, and then I realize what she must have meant as she's thinking how to rephrase it.

"Sucked him off," says Natalie, giggling.

"Honestly," says Dan, "His private life is a public health hazard."

"I've had a very sheltered life," I say, and it's true. I'm more shocked than the others seem to be, but it seems important not to show it.

"So have I," says Doreen, "and I want to keep it that way." I see her the following afternoon in the office when there's no one else around.

"I told him to go and be charming," I say, "I feel a bit responsible."

"Don't," she says, "It's not the first time. Well, maybe the first time with a policeman on the school's premises."

"He has a very welcoming smile," I say, "You can see how it could happen."

"Just stay well away if you know what's good for you," she says, opening her eyes wide, "Seriously. The health service here isn't all it might be, but you really don't want to find out about it through the VD clinics."

"It hadn't entered my head," I say.

"Exactly," she says, "You need to be careful. He has ways of making people do things they never thought they would. I've seen it happen."

"What's going to happen to him?" I say.

"What do you mean?" she says.

"Well," I say, "Will he be expelled or something?"

"Not unless there's a complaint from the Greeks," she says, "We won't mention it again. We'll behave as if it didn't happen."

"Oh," I say, convinced that I'd never be allowed to get away with something like that, "but I was wanting to ask about the Paleoziros project." I pause to see if she changes her expression, but she doesn't, so I go on, "Have there been any architects involved with it before?"

"No," she says, "There was a surveyor in the early days who did a plot of the site, but that was before they'd uncovered anything. You're the first who's been measuring the buildings."

"That's good to know," I say.

"Why's that?" she says.

"Oh, you know," I say, "I'm worried that Winchester expects me to do things like Piet de Jong, and he's going to be disappointed with what I can do. I wondered if he'd sacked uncompliant architects in the past."

"Don't worry about that," says Doreen, "He has Piet on a pedestal. No one else will come close. He's going to be disappointed with anything that anyone can produce, and he'll blame it on the modern world, not you personally."

"It's kind of you to say," I say, "Reassuring, I suppose."

The Lantern is familiar to me now, but I don't suppose I'll ever feel that I belong here. I know the fantastic terrace and the knockout view, but I'll never learn what's OK and what's beyond the pale. There are rumors about the goings-on in the library, which has a large sofa in it, but that's always behind closed doors, so at some times of the day, when the doors are locked, it's a private space. There's nothing personal about my own private space here, and I feel more at home in the city when I revisit cafés and find they haven't changed, and I can sit there and read for a while. There's noise and dust and passers-by, and I disappear into the scenery. That's how I like it.

108

Xander photographed the masks upstairs in the house he was still renovating, in the room with a door onto the terrace and a window looking down into the courtyard. Then the masks were wrapped in muslin, put in sackcloth bags, and passed from hand to hand around the village, hidden in one person's house after another so that everyone was in on it.

Without Luke around, Xander still thought of the house as theirs, and as Xander had done most of the work on it, it seemed to him that he had a right to it. He hadn't quite noticed that Stasia thought of the house as hers, but they kept meeting there and usually ended up in tears together. The ground floor was already set up as Xander's workshop with the expectation of some power tools when the electricity arrived. He could still visit the forge but felt unencumbered by the old tools for ironwork and masonry that were there and by the darkness of the place. The new workshop was a place to face the future.

Xander made three beautiful boxes lined in deep blue velvet. They closed with concealed brass hinges and unlocked with subtle pressure at the corners. They would protect the masks when they traveled. Xander developed the film at home, but to make prints, he needed more equipment. He had started taking pictures of village life and the harbor at Chania and kept visiting Mr Galanakis to print them. Galanakis taught him how to use the equipment, and Xander took the film with the masks with him every time he visited. At first, he needed supervision, and it was impossible even to look at the negatives of the masks in the darkroom. Once he knew his way around the apparatus, Galanakis left him alone, and Xander then looked at the negatives to make sure they had come out. He could always go back and take the photos again if need be. Xander's photography improved with Galanakis's tuition. The Cretan light gave him strong dark shadows. Galanakis showed him how to use them to frame the scene. One day, Galanakis went out and left Xander in the darkroom with only his daughter, Sophie, in reception.

109

In the library of the Lantern of Demosthenes, Ian is wondering if the Voodoo books would all be grouped together or dispersed under their authors' names in some other way. He starts by looking at V in the card catalog. Charles Winchester comes in. They nod to one another, and Ian abandons his search.

"I've been meaning to say," says Ian, "This year, I've been invited to stay at Ziros in the village. I think it will work quite well. I have the drawing machine there, and I'll be able to get more done, I think."

"As you like," says Charles, "You know what's best for you. You can always come back to join us if it doesn't work out as you expect."

He looks appraisingly at Ian. If he's disappointed, he's not going to say so.

"Great," says Ian, I'll see you there in a couple of weeks."

"Do we need to organize someone to pick you up?" says Charles.

"I think that's taken care of," says Ian, "Thank you. I know my way around now, so don't worry. If it doesn't work, I'll find a way to get there. This time, I'm flying to Chania, so a taxi isn't out of the question."

In the office later, when Natalie is busy on the phone, Ian says quietly to Doreen, "I hope Winchester doesn't feel that I've betrayed him."

"Ouf," she says, "Why would he feel that?"

"I wondered if he looked hurt when I told him," says Ian.

"Well," says Doreen, "You're doing the right thing. The students are all new this year, so you won't know any of them, and you do know some of the diggers, which none of the students has ever done. You'll have better company and better facilities, and that can only be good for the project. Don't worry about it."

110

In the darkroom's dim orange light, Xander sees the octopuses one by one in negative, projected on the paper, and then in the developing tray underwater, they darken into a positive presence that's at first quite ghostly, then arresting in its physicality. Three subtly different octopuses with wide eyes and doleful expressions, serpentine tentacles radiating out like haloes. They hadn't been cleaned up, but the incorruptible gold glows across aeons, even in black and white, and every mark of the maker's tool is there just as it was left. Beaten metal sheet, with added solid lumps, indented, pressed, and twisted into shape. There is detail in the working – the suction cups along the tentacles were modeled with a care that shows reverent respect for the octopus original. The tentacles themselves are all different – not schematic and repetitive, but each one curved this way and that to make its own distinct line. Their mouths don't show, so there's no question of their being expressive, but the eyes hold you. The eyes are mournful and look right back at you. It's not an expression of reproach, but it's wary: weighing you up. There's no question that there's intelligence at work on the other side, and it isn't going to trust you right away.

Xander prints the photos of the three masks, four times over. He also prints pictures of young sailors doing their solitary dances at a taverna in Chania. The lighting levels are low, and images dark – a candle flame burns out, over-exposed. The sailors' limbs in dark uniform blur with movement, but chairs and tables come out sharp, as do some of the people watching. The sailor was the thing-not-focused in the image, but it also made it fascinating. Galanakis would be drawn into a discussion about it, and if there was a question about where all the paper had gone, Xander would explain how he'd been trying to print this tricky image repeatedly and now wanted advice. Some prints from the taverna to show to Sophie on the way out, one to leave behind for Galanakis and a dozen sheets of important prints to take back with him, tucked in behind the scenes that he could show.

111

Xander comes to the airport at Chania in his van and picks Ian up. He's on time and relaxed. There's no hurry, and they have a coffee in Chania so Ian can see the harbor again and feel he's arrived. It's there, just as he remembers it. Everyone who lives and works in Chania knows it's going to be hot, so they're staying indoors. There are some tourists out and about, and lots of little shops are selling things that tourists might buy: postcards with garish blue sky, leather bags, straw hats, plastic things for children, flip-flops, and garish beach towels. Xander and Ian sit under an awning with a view across the water to the little Venetian lighthouse at the end of the harbor wall.

"It's good to be here," says Ian, "I don't suppose it's any cooler than Athens, but here the heat feels bearable."

"It's the sea," says Xander, "The sea changes everything. You're still jumpy."

It's true. You can tell from the way Ian sits that he's still in his uptight city way of being, expecting things to happen too quickly. The waiter comes, not too fast. He seems just to be drifting by, and Xander doesn't raise his voice but seems to involve the waiter in the conversation.

"They make their baklava with pistachios here," says Xander, "We should have it."

"Of course," says the waiter, "Sweet coffee? Nes?"

"Sketo," says Ian. He glances at Xander, looking for approval.

The waiter nods.

"Let me see your watch," says Xander to Ian.

Ian holds out his hand so Xander can read the time. Xander gestures to tell him to turn his hand over. Xander undoes the watch, takes it off Ian's wrist, and puts it on the table. Ian looks surprised and puzzled. Xander looks at Ian's wrist and laughs.

"They say when you go on holiday, you should take off your watch," says Xander, "and when you can't see the pale skin that was where your watch strap used to cover it, that's when your holiday really begins. Until then, it's just … what's the word?"

"Winding down?" says Ian, "Preparation?"

"Preparation is good," says Xander, "But look at your wrist! Your English weather's so bad your whole arm is pale. Put your watch in your pocket. You won't need it here."

"I'm here to work," says Ian, "It's not a holiday."

"Of course," says Xander, "But you need to work at the island's pace. Then you'll understand things properly."

"I'm in your hands," says Ian.

"Len's looking forward to seeing you," says Ian, "He thinks this year's students are twits. If you weren't here, he'd have to work with them."

"I'm very pleased he's here," he says, "but what a funny word, 'twits.'"

"That wasn't the word he used," says Xander, "He might have said they were wackers."

"I don't know that word," says Ian.

"That's why I translated," says Xander, "You'll want some water. Oh good, he's brought some."

At the house, they go into the workshop. In the main space there's a half-made boat on the floor, made from sheets of plywood. There's the drawing board on its pneumatic pedestal. Through the courtyard, Ian's room is ready for him.

"You'll want a shower after the journey," says Xander, "Come and say hello to Stasia when you're ready. Take your time."

The room is as bare as a hotel room, with no signs of actual occupation beyond towels and some folded clothes.

"Is Dmitri still living here?" says Ian, looking round the room.

"No," says Xander, "He's in Italy now. He's doing alright. This is your room for as long as you want it."

"Thank you," says Ian, "You know I can always stay at the stoa if you need the room."

"Oh, we don't want that," says Xander, with a sly smile, "We can talk at the meal this evening. I've invited Len, in case you want to chat to prepare for tomorrow. Then tomorrow, for food, we can all can join the polloi at the Megaron."

At the table on the terrace upstairs, Ian finds familiar faces. The air is warm, and the pool of light around the table gives a sense of enclosure that's an illusion. The voices carry into the surrounding night.

"The thing is," says Alice, "In Izmir, people are saying there's a steady stream of small black-market Minoan antiquities. They think the police are on to something, and they don't want to take any more from us."

"Do the police know they're from here?" says Stasia.

"The Turks won't come here," says Len, "Will they trust the Greek police?"

"Good evening, Ian," says Xander.

"I'm not sure I should be hearing this," says Ian.

"We trust you," says Xander, "and by the way, just to be clear, you haven't heard any of it. If anyone asks, which they won't, tell them we were discussing the price of fish."

"What if I told Charles?" says Ian.

"Well, then we'd have to kill you," says Alice, with a shrug, in a matter-of-fact way, not like a threat at all, "The Greek police and the Turkish police work well together when it's antiquities. The Turkish boffins are going to ask the Greek boffins what they make of it. They'll be real experts. They're not going to make the mistake of coming to Charles for advice like the journalists did. In fact, perhaps I need to build Charles's reputation in Turkey so the dealers know his name."

"He's been working on that," says Stasia.

"Minoan Hawaii!" says Xander, and everyone laughs.

"You can imagine how that's going down in Turkey," says Alice.

"How?" says Ian.

"They're not impressed," says Alice, "If there were global explorers in antiquity, they'd have been Huns, they say, definitely not Greek."

"When were you going to start in the morning?" says Len.

"I don't know," says Ian, "I'll come along with the rest of you. When are you going?"

"We set off at dawn," says Len, "You want to be able to see the path, but it's not too hot for the first couple of hours. It's the best part of the day for working."

"Yes," says Ian, "I know the routine."

"You can start later if you want," says Len, "Then I can have a lie in."

"I'd better look keen," says Ian, "Can I borrow an alarm clock? I'm not adjusted to the early start yet, and the daylight isn't going to wake me up in time."

"Listen," says Len, "I'll come and find you. You can leave it till the last minute. You wake up while you're walking and shower when you get back. You'll just want your tools."

"Everything's up at the stoa," says Ian, "I just need my notes and my haversack."

112

It's the photos, not the masks that make the journey first to Istanbul by way of several islands, Jael traveling alone in widow's garb to places she knew well in other times. Istanbul itself is much the place she knew but with different faces there behind the counters. It's less than half a lifetime she's been gone, and there must be people still around – retired perhaps and harder to track down. Someone at the museum – you have to ask the questions carefully – someone at a commercial gallery that sells old things – circumspect as ever – shows interest in her photos – someone at a bar – that feels disreputable – asks to take the photos with him – fixing an appointment at the Pera Palace, where it's cosmopolitan and above reproach. Jael, whose habit is staying out of sight, decided that she'd better rise to the occasion, bought an outfit from the place her mother used to like, ordered tea and sat among the potted palms to wait for the appointment. At the exact moment specified, a young woman walks in, sits down, and, without introduction, opens a document that looks at first like a menu but which is a portfolio with three photos in it. The very ones. There follows a discussion, or maybe a set of instructions, but set out in a calm and reasonable way with seeming friendliness. There's no need to haggle. The merits of the masks are accepted, and their value is high.

"You will understand," says the younger woman, wearing pearls, "that if you suddenly have enormous wealth in your possession, it will awaken interest from the police, and if you have a tale to tell them, then there'll be a ransom to pay in tax."

"What do you propose instead?" says Jael, perfectly composed, "A cup of tea?" She seems to be as interested in the tea as in what the woman says. There are two china teacups, not the Turkish kind, and a Wedgwood teapot decorated with delicate lines linking the palest pink flowers, with groups of pale leaves and – yes – two tiny wild strawberries.

"I don't mind if I do," says the woman with the pearls.

"Let me be mother then," says Jael. She pours the tea and leaves it on the tray for the other woman to pick up.

"What we thought might suit you better," said the woman, "would be an account with the Sargasso Bank with a generous overdraft that we would pay off in installments regularly. That way, if questions are ever asked, you're always owing money, never rich. We have heard about the megaron in your village. We propose to establish it in perpetuity to supplement the modest endowment of the Zimbreans with funds that will pay for food and electricity for the whole village. Also, a telephone. And we will supply workers for the excavation project. What we ask for in return is your cooperation."

"This is not what I expected," says Jael.

"I hope it's better," says the woman, "You can see it's been thought through and is well-adapted to the circumstances."

"I can see that we've been watched," says Jael, "You know all about us."

"I've met your son," says the woman, "I met him in Heraklion when he was with Luke Zimbrean. I've met the lawyers at the port, and Charles Winchester is very well-known to me. We have done our homework. I am here to represent the interests of my client, and in a manner of speaking, those masks are already theirs. We would like to take care of them."

"How can I trust you?" says Jael.

"You have no alternative," says the woman, "We can cooperate, and then your village does well out of it. Or you can refuse, and then you will find that the masks have softly and suddenly vanished away, and you're left with nothing. Having said that; you can trust us. You really can."

"I must go back to talk things over with the others," says Jael.

"Of course, you must," says the woman, "There's no hurry. We will make an appointment. Bring the masks to Venice on the fifteenth of December. We have reasons to be there, then. Bring your son – or send him. We can communicate with him. Send him to the Hotel Danieli. If the masks are there, then the overdraft will be at the bank. Go to the bank. You will find that the account is already there, in the name of the village, which is also, I believe, your name. You might find that ambiguity useful."

"And if I can't persuade them?" says Jael.

"Then there'd be no need to do anything," says the woman, "You'll have nothing to worry about. Soon after Christmas, you'll notice that the masks have disappeared. You'll have nothing. It will all be taken care of."

"We may have another offer," says Jael.

"Good luck with that," says the woman with a pleasant smile.

113

In the event, Ian wakes early and goes out to find the others, who are mustering quietly in the plateia near a harsh, bare electric light. No one says anything much.

"G'day," says Len, not too brightly. There's no noticeable signal, but at some point, there's enough light to move off, and there's an ambling drift of bodies in the direction of the site – all with khaki sun hats, carpenter's aprons and sturdy boots, men and women alike.

"Everyone got the new aprons?" says Len, and there's a murmur or a grumble of assent.

They approach the chain-link fencing at Paleoziros like a sullen revolutionary band, and Ian feels like a class traitor about to storm an enclave of privilege.

"From here, we don't say anything except in Greek," says Len, "Except to you when no one else can hear."

They go to a large sliding door on the entrance side of the stoa where the spades and wheelbarrows are stored.

"I never noticed that door before," says Ian, "I'll go round the other side and find my things."

He goes round the end of the building and up the three timber steps to the open part of the stoa, where the long table is. There are four interchangeable youngsters sitting at it.

"We should get a toaster," says one of them.

"You can use the grill," says another, but that just causes the first one to look puzzled.

"Good morning," says Ian, "How do you do."

There's an indistinct murmuring of how-do-you-dos.

"I'm the architect," says Ian.

"Oh yeah," says one of the interchangeable youngsters, "Mr Winchester said you'd be coming."

Charles himself isn't to be seen, except in the framed photo on the wall, where he and Luke Zimbrean look much like the students do now, "Would you like some coffee?"

"Thank you," says Ian, "I'll help myself. I know my way around." The tape measure, spirit level, and string are where he left them a year ago. He puts them in his yellow canvas shoulder bag with the notebooks and pencils and goes down the three familiar timber steps to the ground.

Ian and Len are making good progress, picking up from last year's notes and making some fresh measurements.

"We should stake out the surveyor's grid on the ground," says Ian, "Then we could take measurements from it without having to triangulate everything."

"What would that take?" says Len.

"The problem is keeping track of it with the slope of the ground," says Ian, "but basically, we just need tent pegs and loads more string and a compass so we can get it going in the right direction."

The sun climbs in the sky, and the heat is too much. They all go back to the shade of the stoa. Len doesn't go up the steps but goes to wait on the shady side of the building near the tool store. Ian goes to put his things back in the cupboard. Charles Winchester is there at the table.

"Hello," says Ian.

"How are you doing?" says Charles.

"It's going well," says Ian, "We're plotting those curves. I think I'm going to need more string. I'd be able to plot the lines more quickly. Or maybe a brightly colored tape, so it's easier to see. Is that OK?"

"I think we can run to that," says Charles, "Would you be able to find it in Chania?"

"I expect so," says Ian, "I can ask Xander."

"Yes," says Charles, "I'm sure he'll know where to go. Go with him – and make sure you get receipts from the shop. Not from Mr Ziros."

"I certainly will," says Ian, "Should I go tomorrow or leave it till the weekend?"

"I don't want it to hold you up," says Charles, "Go tomorrow if it helps."

Ian leaves the stoa through the small door by the kitchen area. Looking to the right, he sees the diggers leaning against the wall in the shade. There's no particular reason for them to wait, but they seem to like to move as a group, and Ian seems to have become part of the group.

"I have permission to go into Chania," says Ian when he meets up with Len, "tomorrow morning if Xander can manage it."

"Ah," says Len, "You could stop for a swim on your way back. We're going for a swim now if you want to come."

"Sure," says Ian, "I'll just need to go to my room first to pick up my swimming things."

"You don't need swimmers, mate," says Len, "We're going to Kladdy. We'll bring plenty of towels."

"Where's Kladdy?" says Ian.

"Kladdisos," says Len, "It's not too far. We go on the bikes."

"Are you telling me it's a nudist beach?" says Ian, "I've led a sheltered life."

"You've been missing out," says Len, "I didn't have you down as a wowser."

There are half a dozen motorbikes in an otherwise unused house, and everyone else seems to be familiar with them. Ian does feel that he's been missing out.

"Hold tight," says Len, and off they go, still in their work clothes.

The siesta is half-and-half on the beach and back at the house, where Ian showers and rests before the evening meal at the Megaron. It's only a few paces away from the house, but he treats it as a leisurely stroll. There are fairly familiar faces to acknowledge, and he feels at home here when he looks around.

"I must get a hat like yours," says Ian when he's sitting at a table with Janey, a tanned young woman with a freckly nose. They both have ouzos. "I have to hold my hat on when I'm on the bike, and then it feels so prissy to be sitting on the beach wearing nothing but a Panama when everyone else is so relaxed."

"There's plenty of hats here," says, "You just help yourself. Tee-shirts and undies too if you're interested. You drop them off in the laundry bin and pick up fresh whenever you like."

"How do you keep track of who's is who's?" says Ian.

Janey laughs.

"It's not an issue, mate," she says, "Just pick up something that fits."

"What about the motorbikes?" says Ian, "I didn't know about them."

"Yeah," says Janey, "They're always there. You can use them. You need to watch the fuel. There's a free bowser by the church. You can go into Chania if you want or go inland. Just make sure you've got enough juice to get back. If you run out, you end up having to pay."

Everything looks the same as it did last year, but now that Ian's based in the village, he's discovering how it works for the diggers. On the site, they're at work, but the village is run as a holiday camp.

The expedition to Venice becomes Xander and Stasia's honeymoon. The wedding felt like something that took shape around them, without either of them quite making a decision about it. They both missed Luke painfully and understood that feeling in one another. They both felt they had rights in the house, and somehow, the marriage resolved everything. Radiant Xander and beautiful Anastasia made a glorious match. Galanakis took the portraits of the day. One he chose for the family, where they looked just the way they should, glowing with pride and happiness. That was the one to frame. The other he chose for Xander, and gave it to him secretly to hide away.

"It's not for the family," he said, "but you'll understand." Both bride and groom had moved, so they came out smudged. The surroundings were sharp, but Stasia's hair had blown about, and she shook her head while Xander's eye looked straight at the lens, but then he turned away. There was something about the piercing directness of the look, combined with the head turned to profile and Stasia's blurry cloudiness, that made them both look ethereal and each quite separate from the other.

"Thank you," said Xander, as if his heart might break.

The megaron is much the same as it was, presided over by the carved bison plaque, the photo of Luke and Xander in their youthful prime, and the three framed photos of the octopus masks from Hawaii. They're good photos printed, so the masks are life-size – not huge things, but with a striking presence in the room. Ian's mesmerized by them.

"Yes," says Xander when Ian asks him about them, "I always liked them. Now they're being cleaned at the Smithsonian, and of course Charles is saying they're Greek."

"Are they Greek?" says Ian.

"Who can say," says Xander with a shrug.

"They might be from Crete," says Ian, "There's plenty of octopus imagery around here."

"Suppose they are from here," says Alice, "How could they have gone to Hawaii?"

"Search me," says Xander, with a shrug.

"Suppose," says Alice, looking up to the ceiling, "they were in the tholos, and Charles found them before the excavation officially started. Suppose he spirited them away to a rich buyer in the 1950s. I bet that's what happened. I remember he didn't want to excavate the tholos. That's because he knew it was there and knew he'd already robbed it. He's very keen on the idea that the director of the excavation takes credit for all the finds. We must make sure that he's held responsible for all the losses. All these seal stones are on sale in Turkey – they're being excavated here right under his nose. I'm confident the police would see that he knows what's going on and is making money out of it."

"Hang on," says Ian, "I'm confused."

"Don't be confused," says Alice, "That's the last thing we want. It's important that you're not confused. We know nothing. You know nothing. Everything happened under Charles's direction. He's responsible. That's the law. It's the director who takes the credit when things are going well and the director who takes the blame when they don't. "

"Is he in trouble?" says Ian.

"This season, Charles is going to be very, very pleased," says Alice, "It'll be the best-ever season for finds, and he'll find a little extra in his bank account."

"How will you do that?" says Ian.

"My dear," says Alice, "It couldn't be easier. The only problem is deciding which bank it will look as if it's come from. I think perhaps a Turkish one. Or maybe Swiss."

116

During the honeymoon, they stay out of sight as much as they can, at a hotel on the mainland for most of the stay, dressed in dowdy clothes that keep out the December chill. They see the city, fall for its sparkling insubstantiality, find their way through its labyrinth of alleyways, eat its food, and find someone in Mestre who'll rent a little boat to them with an outboard motor. It's only once they're in the boat that they start to feel they have a feel for the place and its muddy fragility. Crete has been Venetian, so there's plenty that feels familiar, but here, its light is misty, shifting through clouds, and when it glitters, it glitters without heat. They know, then, what they're doing when they arrive at the appointed date and check in to the Hotel Danieli to wait for something. They've bought some clothes from places fancier than they've ever known before. They have their hair done, and they buy new shoes. Xander wears the sunglasses Luke bought him and feels the way he did the day he first met Galanakis. They look the part as they arrive at the water door of the grand hotel and let the porter deal with their unpretentious little barque. The boxes with the masks in are in neat hessian bags, not hidden but mixed with a good array of luggage that should go up to the room.

"What do we do now?" says Stasia in the room, which looks out across the water to a white church on an island.

"We wait," says Xander, "There'll be a message, maybe at reception. It's not there yet, but we can ask later or in the morning. We could go down for a drink." He opens up the boxes just to see that everything's in order, and it is. The masks look like they've been prepared to go on display in a museum or in a shop window.

"Is it safe to leave them here?" says Stasia.

"I don't know if it's safe to be with them at all," says Xander, "but they've had rich people here at the hotel before with precious things. I'm sure it's quite secure."

They go and sit near the Christmas tree and the enormous fireplace – the most visible place in the hotel – half-expecting to be visited by someone with a message.

"Two Negronis," says Xander when a waiter appears, "It was Loukas who taught me to be comfortable in big hotels. We should raise a glass to him."

"We wouldn't be here without him," says Stasia, who looks at this moment as if she's always been accustomed to such surroundings.

"Gold suits you," says Xander.

117

There's a steady routine at the site, and you'd hardly notice the progress day by day, but when you look back on it after a week or two, you can see that things have moved on. This year, more little things have been found than ever before, and Charles is quietly excited. He doesn't really show excitement, but he's in a good mood more often and more confident about his views. Ian has brought his plans to the stoa. They're drawn on half a dozen pieces of tracing paper, which he's pieced together partly overlapping, lightly fixed to one another and to the long table, with torn-off squares of masking tape.

"You can see how the wavy walls all radiate from the tholos," says Ian.

"It's not like the plan of a palace," says Charles, "I think it must be a temple of some sort."

"Hmm," says Ian, "You don't think it's a village?"

"Nah," says Charles, "It's too well made for that. Especially the tholos."

Something lights up behind his eyes.

"We have the trustees meeting in January," he says, "We've had the best season ever for small finds. We'll fly you out in January. You can present the plan. It will be a triumph."

"That sounds good," says Ian.

"We'll present it as a cult site," says Charles, "It's obvious that it's a snake-goddess cult. Your plan makes it clear that it's Medusa. You can see the tholos is the head, with the snakes radiating out from it."

"Oh," says Ian, "I thought Medusa was a jellyfish."

"No, no, no," says Charles, "Draw it up as a gorgon."

"I'll need to plot the lines accurately," says Ian.

"Of course," says Charles, "I don't want you to falsify anything. Just bring it into focus, as it were. Show it as it looks with the eye of faith."

"This is the one that turned people into stone?" says Ian.

"That's right," says Charles.

"She's a sort of anti-Pygmalion," says Ian, "He brought a sculpture to life. She turned people into sculpture."

"There you go," says Charles, "She should be a patron saint for architects."

"I'm not sure about that," says Ian.

"Well," says Charles, "Have a think about it. If you can draw up the plans and think of something to say about them, you can make a presentation in January. It's about time I had something big for the trustees to see."

118

"What were you dreaming about?" Stasia says in the morning, "You were moving about quite strangely."

"Was I shouting in German?" says Xander.

"No," says Stasia, "Nothing like that. You were moving your arms about as if you were pretending to be seaweed or something."

"I don't remember," says Xander, but as he says it, he has a memory of being underwater, with chandelier-like clumps of golden seaweed hanging from a cellophane ceiling. He has a conviction that he knows what he has to do today, but he doesn't mention it right away.

"Someone might come with a message," says Stasia, "We should have breakfast somewhere they can find us easily. Downstairs."

"I don't need a message," says Xander, "I think I've been told. First I want to go and buy some masks. Where's the harm in that?"

They look in one mask shop after another. Some of them are very garish and won't do at all.

"What about this one?" says Stasia, holding a huge, hooked nose with demon's horns and a big chin in front of her face.

They laugh.

They each try the pretty porcelain doll masks, which look unnervingly creepy and are no fun at all. The grinning, grotesque ones make them both livelier and somehow they're OK.

They end up in a shop with a small and rather dull display of leather masks. They're rather minimal and cover only part of the face, so you think they're hardly going to work as a disguise at all, but yet when Stasia tries one on, she becomes completely unrecognizable. The woman who's serving them has bleached hair and a manner that's protective of the masks. She's clearly proud of them. Her husband, the artisan, hides away in the background, but he seems to make the masks here on the premises. Xander tries one and you can't see that it's him behind the mask, even though nothing much seems to be hidden. The leather's pressed and molded into the shape of the head – a second skin, not so very different from his own. It's these masks where the craftsmanship of their being made is most clearly seen. They're also the ones where the illusion is most difficult to pin down. They're expensive, but they're the ones they buy.

"You might want a box if you're traveling with them," says the woman, gesturing to a pile of buff and pastel-colored hat boxes.

"We'll be OK with the bags, thank you," says Xander. They're good, sturdy carrier bags.

They board a vaporetto, thinking it will take them back towards the hotel, but they're mistaken. It will go there eventually but by way of a great looping route. They go up the Grand Canal and see the showy fronts of the palaces. The labyrinth of alleys goes to the service entrances, so approached by land, the palaces all seem to be unaccountably hidden away, but from the water, everything makes sense. Then the impressive facades stop, and they're at a place where ships come in.

"There's the Giudecca," says Stasia, as they're passing a place where a big yacht is berthed. Cthulu, Honolulu, it says on the stern.

"Hulu Lulu," says Xander to himself.

It has a gold funnel, which reminds Xander of the gold masks. Suppose someone finds them in the room. Would they feel obliged to alert the police?

"We should have organized fake passports," says Xander.

"Don't be silly," says Stasia, "We'll be invisible again after today."

They stay on the boat until it reaches San Marco, and they walk to the hotel. Back in the room, everything is in order. They take the leather masks out of the carrier bags and unwrap the tissue paper around them – some smoothly wrapped around the mask, and then some crumpled to make padding in the bag. They take the gold masks from the boxes and put one in each carrier bag, wrapped just the way the leather masks were. Then, they put one leather mask in each of the three boxes.

"Very good," says Xander, "Now, weren't you wanting to look around the diocesan museum?"

"I don't remember saying anything about it," says Stasia, "but it sounds like a good thing to do."

They take the carrier bags with them.

As they're going past the north side of San Marco, Xander says, "Come, dearest, we don't want to take this heavy old shopping around the museum. Let's check the bags in here."

"Are you all right?" says Stasia.

There's a place for left luggage. It isn't crowded. There's no queue. It's off-season, even though Venice seems perfect for Christmas. The Christmas decorations bring out the place's fondness for tinsel and bling. Instead of three heavy carrier bags, they have a formica disc, rather larger than a coin, with a three-digit number on it. The museum is absolutely deserted. They're the only people here.

119

In England, back at the university, I had Xander's photo of the tiny seal stone made up as a slide so I could project it on the big screen in the lecture theatre. I saw the real thing with my naked eye. Xander took a photo of it with his specially ground lens, and projected the negative on the wall of his gallery, or whatever it is – the room off the terrace above the workshop. I have a sense of that room taking shape around me as I get lost in the image. Are they waves? or flames? They don't look like flames – I'd have given them pointed tops. These are curved. The central figure looks like he's in command, not like someone being burned. It is a man with broad shoulders and muscular thighs. Maybe I was imagining the lions. Maybe it's a waterfall. The man's stick makes him look authoritative. Maybe it's an altar on the left. Maybe all the little buildings are altars. There's another male figure on the right, but he's less important, and his head is a bit lost. The image doesn't make any clear sense. I don't think it's Paleoziros. There's nothing in the image that matches anything we've found. Maybe it's Chania – a cult site at the port. It draws you in. It takes you back to Crete, back to Xander's upstairs room. On the right, there's a window with closed shutters that looks down into the courtyard with my room opposite down below, Xander's study straight across. I'm in the lecture theatre with raked seating and a much larger screen here, but somehow, I can feel myself in both rooms at once, both real, both held in place by the image on the screen. I'm in both places at once, and I'm crying, and I don't know why. There's something wrong, but I don't know what, and something is falling into place or falling apart. Perhaps it's me. Something's missing. I'm missing something in myself, and I think I'll find it at Ziros, but I can't put my finger on it. There's some sort of bond with the place. Have I fallen in love with it like Xander said I would? I must go back there. I can't bear the thought that I won't.

120

"We could see this at home," says Stasia, as they go through a room whose walls are lined with a band of icons, all the same size, all mounted at eye level, repeating a format with slight variations.

There are paintings from the workshops of Venetian master painters. The names are familiar, but it's the brother or the father or the son of the famous painter with that name. There are rooms of reliquaries for souvenirs of minor saints in beautiful glass and gilded brass containers, making them look like anatomical specimens if we can work out what they are.

"Well, this is definitely a hand," says Stasia, "and who's to say it's not Saint Emgydius's? He must have had hands."

"And this," says Xander, "is a fiber of a sponge!"

It's labeled as coming from a sponge that was soaked in vinegar and proffered as a salve to Christ when he was on the cross. There's something wonderful about cherishing something so delicate. It's almost like the filament in an electric light bulb. The glass phial with its brass mount could hold a gas, and the sponge filament could be charged with holiness, and then it could glow.

Xander's mesmerized. Fixated. A sort of tunnel-vision closes in on him. There's just him and this filament of sponge – and it's glowing – very gently, barely perceptibly at first, but there's a tremor of light running through it with a pulse, and it's growing more intense, throbbing, pulsating, definitely illuminating the things around it, and dazzling now – hurting – blinding. He holds up his hand to shield his eyes and feels its heat.

"I'm burning up in the sun," he says. He feels his flesh being cooked, like with sunbathing – miraculated into something that it wasn't before – something more alive than ever, but hardly in his body.

"I'm floating," he says, "I'm looking down on myself from above." He can hear through intense tinnitus – voices – singing.

"Xander! Come on. Are you alright? You went into a seizure," says Stasia. She looks worried but sensible.

"I don't know what happened," says Xander, "It was like when I started seeing Matthias. In fact, the light was the same blue. Something electric. Something like burning gas-jets."

"You're not making any sense," says Stasia, "You need a glass of water."

121

The big plan of Paleoziros is carefully put together with accurate measurements, but it doesn't look very exciting on the page. It's projected now as a negative slide, so the ink lines show up as lines of light on the screen, like chalk on a blackboard, but more precise and brighter. The lines shine light into the darkened room. I've worked over two prints of the plan using charcoal – the side of a broken stick, not the end of it, to get a cloudy shadow. I take care not to smudge it, so it looks quite precise in its way. I can make the charcoal clouds suggest the lines that might be there, extending the lines of the measured stones. I have some curves firmly in place; others are guesswork or free improvisation, but they go with the flow of what's there. It's definitely turning into an octopus. I'm staying with that. The tholos tomb makes the head. There are not enough walls to be clear about the use of the place – I'm not getting the feeling that these were houses, but who's to say? I take photographs of the drawing in three states of its development – with very light sketchy charcoal shading over the plan, then with the lines more firmly in place, then with the addition of the symmetrical "other half" we can infer should be there, if we look for it under the olive trees. I have shadows where the mournful eyes would be, and they fix the image as an octopus. If I have the two versions of the plan in two projectors, both trained on the same screen and if I have a dimmer so I can bring the brightness up slowly, I can show the plan and gradually reveal the octopus staring back at you from the dark.

I've also done one with the gorgon head. The wavy lines, then, aren't tentacles but snakes. There's not nearly enough of them, and I'm not happy with it, but it's what Winchester's determined to see, so I'm humoring him. I can use them in sequence. I'll show this one first and then the octopus can loom into view. As my final slide, it will linger.

Athens in early January is like a proper city, rather than being half taken-over by holiday-makers who seem to have dressed for the beach. Of course, I know my way around, but it feels quite different from usual. I notice the shops – clothes shops, book shops, electric light shops – rather than concentrating on the routes between museums. The trustees' meeting is a big deal for the school. It's an annual thing, and the trustees are not out to sink the institution, but they're substantial people who stand to have to bail the place out if it isn't properly run, so they want to hear a good story about what's been going on. They want to hear that the Lantern is doing good work, and that it's making a success of things in attracting the right sort of attention and some income. There are two Cantacuzene trustees appointed directly by the family, and they have a right of veto, so they have to be courted assiduously. It's Charles's job to court them. He's on the board, but as director, he's answerable to the trustees. There's also a representative of the Zimbrean Trust, who has a right of veto on Zimbrean Trust monies if they're being discussed here, and that has always and only ever been Charles, but this year the widowed Mrs Zimbrean, now in her 90s, will be attending so he will be treating her with respect. The Zimbrean Trust supports the Palaeoziros project, while the Cantacuzene Trust pays for the running of the main building and other activities, but there's always a need for more, and there are ideas about fundraising or income generation from the building to be discussed. There are other trustees who are experts in one thing or another – accountancy, museums, management – and they give advice to make sure the Lantern stays on track, doing good things and remaining solvent. It's not run for profit, but it's healthy if its overheads are less than its income, so there's money to give to good things in the future – publishing projects, exhibitions, conferences, and the like. It's a private meeting in the library, with the furniture rearranged so there's something like a boardroom table in the central double-height space.

I check the blackout and the projectors. Winchester will be showing slides of this season's spectacular finds. A great success. Then I'll take over and show the seal stone with the architecture in it and my plans. Charles can say what he likes about the Medusa's head, and then I'll quietly dissolve to the octopus and leave it up for as long as I can.

Doreen's here, arranging tea cups on trays. There's an urn with hot water in it and several small jugs of milk.

"They always want jammy dodgers," she says, looking woefully at the plates of biscuits, "Help yourself whenever you feel like it. They'll go on all afternoon. We have your short talks – you and Charles – then you'll leave. They'll be discussing Charles's contract, so he'll have to leave while they do that."

"What is there to discuss?" I say.

"How much longer he's going to stay," says Doreen, "They've always been three-year appointments before, but somehow Charles negotiated something different. He's reached the age where they can let him go if they want to replace him."

"So it's a big deal for him," I say, "I imagine after this season there won't be a problem."

"He needed it to be a good one," says Doreen.

"And it was," I say, "No wonder he was so chipper about it."

Dan looks in.

"I'm off to the Grande Bretagne," says Dan.

"OK," says Doreen, "Mrs Zimbrean's there," she says to me, "There's a car booked to bring her here with her wheelchair."

"Let's see what's already in," I say. I switch the projector on. "Do you know how to do the lights?"

I work through the slides in the carousels. Winchester's just using one projector for his slides, which are awful. Whoever took the pictures has used the automatic setting on the camera, so it's adjusted itself for the white paper in the background, and the small objects are underexposed, but you can see the texture of the paper quite clearly. There are three or four objects on each slide, and they have as much impact as a collection of pebbles from the beach. I can't even tell which stone it is that Xander photographed for me, let alone what its engraved lines depict.

"These are disappointing," I say.

I have seven slides, one of them a black blank. I've done one that's a sketchy section showing that if you put a monumental statue on top of the tholos, you'd be able to see it clearly from the sea if you cut down the trees. The tall cypresses give a bit of an idea of how it would show, and there's a picture taken from the beach where we used to go swimming in my first season there. If I'd known I'd want this image I'd have taken the camera out a bit further, in the little dinghy. It didn't seem like a good idea to take the camera to the beach, and I must have taken this shot early on. I'd have been lynched if I'd taken a camera out at Kladissos. I need to adjust the two projectors on their piles of books so the images are in alignment when I have the octopus overlaid on the plan.

122

Xander, in his own mind, is wandering from crisis to crisis across his life. There's a lightning storm, some kind of absolute thrill. If I could go on like this, he thinks, I'd have the most radiantly ecstatic life, but I'd be catatonic – useless to the world but radiating saintly happiness. These life-defining moments tell me what matters most – the eyes of Matthias – the filament of sponge – the ecstatic morning at the Hotel Megaron – the tholos tomb – unrepeatably, they can only take me by surprise. To organize my life around them – that's an addict's problem, always hoping that this next time will be right again. My moments creep up on me and catch me unawares. My fingers feel the edge of the formica disc in my pocket – nothing in itself, but freighted with my moments and all that led me up to them.

A guard smiles and points out that they don't want to miss the cloister – down the stairs here. It's the oldest part of the building – crumbly brick making small arches, not all the same size, with several storeys of building up above, so it feels very enclosed and underlit. It's not richly decorated but has a feeling of good character, as if the work was done honestly and well. It's certainly lasted, with some cracks and doubtless some rebuilding, but it's lasted. They turn a corner, see a woman dressed in navy blue, and think that she's a nun. She's not. She's wearing earrings shaped like seahorses.

Xander takes the formica disc from the left-luggage office
and gives it to her as if she had been begging.

123

Dan found Mrs Zimbrean, and he wheeled her in. She's looking very frail, but autocratic in a dazed sort of way.

"Is Charles here?" she says, "Where's Charles?"

"This is Ian Bell," says Dan, whose eyes are darting around the room.

"How do you do," I say, "I'm the architect on the project."

"Have we met before?" she says.

"No," I say. What else can I say? She seems to lose interest.

"Lovely to meet you," she says to signal that she's moving on.

"Mrs Zimbrean," says Charles.

"Charles, dear. How lovely." He bends over to kiss her on each cheek.

"Should we settle you in the library?" says Charles, "Then you'll be ready for the slide show."

"How exciting," she says, "Of course, I don't see these days, but you'll tell me about the slides, won't you?"

"Of course," says Charles. His summer complexion, which I usually see, has faded back to redness. He's not looking too healthy. Dan signals that it would be a good idea for everyone else to go in, too.

"It has been a remarkable year for the Zimbrean Palaoziros Project," Charles says, "and we want to show you some of the things we've found before the formal meeting. We won't take too long about it – we don't want to try the patience of our very distinguished visitors, but the ZPP is our most important endeavor at the moment, and I'm pleased to say it is going simply splendidly. We have had some years when the finds have been maybe disappointing, but we have stuck to our principles and have excavated in a methodical manner, and I'm pleased to say that we're now getting the results that we were always confident we would get. As Mrs Zimbrean is here today, I'd like particularly to thank her and her late husband for their steady support over the decades and for keeping faith with us when the pickings seem to be lean. In particular, of course, I owe a huge debt to her late son, my dearest friend, Luke Zimbrean, whose vision and insight were – well – it's obviously not going too far to describe him as a genius. The project is, every day, a tribute to him, and with our most recent season, it becomes apparent that he is going to be remembered as a towering figure in the world of Aegean Prehistory."

He's pitched this high, I think, and it's all going to be an introduction to his terrible slides. It's bound to be an anticlimax. But of course, he's saying what Mrs Z wants to hear, and she's not going to be able to see the slides. They're not going to care whether there's any evidence at all to back up the fanciful things I'm going to claim. They'll love it. They'll lap it up. What am I doing? I'm playing into their game. The more outrageous my claims about the settlement, the more they'll love it. The more Charles will love it. The more likely it will be that he'll get the next few years of life funded, whether he retires or not – and let's face it, he really retired some years ago. His job now is just a hobby, but it's a hobby that brings him a decent income and a fabulous place to live. It brings him status. And I've been played. I'm a pawn in his game. The more extravagant my claims for the project, the happier he's going to be. I start to feel almost drunk. Do I want to undermine him? Do I want to help him along? – knowing that he'll help me if I do. Do I have any moral feelings about this? Do I have a backbone? No. I can see the game, and I can see that I'm implicated in it, so I may as well go along with it. The project is going to be more incredible and more fabulous than has yet been imagined. It is the most extraordinary project that the Lantern has ever had.

124

Three octopus masks from Hawaii came to the Smithsonian for restoration work. They've been in the museum on Kaua'i island from before the island was part of the USA, so it's as if they've been there since the dawn of time, but no one really knows whether to put them down as ancient treasures or modern work. They're not at all like anything else from the islands. The octopus imagery fits well enough, but there's none of the characteristic face-pulling with big eyes and fierce mouths. So maybe there was a civilization here before the Polynesians arrived. Could they be Chinese from a thousand years ago? Could they be older than that? The people at the Smithsonian think it looks like the gold mask from Mycenae, which Schliemann found in the nineteenth century. Could there be a link? Maybe some nineteenth-century Hawaiians saw the Greek mask and thought they'd make some like it. That's unlikely. The cost would have been exorbitant – making them in solid gold – and we would have heard about the craftsmen who could do that sort of work if they'd been as recent as that. No. Everything points to something much older.

125

Charles has shown his terrible slides, and it's my turn to speak. I might be drunk, not because of any alcohol but on adrenalin.

"Here's an image from one of the seal stones," I say, and there's a murmur in the room. It's the first slide that shows something you can actually see. I suddenly feel that I'm in Xander's upstairs room, and in the university lecture theatre, as well as here, and I can feel tears rolling down my cheeks as I speak, but it doesn't seem to affect my voice, and in the dark, they can't be seen. I'm wishing that the image showed an octopus, but it doesn't. "We don't know quite what it shows," I say, "but maybe there's some sort of religious ceremony going on, with the priest holding out a staff, standing in a high place. There's a building on the left, which looks like some sort of temple structure or an altar. These might be conventional symbols – heraldic, if you like – not something we'd literally expect to find on the site. There's nothing here to make it clear that we're looking at Paleoziros, but it's the most coherent architectural image we have from the site. It's a tiny thing, so we can't expect too much from the person who made it. There's more in the image than you'd think possible. Maybe we can see a hint of the military side of a city. The ordinary fabric of the town fades from the representation, and you get the idea of a stronghold, a port, an elevated sanctuary."

I'm overdoing it, but it's the best slide. Now, here's the section and the view from the beach, which looks sadly too much like a view of the beach, but I make the point that a figure as big as the one in the seal stone picture would have towered enough to show up from the sea.

"Maybe," I hear myself saying, "it was a lighthouse like the Colossus of Rhodes that showed sailors the way to the port." I hadn't rehearsed that, but it seems to go down well. Here's the plan with the wavy lines. Here's the overlaid image of the unconvincing Medusa, and here's the much more persuasive octopus.

My jaw drops. I feel panic. The octopus on the screen isn't my charcoal drawing but Xander's photograph of the gold octopus mask that's now at the Smithsonian. I lapse into silence. There's a round of applause.

Charles looks puzzled.

"Where did that come from?" he says.

"I've no idea," I say, "I wasn't expecting it."

"And what about the seal stone?" he says, "That's an excellent slide."

"I'm very short-sighted," I say, "It's a super-power."

"Very good," says Charles, still looking puzzled.

126

"Job done," says Xander, "Here's San Zaccaria. The hotel's just up that way."

Back in the hotel room, the new leather masks look rather good against the deep blue velvet. They look redder than they did in the shop. They're much lighter to carry than the ancient masks. From Venice, they'll sail to Brindisi and change there for the crossing to Patras, and then once in Greece, they can decide just what to do.

The masks, meanwhile, are reclaimed with the token and taken to the Hotel Bauer by the woman dressed in navy blue who could be taken for a nun. She sits in the bar by the window on the square in front of Saint Moses' church. She's drinking tea with a friend who wears a well-tailored stone-colored suit. We know her as Alice Cyprian, and it doesn't surprise us in the least when she takes the carrier bags up to her room that overlooks the Grand Canal. She opens the window and looks out but seems not to see what she might have been expecting. She unwraps the masks, then bundles them up with sheets and puts them in a laundry bag. She conceals her smart suit with a nylon housecoat and puts on flatter shoes. She looks out of the window again and waits.

She goes down the service stairs with the bag and to the modest service wharf in the Rio di San Moise. A boat pulls up with a dozen laundry bags just like hers aboard it, and she adds to its load, then goes back inside. She smartens up again and leaves to go and look at shops.

It's months later when the masks arrive at Honolulu, from where they quietly go to Kaua'i Island, where we might say they're hidden, but in fact, they're put on display. There's a good museum, and they find a place where they look at home and as if they've been there forever.

A few years later, Kaua'i, along with the rest of Hawai'i, joins the Union of States, and no one pays much attention to the museum, but the masks are documented as present from before the time that US law came to apply.

127

The gold mask is still on the screen, looking at us all, part octopus, part radiant sunshine. It's mesmerizing, and we hardly notice when the door opens and some more people come into the room.

"I'm from the ephoria," says a sturdy middle-aged woman who's been here all along, "That's a brilliant presentation," she says, "but please excuse me. I haven't been working on the site, but I have been doing some work to help put these discoveries in context."

She says, "I'd like to acknowledge the help of some colleagues who may not be known to you."

She says, "But you can be sure, Mr Winchester, that you are known to us."

Charles smiles benevolently.

The woman says, "The ephoria has been working closely with the police, both on Crete and in Izmir."

She says, "Please change the slide."

I change the slide, and there are new images there, showing the same sort of things that Winchester was showing, but much better photographed.

She says, "It's really the work of the police that I'm showing here."

She says, "These things look very like the things you were shown earlier."

She says, "But these were not found on Crete. They were found where they were offered for sale, in Izmir."

She says, "There has been a steady supply of them for as long as anyone can remember."

She says, "It stopped this year, just when we were tipped off where they were coming from."

She says, "This year when there were better-than-usual finds at the source."

She says, "They stopped appearing in Izmir and started appearing at Paleoziros."

She says, "And then there's the question of the gold masks."

"What are you saying?" says Charles, "Are you implying that I've been buying things on the black market and planting them at Paleoziros to make the project look like a success?"

She says, "On the contrary. I'm saying that you have been finding real things. There are questions. You might have been getting a good price for them."

"That's an outrage," says Charles.

She says, "Just a few questions if you'd be so kind."

"I have important business to attend to here," says Charles.

Six policemen move into position around him. One of them is holding handcuffs. They all have guns, which stay in their holsters, but they're there.

The woman says, "We've been able to match the grains of earth from the treasures with the soil samples from the site. There's no doubt about it. Your laboratory was able to help."

She says, "You can come quietly, or you can struggle, but you will be coming with us."

"This is most unfortunate," says Charles to the room in general, "You will have to carry on without me."

"Thank you," says the chairman of the trustees, "The first item on the agenda is reserved business. We have to ask you to leave. We will manage. I'm sure it will all blow over, and we'll see you later in the day. We'll let the office know when we're ready."

128

Charles Winchester, Director of the Lantern of Demosthenes in Athens, is in charge of an excavation of a Mycenean-era site in Greece. He knows the mask from Mycenae – everyone knows it. It's prominently on display in the National Archaeological Museum in Athens. An American journalist – a bright and serious-seeming young man with a winning smile but no specialist knowledge – tracks him down and asks him for a comment. As an expert, what does he have to say? Winchester sounds serious and looks like an archaeologist should – not too young, pompous, and condescending, but impeccably polite. He speaks with the authority that the journalist lacks. He has not seen the octopus masks except in the excellent photos that the Smithsonian has sent him, but the detailed handling of the metal and the way it has been shaped make him think that they belong to the same tradition as the Mycenean mask.

"You wouldn't want to go so far as to say that it's the same goldsmith that worked on them both," says Winchester, sounding cautious and scholarly, "but I would certainly say that they belong to the same culture."

"What does that say about them then?" says the journalist, who's furrowing his brow because this is an important question.

"How do you mean?" says Winchester.

"Does it mean that Greek craftsmen came to Hawaii thousands of years ago?" says the journalist.

"It could mean that," says Winchester, and he might have been intending to say more, but the journalist turns to the camera and says:

"Thank you, Professor Winchester. There you have it: the ancient Greeks discovered America two thousand years before Columbus."

"I really didn't say that," says Winchester, altogether too late. The camera isn't on him now. He rather likes being called professor, and the young man is quite charming.

"Don't worry about it," says the journalist, "People like that sort of thing," and Winchester finds himself on the front page of the Athenian newspapers the next day. His standing is enhanced further by a knighthood that some of the journalists have given him. Professor Sir Charles Winchester, Director of the important excavation at Paleoziros on Crete, says that Bronze-Age Greek navigators knew their way to the South Pacific and settled there. Winchester modestly demurs whenever he is questioned directly, but he likes the attention, and with his polite manner, he seems to accept the basic truth of the assertion even as he's repudiating it. It seems to be going down well, and it would be churlish to stamp out the goodwill.

129

"I've done nothing," says Charles, quietly exasperated.

The woman from the ephoria says, "As director of the project, you are responsible for the site's security and integrity."

She says, "You know that."

She says, "Clearly, something has gone wrong, and we will need to find out exactly what has happened. Maybe you turned a blind eye. Maybe you were blind. Maybe not. But you are legally responsible, and there are questions to answer."

She says, "I expect you would prefer to answer them in private."

She says, "You might want to have your lawyer with you."

All this has gone on in the subdued golden light reflected from the screen, with the mask looking on. Their voices are quiet, but there's silence in the room, and everyone can hear everything.

"Could we have the lights up," says one of the trustees, as an instruction, not a question.

People start talking once the lights come on. It's not until the lights are on that I realize that Alice has been sitting just beside me, behind and to the right. She's wearing her seahorse earrings.

"Hello," says Alice.

"Not a word of this outside this room," says the chairman, "Not a word."

"We'd better leave," says Alice.

130

Alice and I go to a cafe where we both become invisible.

"Well," I say, "I don't suppose they'll be renewing his contract."

"I don't suppose they will," says Alice, "It's all for the best."

"What's going to happen?" I say.

"Who can say?" she says.

"Is he guilty?" I say.

"It looks bad," she says, "That statement is pretty incriminating."

"You've seen it?" I say.

"I wrote it," she says.

"What did you say," I say.

"The truth," she says, "or something like it."

She says, "When I first went to Palaeoziros, Winchester behaved very strangely."

She says, "It was obvious that the tholos was there to excavate, but Charles actively resisted excavating it."

She says, "He pretended it was a nineteenth-century sheepfold when it made no sense as one."

She says, "He excluded it from the archaeological site and said it was a matter of principle to work methodically through the squares of a grid when anyone could see the tholos was the central thing and should be a priority."

She says, "I was scandalized that he set the site boundary where he did. But it left that ground free for me to have a go at it."

She says, "He, of course, was furious."

She says, "I knew he would be, but I was vindicated."

She says, "I was, of course, disappointed to find that the place had already been robbed."

She says, "Charles took all the credit for the discovery of the tholos because he was the project director, so I left the place embittered, and he's never seen me since."

She says, "He didn't even see me today when I was in the same room for your talk."

She says, "At first, I believed him when he tried to work out the dates for the robbery, but then it dawned on me. Charles was the robber. He robbed it before he started the excavation, and that's why he wanted to avoid it."

She says, "I think he visited with Luke. It's my hunch that they robbed it together."

She says, "Imagine it. Charles and Luke, reckless budding archaeologists, secretly plunder the tomb and smuggle the masks out. It's 1950 – still the aftermath of war. Public services are zilch. No one cares about antiquities. They don't have the resources to police them. There were still hardly any men in the village because they'd all been shot. When Charles and Luke show up, they know there's a settlement there because they've already robbed it of its main treasure, maybe the previous summer. Maybe earlier than that. They come back pretending it's the first time. Then Luke, with his family connections, manages to buy the land to do a legitimate excavation."

She says, "Now I'm beginning to wonder if there's a story to be told about Luke's death. Was it an accident? He fell off a cliff. Who benefitted from that?"

She says, "Think about it."

She says, "Do you think Stasia killed him? She was distraught and married Xander on the rebound."

She says, "Do you think it was Xander? He was doing very well out of the link with Luke. You've seen the picture of them together. They were the best of friends."

She says, "They were more than that."

She says, " Stasia and Xander were both in love with Luke. Their grief was what they had in common. It was real. It brought them together."

She says, "Do you think it was someone from the village who resented him making them prosperous and bringing them electricity and a good water supply?"

She says, "Or do you think it was Charles who was put in charge of all Luke's work and given the money to see it through?"

"You think it was murder," I say.

She says, "I don't know. I just know that if you ask who benefitted from Luke's death, you have to see that Charles benefitted more than anyone else."

She says, "I've told the police it would be a good idea to have a think about it."

The bustle of the city folds itself around them. They're not hiding, but they can't be seen. In principle, they're easy to trace, but no one's looking for them. They can melt away and do whatever they had in mind to do.

131

"How can we trust them?" says Stasia.

"We have to trust them," says Xander, "We won't trust them more than we need to. Unfortunately, when you're working outside the law, you don't have the protection of the law. It makes you realize why we have it."

"I don't like it," says Stasia, "We've handed over all we had. Now we have nothing except their promise."

"My mother thinks they're honorable people," says Xander.

"Do you understand how feeble that sounds?" says Stasia.

"It's all set up," says Xander, "You know it is. We keep a distance now. You trust Maria, don't you?"

"Of course I trust Maria," says Stasia, "She's one of us. She might be cheated. Then we have problems."

"We won't have any real problems," says Xander, "just disappointment. We'll be no worse off than we were before. We'll have lost the masks, but we didn't have them before."

They look at the three Venetian masks, now displayed on Stasia's blue velvet in the three boxes, ready to be closed up and taken on the journey back to Ziros. They're nicely made leather masks and, displayed like this, they look like the crown jewels of the Venetian empire.

"This journey has cost more than we can afford," says Stasia, "People like us don't stay in hotels like this."

"You're forgetting," says Xander, "You're my bride. This is our honeymoon. Nothing is too good for you for once in your lifetime. For these few days, you are a princess."

They go through the arrangements for the money as though they are saying a catechism. The payment is not a payment. It's an overdraft facility. The person in charge of the account is Maria. Maria is in charge of the megaron and in charge of explaining to the electric people which houses need to be supplied. The company will insist on individual meters for each house, but the village will pay the bills. The megaron will provide food for the village when it's wanted. We will go to eat with Maria as we always did, but the megaron will supply the food. There will be archaeologists coming with Winchester, and they will be fed also. The overdraft will grow. If we do something disobliging to the agreement, the bank will ask to be repaid, but we won't be able to pay, so the village will be bankrupt, and that will be the end of the arrangement.

"So we trust the buyer and avoid the police," says Stasia.

"We must assume that the police are watching us," says Xander, "but we can make ourselves difficult to follow. We can take our boat back to Mestre tomorrow. Our boxes of ordinary clothes are there, and we can be invisible again.

Maybe we should change our sailing. Does it draw attention to us if we make a last-minute change?"

"What does it matter?" says Stasia, "We have nothing."

"This evening, we can be seen," says Xander, "Let's enjoy being here. Tomorrow, we disappear, and our honeymoon is a treasured memory. We must take photos that show us here and that show how much we're in love."

"So romantic," says Stasia, "and so practical."

"The dark blue was a good idea," says Xander, "Even these masks look good against it."

"You can never go wrong with navy blue," says Stasia.

132

Each June, there's an impossible pile-on of stuff – students, marking, setting things up for next year. By the end of each June, I lose the will to live. I shut myself off, hide away, and write. It's easy to forget about the Lantern of Demosthenes and the people there. It wasted my time and I don't want to be linked with the place. I don't want to be linked with Charles Winchester. I've heard he's back in England now, but there's been no recent news. That's all part of what I want to shut out and put behind me.

But Crete beckons.

Sitting by the harbor at Chania, wristwatch in pocket, I'm too hot and wearing too many clothes. The suitcase is here, sunglasses still in it. I'm a couple of hours off-kilter with the day, but I'm here.

"Mia kafe sketo and baklava," I say, trying to sound like I belong here.

"Certainly, sir," says the waiter, in English.

The water's still too close to the quay, under the impression that it's in a Venetian canal. The lighthouse at the end of the harbor wall hasn't changed. Nor has the baklava, which is still made with pistachios. I look at my wrist, which is no paler than the rest of my pale arm. I should have phoned Alexander Ziros. The phones must be better than they were. I looked up a number, and I have it here. I imagined his wife picking up and being confused by my English. I imagined him not remembering me. It wouldn't have been right to ask him to come to the airport. I wouldn't have wanted to ask if I could stay at his house.

I take the bus to Gerani. The road has improved. We used to come along here to get to Kladdy on the motorbikes, swerving around potholes. Gerani is nothing but tourism, but I can easily walk to Ziros. I get some paracetamol from a pharmacy with an illuminated sign, which has an unilluminated sign saying something about a hotel.

"Is there a room here?" I say to the pharmacist.

"I'll ask my wife," he says.

She looks sensible, with permed grey hair and a pale yellow nylon housecoat. She takes me around the outside, where there's a stair up to a balcony and a room that looks out onto the beach. It will suit me. I hardly need to take a stroll. I can just stand here and feel the warm breeze and look out to the clean horizon, everything washed away by the sea, even the clouds washed out of the sky. I feel drained, washed out myself. I lie face down on the bed. I don't know what I want to do. I just want to switch off and let go. I tell myself I'm just where I want to be, and things couldn't be better, but there's a feeling of despair that doesn't lift right away.

In the morning, there's a café next door that might as well be part of the hotel, if it is a hotel, and if I want breakfast, there it is. I have Nescafé, nostalgically, yoghurt with a spoonful of honey and some bread. The day is all set to be perfect.

"Ziros," says the pharmacist's wife, "Yes. That's easy. Follow the motorway and then go underneath it. You'll find the way."

"Thank you," I say, "I'll recognize it. I've been there before."

But I don't recognize it. The motorway is a new road that doesn't connect with my memory. It's not much like a motorway. It's not in exactly the same place as the old road, but the view out to sea looks the same. It's confusing. The place isn't playing by the rules. Am I heading in the right direction?

"Ziros," says a sign, pointing to the left. The path goes under the road. My confidence returns with a rush of dopamine, and there's a spring in my step for a moment, but even now, the smaller road doesn't feel right. There are more trees than there used to be and assemblies of stopcocks and hefty pipes. The lemon trees are being watered properly, and they're flourishing. There's far more of them, and the whole feel of the landscape has changed. Ziros village seems to have grown, too. The houses don't look like ruins, and there are some new ones. Every house has a car, but there's no sign of anyone, even at the plateia, just the cats languidly keeping an eye on things.

133

Outside, it's going dark, but the water still reflects fractured images of buildings and boats and makes magic of them. The whole place is a shimmer of illusions, and if you're not prepared to play along with its hallucinations, you miss the point of the place. Venice, without illusions, is a city of baked mud, covered in jewels, sitting in mud and filth. You have to concentrate on the surfaces and the reflections and not ask too many questions about the past. There's plenty of Greek stones here, from Constantinople, and the golden horses, of course, and you can be sure they weren't just given to Venice as gifts, but they make Xander and Stasia feel at home here, even though it's a much more fabulous home than they're used to.

"I've grown up with stories about this sort of thing," says Xander, "Venetians and pirates, foreign rulers and marauders."

"So have I," says Stasia.

"Of course," says Xander, "but my mother's versions of things get even more confused. Before she was declared Greek, she was fed with stories about dashing Corsairs, who were Ottoman admirals, but in Crete, we know them only as pirates. The Venetians make the laws around here. I don't suppose there's any stories about Venetian pirates."

"Well, no, not in Venice," says Stasia, "and when you think about it, the Venetians were richer than anyone, so they were the ones who were there to be robbed."

"Good point," says Xander, "Mind you, 1204's a story about piracy, isn't it? It's just that it's on a huge scale, and it's a city rather than a ship. They bring all that gold and all those jewels and all those holy relics to sit and glimmer here in their open septic tank. No one talks about sending things back. Napoleon stole the horses from here, and when Napoleon was deposed, they came back here. But why doesn't Constantinople have a claim on them? They're my heritage as a Greek and a craftsman, my heritage as a Constantinopolitan descendent in exile."

The megaron's open but deserted. Everything's still in place, but I have no business here, and no one's expected. Xander and Luke look out of the photo from another epoch of the world. The bison plaque looks like it came from the Festival of Britain, nicely done in its way and quite gracefully dated. Up above is the frieze of photos of the gold octopus masks, beautifully framed with Xander's intricate jointing. They look good there. They belong here. It's a good judgment.

A chill runs through me.

The Venetian masks that used to be there were place-holders. They were only ever place-holders. Xander knew all along that it should be these gold masks here. It's nothing to do with them coming to light when they went to the Smithsonian. He knew about them before. He kept these pictures already framed in his gallery room, waiting for the day when they could go out on public display.

"Boró na se voithíso?" says a voice that I immediately know as Xander's.

I turn and look at him. He smiles when he recognizes me. He's put on some weight and looks powerful. His hair has receded quite a bit. He's let it grow long, and it's turned grey, but he's still the same person. A little more gaunt in the face somehow, with his eyes set deeper than they were.

"I knew you'd come back," says Xander. We hug – long and close enough to feel the heat of his body. He's watching me intently.

"These are good photos," I say, "I remember them?"

"You know the Smithsonian found traces of earth on the masks that they say means they came from here," says Xander, "It's official now. They belong here. We've started a petition to have them brought here. You can sign."

"When did they go away?" I say.

"They were stolen," says Xander, looking me right in the eye, "We think Charles Winchester did it, but we can't prove it."

"Good luck with that," I say, "but you knew about these masks before they went to the Smithsonian."

"Alice showed me pictures from Hawaii," he says, "Years and years ago. As soon as I saw them, I knew they belonged here, but it was just a feeling. I couldn't explain it. Your work with the site plan was extraordinary. They, more than anything showed they belonged here. Octopus masks in an octopus town. Charles didn't spot it. He wanted to turn it into snakes and gorgons. Now we know why. He already knew it was an octopus place, and he was trying to put us – put everyone – off the scent."

"Have the police brought any charges against him?" I say.

"They will when they can," says Xander, "They want to. They've lined him up with Lord Elgin and the other robbers we've had here over the centuries. They know it's their patriotic duty to convict him, but he's been too clever for them. Cleverer than I thought he could be."

Xander's trying to see whether I believe him. I don't believe him, and I think he knows it. I'm sure he took the pictures himself. He's never mentioned going to Hawaii. He must have taken the pictures of the masks when they were here.

"I hear he's back in England these days," I say, "He's gone back to Gloucestershire to be with his wife."

"That's a good idea," says Xander, "He should have been a schoolteacher there. He was out of his depth here."

"There's never going to be any real evidence against him," I say. "is there?"

"Well," says Xander, "There are things he can't explain. How did small finds from the site end up on the black market in Turkey? And how come there were regular payments, going back years, from a Swiss bank?"

"You can explain that," I say, "Alice can explain that."

"They're not asking us," says Xander.

"So everyone thinks he's guilty?" I say.

"Pretty much," says Xander, with a wry smile.

"But you don't," I say, "You know he's not."

"I know they're never going to be able to convict him on the big things," says Xander, "but he can't return to Greece. He's guilty enough because of the smaller things. If he comes back to Greece, he'll be put in prison."

135

I can work myself up into feeling bitter and feeling cheated and feeling self-righteous, but then, outside again, seeing the white temple-fronted church across the water, seeing the bobbing gondole at the quayside, hearing the seagulls' cries, and the rattle of stays on masts, and the seething hiss of the waves, and the sea breeze, which is actually fresh, and above all the glittering broken light that makes things tremble out of the darkness and seem insubstantial after all – how can I resist this? Why would I want to resist it? It's a pure magical rapture that makes every criticism feel tetchy and ill-judged, and it's here for me, that rapture if I let it in.

"I'm going to stop feeling that things are in the wrong place," says Xander, "I need to wake up and change so I know that I belong here. The world that has been so shimmeringly put in place here is a fragile assembly of my destiny. It's here to make me feel at home once I've found my way here. There's something about the way the water meets the pavements that put me in mind of the harbor at Chania. It's as though I've turned a corner into an unfamiliar part of town."

"This place is doing strange things to you," says Stasia. "I think we're lost again."

We're in a tall space that feels like a courtyard, but it's between buildings, with a walk along one side, two small bridges connecting one another, steps everywhere, and water. There's no view out and no sense of which way to go. A bearded man comes through.

"Excuse me," I say in English, "Can you point us in the direction of the Academia Bridge?"

"Of course," he says, "I'm going that way myself." and he walks us briskly along. We go into a passage that seems impossibly narrow. I'd have assumed it went nowhere had I been by myself or just to somewhere private and a dead end. It's barely wider than my shoulders. "When you're with a Venetian, you take narrow paths," he says as if it's proverbial. Now we're at San Stefano, a plateia, and the bridge is just across the square. "Where are you from?" he asks.

"Crete," I say, wondering if I should have said something vaguer or told him a lie just so he wouldn't know the truth about me.

"I love Crete," he says, "It's a shame we lost you to the Ottomans."

"We're lost to Athens now," I say.

He laughs, not as if he finds the remark funny, but as if to acknowledge that I might have intended it as a joke, which I didn't. Not really. He's curious about us and doesn't want to let us go just yet.

"What do you do?" he says.

"I make furniture," says Xander, "and my wife makes clothes."

"You're valuable people," he says, "I'm an architect. There's lots of architects in Venice. There's lots of work to be done here. Everything's falling down. Have a coffee," and he gestures to the tables set out in the square. Stasia and Xander exchange glances and wonder if they should know better, but they sit down. There's a statue looming over them. A bearded nineteenth-century man with a pile of books behind him, disappearing up under the hem of his loose coat.

"As school kids, we'd say he's shitting books," he says, and he does his little laugh-that-isn't-quite-a-laugh, "Espresso? Beer?" He's called Carlo. "Do you make furniture to order? Or are you in a big workshop?"

"It's just me," says Xander, "It was my father's business. I do commissions and repairs."

"You must be doing well," he says, "for you to be traveling to Venice."

Xander smiles, seeming to accept that he's a success.

"It's our honeymoon," says Xander, "we're leaving tomorrow. It's just a short stay."

"For all of us," says Carlo. He turns and points out that at the corner of the square, there's what looks like an alleyway, but it's an alleyway with a canal in it. "You'll get this. Look along there. You see how the walls are all crumbling. The saltwater gets drawn up by the bricks, then it evaporates and leaves salt deposits. They bring off the surface. Every generation needs to replace the first forty courses, or the building's lost. No one who lives here thinks it's going to last forever, but we're living the dream, so we want to go on dreaming it."

"I should have brought my portfolio with me," says Xander, "but we were just going out for a stroll."

"Here's my card," says Carlo, "Send me something."

"I liked him," said Stasia.

"He liked us," says Xander, "I hope we didn't give too much away just by being here."

"I'm cold," says Stasia, "It's all very well your mother telling me to get good shoes for the hotel, but what I really want is some really solid underwear."

"Where did you find that perfume?" says Xander, "You should have some to take home."

It smells of the sea, of salt-spray with the iodine of seaweed. She'll be a mermaid when she wears it.

"That was back near San Marco," says Stasia.

"We could get a boat," says Xander, "Will you be OK getting into the boat with those heels?"

"In Venice," says Stasia, "anything is possible."

136

"What are you working on now?" I say.

"Step this way, Ian," says Xander, "Come and see."

We go across to the workshop. There's a boat in pride of place.

"I remember this," I say.

"It must have been at an early stage," he says, "It's in production now. In Germany. You buy it as a kit and assemble it yourself."

"Is it fiberglass?" I say.

"Plywood," he says, "I fine-tuned the shape with Stasia. It's the same idea as her dress patterns. You cut them flat but then bend the plywood. She helped me to get the sheets the right shape. They're held together with fiberglass seams. You can have the boat delivered by post."

"Wow," I say.

"Have you been to see Palaeoziros?" he says.

"Not yet," I say.

"I'll walk there with you if you like," he says.

"I'd like that," I say.

It's a familiar walk, but something's changed.

"I can hear traffic," I say.

"It's the new motorway," says Xander, "It comes close."

"There was a time," I say, "when I thought part of an ancient city was there, spreading from the tholos down to the sea."

"Well," said Xander, "If they'd found an ancient city, they'd have stopped the work."

"So it isn't there," I say.

"They wanted the work to go ahead," he says, "They thought it was better not to find it."

"What?" I say.

Xander shrugs.

"Are you telling me it's there, but they chose not to investigate it?" I say.

"Maybe," he says, "Or maybe there wasn't anything there to find. Who can say? In principle, if you start here and go west and follow the motorway all the way, you will end up in Norway. It's a big project to hold up."

The Paleoziros site's border fence is intact, and the gate's locked up. The stoa where I lived for a few weeks is still in there, but completely closed, as it never was when I was here – which was at this time of year.

"Have they stopped work on it altogether?" I say.

"No one's been here since Winchester was taken off the project," says Xander.

"That's sad," I say, "I'm sure there was lots more to discover."

"It can wait." says Xander, "It's been there for four thousand years. Another generation or two won't hurt it."

"Those photos in the megaron," I say, "You took them, didn't you? They're good. They're lit the way you'd light them."

Xander hesitates. He's wondering whether to admit it or not.

"And you took them here," I say, "When you see them now, you can see they've been cleaned up. They're bright gold. In your photos, they're not like that."

I look at him to register any reaction. I'm half-expecting a look of murderous rage. I might have to defend myself or run. But there's nothing like that. He's completely controlled. He doesn't twitch. He admits nothing, but he looks relieved. He slowly turns his head and smiles as though he's fallen in love with me.

"You're better than the rest of them," he says, and a faraway look comes into his eyes.

They've cut down quite a few trees for the road, and from this ridge, you can see the sea glinting now between the branches.

"You can't begin to know what I've lost," he says.

"Tell me," I say.

"You have no idea," he says, and I can see he's stopping himself from showing emotion.

I want to kiss him gently on the forehead. I want to hold him. I find his fingers, but he seems remote as if he's lost somewhere on the far horizon or trapped somewhere in his past I hold his hand, and move ahead. He lets me lead him on, but his mind's on other things.

"Beautiful. Beautiful," he says, and I know he isn't talking about me, "He fell from the sky."

"Who? Luke?" I say.

He smiles, amused, through other emotions.

"No, no, no. Not Loukas," he says.

"Icarus?" I say.

"That might be closer," he says.

We walk on a bit further, and he's himself again.

"Here," he says, "You'll like this."

We go down to the road, and there's a sign there with a silhouette of a cow.

"There you go," he says.

"It's just a road sign," I say, "Why would I like it?"

"The beautiful thing," he says, "is that there are no cows on Crete."

"So," I say, "Why would I like it?"

"There are sometimes stray goats," he says, "and we bought the signs cheap from a German company that had made too many. They're all over the island. The information isn't quite correct, but it's the right result. People are warned about the animals."

"Is Stasia here?" I say.

"Yes, she's around," he says, "She's doing well. Come and have a drink with us. Something to eat if you like. How long are you here?"

"Oh," I say, "just a few days."

"Then you must stay," he says, "You can have your old room back."

I feel like I'm dreaming, connecting, and not quite connecting with the place. Xander's old now, and maybe he seems older than he is, but he's being moved by things that happened when he was young, and I can't connect with them. I want him to talk about things he's going to keep secret.

137

The cold, dank air of the canal isn't foul, but it is oppressive – invasively damp. The water laps at the walls, and the chill starts to penetrate bones. Where there are lights, you can see a mist forming – a miasma – that's at exactly human level, close to the water, and you can see exhaled breath. The warm air in the hotel comes as a relief.

In the middle of the night, Xander dreams or does something that feels like dreaming.

There's someone wearing a white lab coat. The three gold masks are laid out on the table. The white-coated figure turns, and it's a man with a white beard and metal-rimmed glasses.

"Dr Kabalevsky tells me they're the real thing," says a voice from the other side of the table, beyond the glare of the screen.

"I know they're real," says Xander.

"You have done well," says the voice, "You've done the right thing." He comes round the table, and Xander can see him now. He's looking him in the eye. Xander knows he has to look straight back. Everything else goes away. There's a pounding in his head and some background flickering, but it's his eyes that take over, and he knows that if he glances away, even for a moment, everything is lost. There's something looking back at him, but he doesn't know what it is. The eyes are extraordinary. They're orange. Their gaze searches around inside him. Their dark center dilates, and he's lost in their darkness. He has a sense of swimming. Of drowning. Of coming up for air. There are sparkling lights and flickering sheet lightning. There's a high-pitched whistling going on through the throbbing. He can hear the leaves of the plants in the garden start to rustle. He can hear the currents in the oceans. He can hear the moon start to sing. He moves a finger in front of his face, blocking the view of one eye and then the other, and they're in the hotel room again, and Xander relaxes.

"Go back to your village," he says, "One of our banks is dealing with the arrangement. These are my ancestors. Their story might never be known, but the story I tell is that they left their great cities and took to the sea. We're water people, and if land people don't quite notice us, that's fine. When they do notice us, they get it wrong. Always remember that. I have a special bond with your village, and I want to honor that in perpetuity – be assured of that. The village is special, and it deserves to prosper, but it mustn't attract attention to itself. Don't draw attention to the money. It will come gradually, as if the soil there is more fertile than in other places – which, in a way, it has proved to be."

Xander reaches out to shake his hand. He reaches out his hand and touches the back of Xander's hand with the back of his and strokes it gently.

"We might meet again, one day," he says, "who knows? But be assured, I'll hear about what you're doing."

"I know that he knows what it's like to be a god," says Xander, to Stasia, who is fast asleep, "And he knows that I know it too. He knows that I'm the real thing."

138

"Ah!" says Stasia, and she carries on in Greek, when we get back to the house. She looks at me.

"You remember Ian," says Xander in English.

"Of course," she says, as if she's only just recognized me, "I hope Xander has invited you to eat."

"He has. Is that OK," I say.

"It's lovely," she says.

"Thank you," I say.

We will be out on the terrace, but I go into the house with Stasia in case I can help and so I can look around. Some of the furniture is in different places, but it all looks familiar – rather sparse. I want to go into the study. I feel I have a bond with this place that isn't being altogether acknowledged. I don't have a right to walk in here, but I feel as if I should have. It's part of my past, too. I was changed by being here. I'm part of the family, but I'm an outsider who has to stay outside it.

"I remember when you had the only phone in the village," I say as if the telephone is drawing me into the study. I want to see if the wedding-day photo is still there. I remember the way it caught Xander's remoteness. Maybe I have to make do with the memory. In his place, I guess I'd keep it hidden.

"Oh," he says, "everyone has them now."

We can see the sea from the terrace, over the roofs of the houses lower down the slope. It's a dark band below the sky. Flat and uninformative. The sun goes down as we eat. Xander brings out some candles.

"The electric light is convenient," he says, "but these are better for eating in the dark. They used to be all we had. I can't say things were better then, but I like the light they give."

"It's gentle," says Stasia, "and flattering."

"Ziros used to be a very different place," says Xander, "It used to be very isolated. Everyone knew one another in the village, but hardly anyone outside it. That's what drew my mother's parents here. Now I can do furniture designs and send them to Milan and Basel. I can have an international career without leaving the village. I need to be able to imagine Milan – or the factory – or the machines – but I've been there. I can remember. I can sit here and look at the sea, and I can know that I'm in Venice, or on a ship, or with my mother."

It's dark, and the sea is no longer visible, but he knows it's there, and that's all he needs.

"How is your mother?" I say.

"She died a few years ago," he says.

"I'm sorry," I say.

"She was old," he says, "It happens. You have to accept it. She was ready when the time came. Is there news about Winchester? How's his health?"

"I've heard nothing," I say, "But then I haven't asked. His great work on Palaeoziros doesn't look like it's ever going to appear."

"Of course it won't," he says, "It's beyond him. He never had the vision. He'll always live in his own little hell and always think it's because of other people. You and I – we see a bigger picture. I'll always be somewhere there in your thoughts, and you'll always be part of mine. You're always welcome back here, you know that, but I don't expect you to come again – and I think you're OK with that now."

I wonder what it is he thinks he's reading in me, and my first reaction is to protest.

"Of course, I'll come back," I say.

"You'll be welcome," he says, "but I'll be surprised."

Ten years have passed since I was last here, and if there isn't a project to bring me here, it could easily be another ten, and by then – well, who's to say that he'll still be alive? Or me. I have a life of my own to live. Xander saying these things makes it seem that this is the whole of me – my memories of him, his memories of me – but that's just one fiber. I have other lives to live. I'm woven into other stories.

"I'll take you back to your hotel," says Xander, "You can't walk in the dark. You can stay here if you want to, but I expect you want to get back to your toothbrush."

"That's probably best," I say with some reluctance. I can take a hint. And anyway, it won't be the same without the diggers here. That immersion in some sort of psychic ocean together as we slept in different spaces not so far apart. I'll hold on to the memory of it.

"I have some boxes for you," says Xander, "They're not heavy. The hotel can arrange to have them sent to England."

"It's not that sort of hotel," I say.

"Then stay at a better one the night before you fly," he says, "Or take them on the plane. They're quite robust. They're designed to travel. They'll go in the hold. I made them about 40 years ago. I don't have a use for them now. I'd like you to have them. You'll appreciate them. Come downstairs."

In the workshop, things are tidy at the front and cluttered at the back.

"How's business?" I say.

"Oh, it's OK," says Xander, "We're doing alright. I've never had to work at this if I didn't want to. I forget how frantic some people's lives are. I've always kept my overheads low. Even when I had nothing, it didn't feel as if I needed anything. I dream of living at sea. I'd like to die at sea. But it's a dream, and dreaming it is enough. I can see the bigger picture. The island is at sea. The waves are close enough. I can see them from the terrace, but they're in my mind, and in my veins. I'm at sea here already."

"Look," he says, "Here they are."

He moves some cardboard boxes and some lengths of timber to expose some well-made timber boxes with neat dovetails zipping up the corners. He passes them to me, one at a time, and I put them on a nearby workbench.

"Excellent," he says, "Let's take them out to the van. You can open them when you're at the hotel, but don't open them here."

I carry two boxes to the van. He carries the other one. He balances it on his hip, while he finds the key and opens the back doors one-handed.

"Thank you," I say, "I'm sure I'll find a use for them."

Xander smiles. I want to say he smiles mysteriously, but that isn't quite it. It's not a smile for me. It's a smile for himself. He knows he's done the right thing, and he believes he'll never see me again, so there's maybe something rueful about it, but maybe I can't really see that.

It's only a few minutes back to the hotel. I wish it were a longer journey.

There's some light in the street outside the hotel, but not enough to see very clearly. So we say goodbye and shake hands at the foot of the outdoor stairs. He grips my shoulder.

He wants to see me open the boxes, but he doesn't want to
be there.

"I'll write," I say, and honestly that's my intention when
I say it.

139

The journey back to Mestre is cold, chugging back through mist, following the straight line of the long bridge. An illicit adventure. A hallucination. Xander and Stasia are calm and silent. It's as if talking about it – putting it into words – is just going to show how mad and impossible it all was. Our host at the little hotel greets us like old friends. The boat's returned. They've learnt their lesson – how easy it is in Venice to live beyond your means – and they've come crashing back to reality in Mestre so he can help them out, which he's happy to do.

"No wonder you went through your money if you've been buying clothes like that," he says.

They open the boxes that they left here and change into their old clothes that make them invisible. Then they take the train back to Venice and the port. They find the luggage that was sent directly there from the Hotel Danieli. It's being guarded by a policeman.

"This is our luggage," says Xander.

The policeman looks them up and down, skeptically. These people couldn't afford the Danieli.

"Identity papers, please," he says. He checks the name against the paper he has and seems surprised to find that it matches.

"Are these your boxes, sir?" he says.

"Yes," says Xander. Stasia is barely distinguishable from the background and will melt into it if there's trouble.

"Would you mind opening them up for us?" says the policeman.

"Not at all," says Xander, and he makes a start on the string. One. Two. Three. The leather masks look splendidly important, presented as if they're royal diadems set on the deep blue velvet. "Do I need a license for them? The guy at the shop said it would be OK without."

The policeman can see right away that they're ordinary tourist fare.

"I liked the craftsmanship," says Xander, "The way the leather's pressed into shape and bonded."

"Yes," says the policeman, without sounding convinced, "You don't normally get them in boxes like this."

"I was told they were very old masks and might be quite valuable."

The policeman laughs drily.

"You've been had, mate," he says, "But he's given you good boxes. Look after them. They're worth more than the masks."

Xander looks calm and disappointed.

Behind the appearance, he's ecstatically losing himself in the glitter of the waves. Each individual wave makes its exact negotiation between the deep currents of the oceans and the gaseous maneuverings of the air. The pull of the earth, its restless iron core, the pull of the moon, the hidden movements in the depths, the tension on the surface. Salt spray. Iodine. Ozone. The sun, beaming without heat, makes the water's surface look metallic – quicksilvers it. It's sending its rays into him by way of the minutely configured interaction of great forces softened by the atmosphere. He's irradiated but cold. He's hyper-alert to the nuances of the chill air and the mesmeric, insistent twinkling of the distant waves, but from outside, he seems quietly stunned.

"Oh yes," he says, in a voice that no one hears, "I've been had."

I'll maybe have a day at the beach tomorrow and then see how I feel. I might go back to Heraklion and check in at a big hotel. Or maybe take a boat to another island, just to be on the water so I can carry that sensation around with me. I take one box up to my room. I reach my balcony, which looks out over the sea. I unlock my door and switch on the too-bright fluorescent lamp. It's still hurting my eyes as I open the box. It's lined with navy blue velvet, and there's a Venetian mask in it, made of leather, lightly gilded.

Minutes later, the three masks in their display boxes are sitting side by side. The deep folds of the velvet are the folds of the soul that Xander opened up to me. I've never felt this close to someone, and he's not even here. It's a confession so cryptic it can't be used against him. It makes me complicit in what he's done, and I'm OK with that, and he knows it. The masks look at me, and they know everything. I look inside myself and there's my Minotaur, not knowing what to do, not knowing whether to bellow or cry or curl up in a ball.

I take off my clothes, put a towel round my waist, some flip-flops on my feet, and go down to the beach. The sea is seething through the pebbles, and it's quite difficult to stay steady on my feet even before I reach the water. I put the towel down, with the flip-flops and my glasses on it, and hobble painfully the last few steps into the water. Once it's deep enough to float, I swim, sculling on my back to begin with, then doing proper strokes when the water's deeper. I swim without breaking the surface of the water, without splashing. Silent. Invisible. Not too far, but out of my depth so I'm properly held in the water. Saline solution. Amniotic fluid. All the tears I've been holding back, are already there with no need to cry them. I can lose my body in the water – my body, which is mainly water – I can look out to sea and see precisely nothing. It's dark above and dark below. And turning round, I can see the lights along the waterfront. Not many of them. Everyone's asleep, I hope, or indoors. The lights glitter in the waves, broken up by their movement. Without my glasses, I can't see any stars, but they're there – it's a clear night. I just want to stay here long enough to fix this moment forever in my memory as something that really happened to me – suspended between telluric currents and the pull of the moon, water inside and out, air inside and out, floating weightless without effort – between one life and another – cleansed, trusted, blessed.